OPEN CITY

New York City, Winter 2007–2008
Number Twenty-Four

OPEN CITY

Actual Air
Poems by David Berman

"David Berman's poems are beautiful,
strange, intelligent, and funny. They are
narratives that freeze life in impossible
contortions. They take the familiar and
make it new, so new the reader is
stunned and will not soon forget. I
found much to savor on every page
of *Actual Air*. It's a book for everyone."
— James Tate

"This is the voice I have been waiting so
long to hear . . . Any reader who tunes
in to his snappy, offbeat meditations is
in for a steady infusion of surprises and
delights."
— Billy Collins

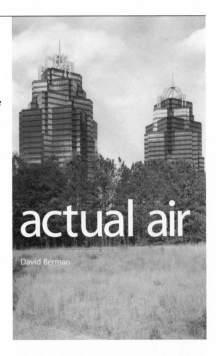

My Misspent Youth
Essays by Meghan Daum

"An empathic reporter and a provocative
autobiographer . . . I finished it in a single
afternoon, mesmerized and sputtering."
— *The Nation*

"Meghan Daum articulates the only
secret left in the culture: discreet but
powerful fantasies of romance, ele-
gance, and ease that survive in our
uncomfortable world of striving. These
essays are very smart and very witty
and just heartbreaking enough to be
deeply pleasurable."
— Marcelle Clements

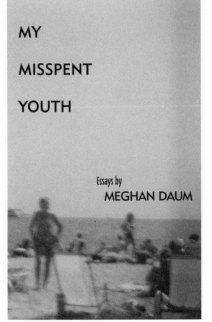

BOOKS

Open City Books are available at fine bookstores or at **www.opencity.org**, and are distributed to the trade by Publishers Group West.

Venus Drive
Stories by Sam Lipsyte

"Sam Lipsyte is a wickedly gifted writer. *Venus Drive* is filled with grimly satisfying fractured insights and hardcore humor. But it also displays some inspired sympathy for the daze and confusion of its characters. Above all it's wonderfully written and compulsively readable with brilliant and funny dialogue, a collection that represents the emergence of a very strong talent."
—Robert Stone

"Sam Lipsyte can get blood out of a stone—rich, red human blood from the stony sterility of contemporary life. His writing is gripping—at least I gripped this book so hard my knuckles turned white."
—Edmund White

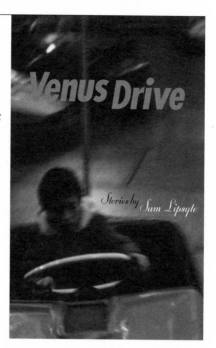

Karoo
A Novel by Steve Tesich

"Fascinating—a real satiric invention full of wise outrage."
—Arthur Miller

"A powerful and deeply disturbing portrait of a flawed, self-destructive, and compulsively fascinating figure."
—*Kirkus Reviews* (starred)

"Saul Karoo is a new kind of wild man, the sane maniac. Larger than life and all too human, his out-of-control odyssey through sex, death, and show business is extreme, and so is the pleasure of reading it. Steve Tesich created a fabulously Gargantuan comic character."
—Michael Herr

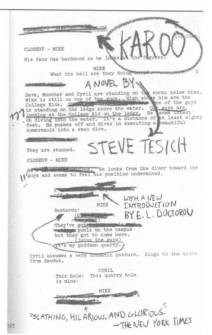

Some Hope
A Trilogy by Edward St. Aubyn

"Tantalizing . . . A memorable tour de force."
  —*The New York Times Book Review*

"Hilarious and harrowing by turns, sophisticated, reflective, and brooding."
  —*The New York Review of Books*

"Feverishly good writing . . . Full of Algonquin wit on the surface while roiling underneath. *Some Hope* is a hell of a brew, as crisp and dry as a good English cider and as worth savoring as any of Waugh's most savage volleys."
  —*The Ruminator Review*

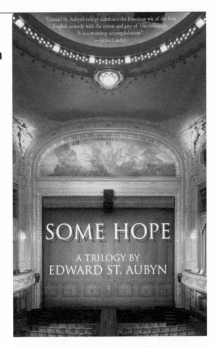

Mother's Milk
A Novel by Edward St. Aubyn

"St. Aubyn's caustic, splendid novel probes the slow violence of blood ties—a superbly realized agenda hinted at in the novel's arresting first sentence: 'Why had they pretended to kill him when he was born?'"
  —*The Village Voice*

"Postpartum depression, assisted suicide, adultery, alcoholism—it's all here in St. Aubyn's keenly observed, perversely funny novel about an illustrious cosmopolitan family and the mercurial matriarch who rules them all."
  —*People*

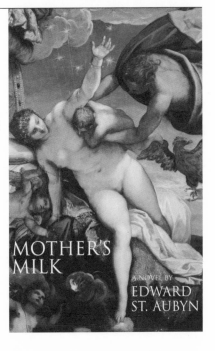

Goodbye, Goodness
A Novel by Sam Brumbaugh

"Goodbye, Goodness is the rock n' roll
Great Gatsby."
—New City Chicago

"Sam Brumbaugh's debut novel couldn't
be more timely. Goodbye, Goodness
boasts just enough sea air and action to
make an appealing summer read without coming anywhere near fluffsville."
—Time Out New York

"Beautifully captures the wrung-out feel of
a depleted American century."
—Baltimore City Paper

The First Hurt
Stories by Rachel Sherman

"Sherman's writing is sharp, hard, and
honest; there's a fearlessness in her
work, an I'm-not-afraid-to-say-this quality.
Because she knows that most of us
have thought the same but didn't have
the guts to say it."
—Boston Phoenix

"Rachel Sherman writes stories like splin-
ters: they get under your skin and stay
with you long after you've closed the
book. These haunting stories are both
wonderfully, deeply weird and unset-
tlingly familiar."
—Judy Budnitz

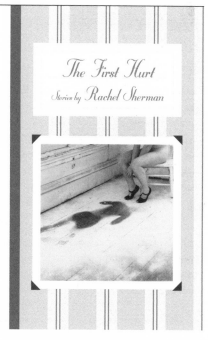

 **OPEN CITY**

Long Live a Hunger to Feed Each Other
Poems by Jerome Badanes

"Reading Jerome Badanes's poems is not so much reading a voice from the heartfelt past as reading a poet whose work is very much alive and yet reflects a lost—and meaningful—age. He is one of our good souls; he is one of our poets. I treasure his work."
—Gerald Stern

"The best best book publishing story of the year."
—*Poetry*

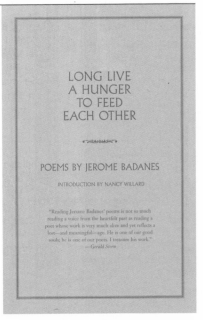

Love Without
Stories by Jerry Stahl

"[Stahl]…knows how to shock us into laughter, and his best work mines the grotesque for pathos, a tradition that includes Flannery O'Connor, Barry Hannah, and Denis Johnson . . .The key isn't whom he writes about, but at what depth . . . Stahl plunges us into depraved worlds with a keen intensity of purpose, and his addled protagonists run up hard against the truth of their desires."
—*Los Angeles Times*

"Tender and gut-busting."
—*L.A. Weekly*

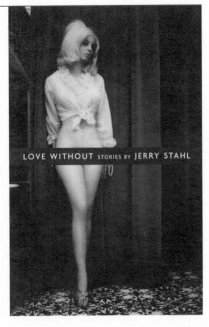

BOOKS

Why the
Devil Chose
New England
for His Work

Stories by
Jason
Brown

"Stories so beautiful, faceted,
and durable, they feel excavated from
a mine. A collection of subtle gems."
—Aimee Bender

"An inchoate evil is hard at work in each of these eleven
stunning, loosely linked stories . . . Brown's deep sympathy
for his flawed characters endows these polished shorts with
brilliant appeal."
—*Publishers Weekly* (starred review)

"*Why the Devil Chose New England for His Work* links gem-
cut stories of troubled youths, alcoholics, illicit romances, the
burden of inheritance, and the bane of class, all set in the
dense upper reaches of Maine, and delivers them with hope,
heart, and quiet humor."
—Lisa Shea, *Elle*

LINCOLN PLAZA CINEMAS

Six Screens

63RD STREET & BROADWAY
OPPOSITE LINCOLN CENTER
212-757-2280

OPEN CITY

CONTRIBUTORS' NOTES xxiv

JEFF JOHNSON 1 The Breather

JAMES HANNAHAM 15 Loss Prevention

KATE HALL 33 Remind Me What the Light Is For

MALERIE WILLENS 35 The Elegant Rube

IAN MARTIN 47 The Devanes

NOELLE TAN 61 Photographs

MARK HARTENBACH 69 Three Poems

CLAIRE KEEGAN 73 Surrender

GERARD COLETTA 85 Two Poems

WAYNE CONTI 89 Brooklyn

DOUG SHAEFFER 93 Withdrawn

ERIN BROWN 99 Reckoning

ALEX LEMON 103 Two Poems

DINAW MENGESTU 107 Home at Last

BARON WORMSER 113 Two Poems

JAY BATLLE 119 People Like This Hate People Like You

JONATHAN BAUMBACH 125 Travels with Wizard

STANLEY MOSS 137 Satyr Song

147 Index

AMERICAN SHORT FICTION

Fall/Winter 2007

vs us,"
t to reme
nt places. A

er trav
ny tow
neir ringi
the begi
oled up
ase, now rumored t
tic, often

New Writing From

M.O. Walsh
Maud Casey
James Scott
Chris Bachelder
Naomi J. Williams
Jasmine Beach-Ferrara

Art by
Wuon Gean Ho

AN INTERNATIONAL BESTSELLER

"One reads this book almost breathlessly, can hardly put it down . . . A handbook for the soul, intellect, and heart." —*Die Welt*

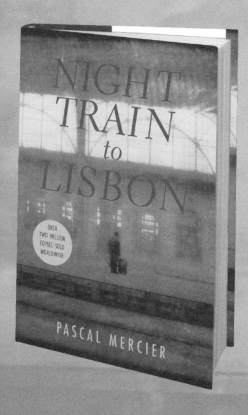

NIGHT TRAIN to LISBON

by

Pascal Mercier

"One of the great European novels of the past few years."
—*Page des Libraires*

"A sensation. The best book of the last ten years . . . A novel of incredible clarity and beauty."
—*Bücher*

GROVE PRESS
an imprint of Grove/Atlantic, Inc.
Distributed by Publishers Group West
www.groveatlantic.com

OPEN CITY

Open City is published by Open City, Inc., a nonprofit corporation. Donations are tax-deductible to the extent allowed by the law. A one-year subscription (3 issues) is $30; a two-year subscription (6 issues) is $55. Make checks payable to: Open City, Inc., 270 Lafayette Street, Suite 1412, New York, NY 10012. For credit-card orders, see our Web site: www.opencity.org. E-mail: editors@opencity.org.

Open City is a member of the Council of Literary Magazines and Presses and is indexed by the American Humanities Index.

Open City gratefully acknowledges the generous support of the family of Robert Bingham. We also thank the New York State Council on the Arts. See the page following the masthead for additional donor acknowledgments.

State of the Arts

NYSCA

Front cover: *Tents in the Woods #1*, oil on canvas, 2006, by Amy Bird. Page one: *Surfers #3*, oil on canvas, 2004, by Amy Bird. Both images courtesy of Milo Gallery.

Back cover: *Withdrawn*, collage, 2004, by Doug Shaeffer. Courtesy of the artist.

OPEN CITY

EDITORS
Thomas Beller
Joanna Yas

ART DIRECTOR
Nick Stone

EDITOR-AT-LARGE
Adrian Dannatt

CONTRIBUTING EDITORS
Jonathan Ames
Elizabeth Beller
David Berman
Aimée Bianca
Will Blythe
Sam Brumbaugh
Amanda Gersh
Laura Hoffmann
Jan de Jong
Kip Kotzen
Anthony Lacavaro
Alix Lambert
Vanessa Lilly
Sam Lipsyte
Jim Merlis
Honor Moore
Robert Nedelkoff
Parker Posey
Beatrice von Rezzori
Elizabeth Schmidt
Lee Smith
Alexandra Tager
Tony Torn
Jocko Weyland

INTERNS
Caroline Gormley
Lina Makdisi
Jamie L. Parra

READERS
Terra Chalberg
Michael Hornburg
Jessa Lingel
Chris Peterson
Aaron Rich
Ben Turner
Kyle Wilson

FOUNDING EDITORS
Thomas Beller
Daniel Pinchbeck

FOUNDING PUBLISHER
Robert Bingham

OPEN CITY WOULD LIKE TO THANK THE FOLLOWING FOR
THEIR GENEROUS CONTRIBUTIONS TO OUR SPRING BENEFIT
AT HOUSING WORKS BOOKSTORE CAFÉ IN
NEW YORK CITY, MAY 9, 2007

Patrons ($1,000 or more)
Clara Bingham
Joan Bingham
Belle & Henry Davis
Vanessa & John Lilly
Eric Lindbloom & Nancy Willard
Eleanor & Rowland Miller
Dorothy Spears
Mary & Jeffrey Zients

Donors ($500 or more)
Robert Scott Asen
Hava Beller
Holly Dando
Laura Fontana & John J. Moore
Alex Kuczynski
Nancy Novogrod
David Selig (Rice Restaurant)
Scott Smith

Contributors ($150 or more)

Joe Andoe
Molly Bingham
Paula Bomer
Arlette P. Brauer & George Bria
Elizabeth Brown
Cheryl Chapman & Josh Gilbert
Nina Collins
Joe Conason & Elizabeth Wagley
Paula Cooper
E. V. Day and Ted Lee
Edward Garmey
Melissa Grace
Pierre Hauser
Edward Lee

Miranda Lichtenstein &
    Cameron Martin
William Morton
Wendy Mullin
Richard & Nicole Murphy
Robert & René Nedelkoff
Alexa Robinson & Steven Johnson
Rick Rofihe
Robert Soros &
    Melissa Schiff Soros
Georgia & Terry Stacey
Jennifer Sturman
Elizabeth Wagley & Joe Conason
Shelley Wanger

Friends

Alex Abramovich
Lucy Anderson
Harold Augenbraum
Caroline Baron
John Barr
Noah Baumbach
Elizabeth Beller
Jessica Bertel
Betsy Berne
Aimée Bianca
Andrew Blauner
Theodore Bouloukus
Sam Brumbaugh
Michael Carroll
Jocelyn Casey-Whitman
Bryan Charles
Winthrop Clevinger
Simon Constable
Hilary Metcalf Costa
Adrian Dannatt
Gerald Dillon
Sarah Dohrmann
Aaron Fagan
Mike Fellows
Jofie Ferrari-Adler
Nick Flynn
Tiffany Foa
Mike Gardner
Deborah Garrison
John Glassie
David Goodwillie
Melissa Gould
Rebecca Green
Gerald Howard
Amy Hundley

Brendan Kelly
Porochista Khakpour
Anthony Lacavaro
Deborah Landau
Matt Lee
Ariel Leve
Sam Lipsyte
Tzipora Lubar
Bruce Mason
Vestal McIntyre
Paul Morris
Carolyn Murnick
Christopher Nicholson
Ethan Nosowsky
Vince Passaro
Beatrice von Rezzori
Isabel Sadumi
Saïd Sayrafiezadeh
Elizabeth Schmidt
Richard Serra
Claudia Silver
Debra Singer
Betsy Smith
Joanna Spinks
Valerie Steiker
Ben Stiller
Nick Stone
Chaya Thanhauser
Ben Turner
Shawn Vandor
Marissa Walsh
Dean Wareham & Britta Phillips
Susan Wheeler
Zach Wiggin
Malerie Willens

EPOCH

a magazine of contemporary literature

Waiting Boat, oil on panel, 31" x 44", by Treacy Ziegler

published three times per year
sample copy: $5
one year subscription: $11

EPOCH MAGAZINE
251 Goldwin Smith Hall
Cornell University
Ithaca, NY 14853-2301

ANNA
CLOTHES FOR WOMEN

150 East 3rd Street at Avenue A
New York City
212.358.0195
www.annanyc.com

NICK STONE DESIGN

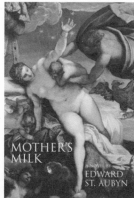

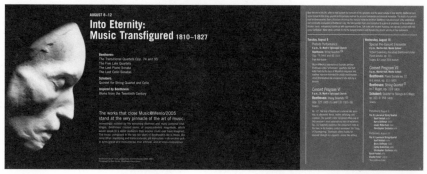

www.nickstonedesign.com
stone@nickstonedesign.com
tel: 212.995.1863

anderbo.com "Best New Online Journal"
—storySouth Million Writers Award

anderbo.com

fiction   poetry   "fact"   photography

RROFIHE TROPHY!

2006 WINNER
ERIN BROWN

FOR HER STORY
"RECKONING"

There were 180 stories submitted to the
2006 RRofihe Trophy Contest.

"Reckoning" by Erin Brown
of Charlottesville, Virginia
is published in this issue.
She will also receive $500 and a trophy.

2008 RRofihe Trophy guidelines at www.opencity.org/rrofihe

Rick Rofihe is the author of Father Must, a collection of short stories published by Farrar, Straus & Giroux. His fiction has appeared in *The New Yorker*, *Grand Street*, *Open City*, *Swink*, *Unsaid*, and on epiphanyzine.com. His nonfiction has appeared in *The New York Times*, *The Village Voice*, *Spy*, and *The East Hampton Star*, and on mrbellersneighborhood.com. A recipient of the Whiting Writers' Award, he has taught writing at Columbia University and the Writer's Voice of the West Side Y. He currently teaches privately and at Gotham Writers' Workshop in New York. He is the editor of the new online literary journal, anderbo.com.

IT WAS LIKE MY TRYING TO HAVE A TENDER-HEARTED NATURE

A Novella and Stories

DIANE WILLIAMS

FC2
The University of Alabama Press
http://fc2.org

CONTRIBUTORS' NOTES

JAY BATLLE is an artist who spends his money between Brooklyn and Paris. Recently he got his New York state real estate license to understand the market. His artwork was on the NBC morning show for best steak tartar in Brooklyn.

JONATHAN BAUMBACH's new novel, *You: The Invention of Memory*—his fifteenth book—has just been published.

AMY BIRD grew up as a faculty brat at the Thacher School in Ojai, California. She has a BA from Dartmouth and an MFA from Rhode Island School of Design. She currently lives in Los Angeles and will be included in the 2007 Pacific Coast edition of *New American Paintings*. For more information, go to www.amy-bird.com or www.milogallery.net.

ERIN BROWN has had work published in the *New York Times* and the *Northwest Review*. She lives in Charlottesville, Virginia.

GERARD COLETTA is a recent graduate of Harvard, where he majored in English. The poems appearing in this volume are his first to be published.

WAYNE CONTI lives and writes in New York City, where he is the proprietor of Mercer Street Books. He is contributing editor of the online journal anderbo.com, where two of his stories appear. He has also been published online at Pindeldyboz.com.

KATE HALL's poems have recently appeared in journals such as *Boston Review*, *Colorado Review*, *jubilat*, *Swerve*, and *Denver Quarterly*. Her chapbook, *Suspended*, is forthcoming with Greenboathouse Books. She is coeditor of Delirium Press and is currently living in Paris.

JAMES HANNAHAM's fiction has appeared in *The Literary Review*, *Nerve*, and *Fresh Men*. He has written for the *Village Voice*, *Spin*, *Interview*, *New York Magazine*, *Time Out New York*, and others. He holds an MFA from the Michener Center at UT Austin and has been a colony rat at Yaddo, the MacDowell Colony, the Blue Mountain Center, and Chateau de Lavigny.

MARK HARTENBACH lives in a small town along the Ohio River where he constantly strives to transcend his surroundings. Among his books are *March* from Pudding House Publications and *The Sound of Music* from Hcolom Press. He has also published numerous chapbooks.

JEFF JOHNSON lives at the bottom of Manhattan with his family. His writing has appeared in *Vice*, *The Minus Times*, *Fence*, *Jane*, *ESPN*, and many other outstanding periodicals. Check fittedsweats.blogspot.com for warm fuzzies.

CLAIRE KEEGAN was raised on a farm in Wicklow, Ireland. A former Wingate Scholar, she lives in rural Ireland. Her second story collection, *Walk the Blue Fields*, is forthcoming from Black Cat in the spring.

ALEX LEMON's books of poems include *Mosquito* (Tin House Books) and *Hallelujah Blackout* (forthcoming, Milkweed Editions). A memoir is also forthcoming from Scribner.

IAN MARTIN is a Chicago-based writer and filmmaker. "The Devanes" is his first published story. He recently completed a Yaddo fellowship and is at work on a novel.

DINAW MENGESTU was born in Addis Ababa, Ethiopia, in 1978, and is the author of the novel *The Beautiful Things That Heaven Bears*. The recipient of a 2006 fellowship in fiction from the New York Foundation for the Arts, he lives in Brooklyn. His essay in this issue will be published in *Brooklyn Was Mine*, a forthcoming anthology.

STANLEY MOSS's collections of poetry include *New & Selected Poems 2006*, *A History of Color*, *Asleep in the Garden*, *The Intelligence of Clouds* and *The Skull of Adam*. A new *New & Selected* will be published by Anvil Press in the UK in 2008. He was educated at Trinity College and Yale University. He makes his living as a private art dealer, largely in Spanish and Italian Old Masters, and is the publisher and editor of the Sheep Meadow Press, a nonprofit press devoted to poetry.

Artist **DOUG SHAEFFER** has lived in Chicago since 1984. He has shown his work at Standard, 65Grand, Lisa Boyle, the Chicago Cultural Center, ArtChicago, and, most recently, Green Lantern.

NOELLE TAN received her BFA from New York University and her MFA from the California Institute of the Arts. Her work is in the collections of the Hirshhorn Museum and Sculpture Garden, the Corcoran Museum of Art, and the Center for Photography at Woodstock. She received a Creative Capital Grant in 2005. She currently resides in Washington, D.C.

MALERIE WILLENS grew up in Los Angeles and lives in New York City. She has an MFA in fiction from Sarah Lawrence College. This is her first published story.

BARON WORMSER's *Scattered Chapters: New and Selected Poems*, is forthcoming from Sarabande in 2008.

RICE

292 ELIZABETH ST

N O H O

212-226-5775

RICENY.COM

PETE'S CANDY STORE

Pete's Reading Series

HOSTED BY MIRA JACOB AND ALISON HART

Come see today's literary icons and tomorrow's stars take the stage.

Jan 24	Jim Shepard
Feb 7	André Aciman
Feb 21	Samantha Hunt

**Every other Thursday
@ 7:30pm
September – June**

Pete's Candy Store
709 Lorimer Street
Brooklyn, NY

www.petescandystore.com

OPEN

"The Crazy Person" by Mary Gaitskill, "La Vie en Rose" by Hubert Selby Jr., "Cathedral Parkway" by Vince Passaro. Art by Jeff Koons and Devon Dikeou. Cover by Ken Schles, whose *Invisible City* sells for thousands on Ebay. Stan Friedman's poems about baldness and astronomy, Robert Polito on Lester Bangs, Jon Tower's real life letters to astronauts. (Vastly underpriced at $300. Only three copies left.)

ISSUE # 1

A first glimpse of Martha McPhee; a late burst from Terry Southern. Jaime Manrique's "Twilight at the Equator." Art by Paul Ramirez-Jonas, Kate Milford, Richard Serra. Kip Kotzen's "Skate Dogs," Richard Foreman's "Poetry City" with playful illustrations by Daniel Pinchbeck, David Shields' "Sports" and his own brutal youth. (Ken Schles found the negative of our cover girl on Thirteenth Street and Avenue B. We're still looking for the girl. $25)

ISSUE # 2

Irvine Welsh's "Eurotrash" (his American debut), Richard Yates (from his last, unfinished novel), Patrick McCabe (years before *The Butcher Boy*). Art by Francesca Woodman (with an essay by Betsy Berne), Jacqueline Humphries, Allen Ginsberg, Alix Lambert. A short shot of Lipsyte—"Shed"—not available anywhere else. Plus Alfred Chester's letters to Paul Bowles. Chip Kidd riffs on the Fab Four. (Very few copies left! $25)

ISSUE # 3

Stories by the always cheerful Cyril Connolly ("Happy Deathbeds"), Thomas McGuane, Jim Thompson, Samantha Gillison, Michael Brownstein, and Emily Carter, whose "Glory Goes and Gets Some" was reprinted in *Best American Short Stories*. Art by Julianne Swartz and Peter Nadin. Poems by David Berman and Nick Tosches. Plus Denis Johnson in Somalia. (A monster issue, sales undercut by slightly rash choice of cover art by editors. Get it while you can! $15)

ISSUE # 4

Change or Die
Stories by David Foster Wallace, Siobhan Reagan, Irvine Welsh. Jerome Badanes' brilliant novella, "Change or Die" (film rights still available). Poems by David Berman and Vito Acconci. Plus Helen Thorpe on the murder of Ireland's most famous female journalist, and Delmore Schwartz on T. S. Eliot's squint. (Still sold-out! Wait for e-books to catch on or band together and demand a reprint.)

ISSUE # 5

CITY back issues

Make an investment in your future...
In today's volatile marketplace
you could do worse.

The Only Woman He's Ever Left

Stories by James Purdy, Jocko Weyland, Strawberry Saroyan. Michael Cunningham's "The Slap of Love." Poems by Rick Moody, Deborah Garrison, Monica Lewinsky, Charlie Smith. Art by Matthew Ritchie, Ellen Harvey, Cindy Stefans. Rem Koolhaas project. With a beautiful cover by Adam Fuss. (Only $10 for this blockbuster.)

ISSUE #6

The Rubbed Away Girl

Stories by Mary Gaitskill, Bliss Broyard, and Sam Lipsyte. Art by Jimmy Raskin, Laura Larson, and Jeff Burton. Poems by David Berman, Elizabeth Macklin, Stephen Malkmus, and Will Oldham. (We found some copies in the back of the closet so were able to lower the price! $25 (it *was* $50))

ISSUE #7

Beautiful to Strangers

Stories by Caitlin O'Connor Creevy, Joyce Johnson, and Amine Wefali, back when her byline was Zaitzeff (now the name of her organic sandwich store at Nassau & John Streets—go there for lunch!). Poems by Harvey Shapiro, Jeffrey Skinner, and Daniil Kharms. Art by David Robbins, Liam Gillick, and Elliott Puckette. Piotr Uklanski's cover is a panoramic view of Queens, shot from the top of the World Trade Center in 1998. ($10)

ISSUE #8

Bewitched

Stories by Jonathan Ames, Said Shirazi, and Sam Lipsyte. Essays by Geoff Dyer and Alexander Chancellor, who hates rabbit. Poems by Chan Marshall, Lucy Anderson, and Edvard Munch on intimate and sensitive subjects. Art by Karen Kilimnick, Giuseppe Penone, Mark Leckey, Maurizio Cattelan, and M.I.M.E. (Oddly enough, our bestselling issue. ($10))

ISSUE #9

Editors' Issue

Previously demure editors publish themselves. Enormous changes at the last minute. Stories by Robert Bingham, Thomas Beller, Daniel Pinchbeck, Joanna Yas, Adrian Dannatt, Kip Kotzen, Geoffrey O' Brien, Lee Smith, Amanda Gersh, and Jocko Weyland. Poems by Tony Torn. Art by Nick Stone, Meghan Gerety, and Alix Lambert. (Years later, Ken Schles's cover photo appears on a Richard Price novel.) ($10)

ISSUE #10

OPEN

Octo Ate Them All
Vestal McIntyre emerges from the slush pile like aphrodite
with a brilliant story that corresponds to the tattoo that
covers his entire back. Siobhan Reagan thinks about
strangulation. Fiction by Melissa Pritchard and Bill Broun.
Anthropologist Michael Taussig's Cocaine Museum. Gregor
von Rezzori's meditation on solitude, sex, and raw meat.
Art by Joanna Kirk, Sebastien de Ganay, and Ena
Swansea. ($10)

Equivocal Landscape
Sam Brumbaugh, author of *Goodbye, Goodness*, debuts with
a story set in Kenya, Daphne Beal and Swamiji, Paula Bomer
sees red on a plane, Heather Larimer hits a dog, and Hunter
Kennedy on the sexual possibilities of Charlottesville versus
West Texas. Ford Madox Ford on the end of fun. Poetry by
Jill Bialosky and Rachel Wetzsteon. Art by Miranda
Lichtenstein and Pieter Schoolwerth; a love scene by Toru
Hayashi. Mungo Thomson passes notes. ($10)

Hi-fi
Sam Lipsyte introduces Steve. Nick Tosches smokes with
God. Jack Walls remembers the gangs of Chicago. Vince
Passaro ponders adult content. Poetry by Honor Moore,
Sarah Gorham, and Melissa Holbrook Pierson. Mini-screen-
play by Terry Southern. Art by Luisa Kazanas, Peter
Pinchbeck, and Julianne Swartz. Special playwrighting sec-
tion guest edited by Tony Torn. ($10)

Something Like Ten Million
The defacto life and death issue. Amazing debut stories
from Nico Baumbach, Michiko Okubo, and Sarah Porter;
Craig Chester writes on why he has the face he deserves;
a bushy, funny, and phallic art project from Louise
Belcourt. Special poetry section guest edited by Lee Ann
Brown. A photo essay of fleeing Manhattanites by Ken
Schles. The cover is beautiful and weird, a bright hole in
downtown Manhattan. ($10)

That Russian Question
Another excerpt from Amine Wefali's *Westchester
Burning (see Open City #8)*. Alicia Erian in *Jeopardy*.
Jocko Weyland does handplants for an audience of elk.
James Lasdun on travel and infidelity. Lara Vapnyar's
debut publication. Poetry by Steve Healy, Daniel Nester,
Lev Rubinshtein, and Daniel Greene. ($10)

CITY

Please send a check or money order payable to:

Open City, Inc.
270 Lafayette Street, Suite 1412
New York, NY 10012

For credit-card orders, see www.opencity.org.

I wait, I wait.
A brilliant outtake from Robert Bingham's *Lightning on the Sun*. Ryan Kenealy on the girl who ran off with the circus; Nick Tosches on Proust. Art by Allen Ruppersberg, David Bunn, Nina Katchadourian, Matthew Higgs, and Matthew Brannon. Stories by Evan Harris, Lewis Robinson, Michael Sledge, and Bruce Jay Friedman. Rick Rofihe feels Marlene. Poetry by Dana Goodyear, Nathaniel Bellows, and Kevin Young. ($10)

ISSUE # 16

They're at it again.
Lara Vapnyar's "There Are Jews in My House," Chuck Kinder on Dagmar. Special poetry section guest edited by Honor Moore, including C. K. Williams, Victoria Redel, Eamon Grennan, and Carolyn Forché. Art by Stu Mead, Christoph Heemann, Jason Fox, Herzog film star Bruno S., and Sophie Toulouse, whose "Sexy Clowns" project has become a "character note for [our] intentions" (says the *Literary Magazine Review*). See what all the fuss is about. ($10)

ISSUE # 17

I Want to Be Your Shoebox
Susan Chamandy on Hannibal's elephants and hockey, Mike Newirth's noirish "Semiprecious." Rachel Blake's "Elephants" (an unintentional elephant theme emerges). Poetry by Catherine Bowman and Rodney Jack. Art by Viggo Mortensen, Alix Lambert, Marcellus Hall, Mark Solotroff, and Alaskan Pipeline polar bear cover by Jason Middlebrook (we're still trying to figure out what the bear had for lunch). ($10)

ISSUE # 18

Post Hoc Ergo Propter Hoc
Stories by Jason Brown, Bryan Charles, Amber Dermont, Luis Jaramillo, Dawn Raffel, Bryan Charles, Nina Shope, and Alicia Erian. Robert Olen Butler's severed heads. Poetry by Jim Harrison, Sarah Gorham, Trevor Dannatt, Matthew Rohrer & Joshua Beckman, and Harvey Shapiro. Art by Bill Adams, Juliana Ellman, Sally Ross, and George Rush. Eerie, illustrated children's story by Rick Rofihe and Thomas Roberston. Saucy cover by Wayne Gonzales. ($10)

ISSUE # 19

Homecoming
"The Egg Man" a novella by Scott Smith, author of *A Simple Plan* (screenplay and book); Ryan Kenealy does God's math; an unpublished essay by Paul Bowles. Stories by Rachel Sherman, Sam Shaw, and Maxine Swann. Art by Shelter Serra, William McCurtin (of *Story of My Scab* and *Elk* fame). Poems by Anthony Roberts, Honor Moore, and David Lehman. ($10)

ISSUE # 20

OPEN CITY
back issues

Ballast
Matthew Zapruder's "The Pajamaist," David Nutt's "Melancholera," fiction by Rachel Sherman, a Nick Tosches poem, Phillip Lopate's "Tea at the Plaza," David A. Fitschen on life on tour as a roadie. Poetry by Matt Miller and Alex Phillips. Art by Molly Smith, Robert Selwyn, Miranda Lichtenstein, Lorenzo Petrantoni, Billy Malone, and M Blash. ($10)

ISSUE #21

Fiction/Nonfiction
A special double-sided issue featuring fiction by Sam Lipsyte, Jerry Stahl, Herbert Gold, Leni Zumas, Matthew Kirby, Jonathan Baumbach, Ann Hillesland, Manuel Gonzales, and Leland Pitts-Gonzales. Nonfiction by Priscilla Becker, Vestal McIntyre, Eric Pape, Jocko Weyland, and Vince Passaro. ($10)

ISSUE #22

Prose by Poets
Prose and poetry by Anne Sexton, Nick Flynn, Jim Harrison, Wayne Koestenbaum, Joe Wenderoth, Glyn Maxwell, Rebecca Wolff, Vijay Seshadri, Jerome Badanes, Deborah Garrison, Jill Bialosky, Cynthia Kraman, Max Blagg, Thorpe Moeckel, Greg Purcell, Rodney Jack, Hadara Bar-Nadav, and Nancy Willard. ($10)

ISSUE #23

SUBSCRIBE

One year (3 issues) for $30; two years (6 issues) for $55.
Add $10/year for Canada & Mexico; $20/year for all other countries.

Please send a check or money order payable to:
Open City, Inc.
270 Lafayette Street, Suite 1412
New York, NY 10012
For credit-card orders, see www.opencity.org

The city has a thousand stories...What's yours?
Tell your New York stories

www.mrbellersneighborhood.com

Attention Teachers:

Mapsites.net is a web based teaching tool that allows students to post historical presentations, personal essays, and creative writing onto an interactive map of their neighborhood.

Mapsites.net is ideal for American History and Urban history courses, as well as English courses in which creative writing or personal essay composition, or even photography, play a role. Any class which encourages students to think about their physical environment in terms of the past or the present could make excellent use of Mapsites.

www.mapsites.net

TWO DOCUMENTARIES

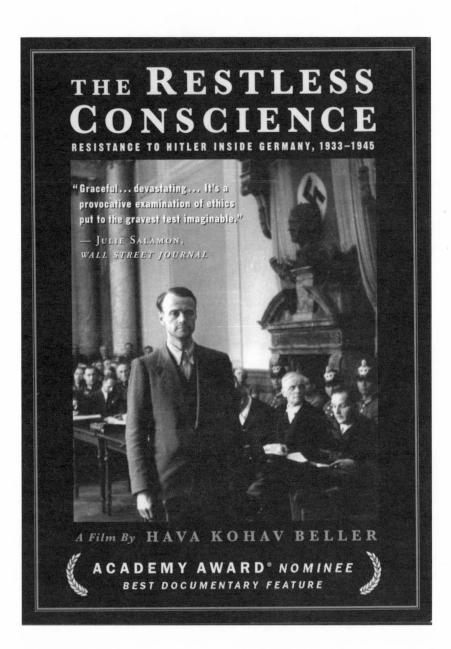

THE **RESTLESS CONSCIENCE**

RESISTANCE TO HITLER INSIDE GERMANY, 1933–1945

"Graceful... devastating... It's a provocative examination of ethics put to the gravest test imaginable."

— JULIE SALAMON,
WALL STREET JOURNAL

A Film By HAVA KOHAV BELLER

ACADEMY AWARD® NOMINEE
BEST DOCUMENTARY FEATURE

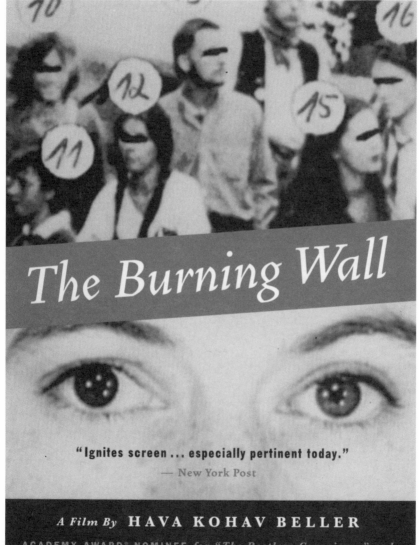

The Burning Wall

"Ignites screen ... especially pertinent today."
— New York Post

A Film By **HAVA KOHAV BELLER**

ACADEMY AWARD° NOMINEE *for "The Restless Conscience" and*
Recipient of THE COMMANDER'S CROSS OF THE ORDER OF MERIT

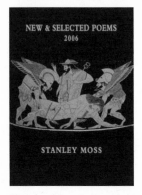

THE SILENCING
Alix Lambert

PERCEVAL PRESS

The Breather

Jeff Johnson

I.

THE ADMIRAL IS KNOWN AS SUCH BECAUSE HE RAN A PONTOON boat full bore into a dock loaded with Cub Scouts ten or fifteen summers ago. It was a humid night, supposedly. Brutally hot. Zero wind. Swarms of mosquitoes. A dense cloud of *something*—I'm terrible at identifying meteorological phenomena—covering the lake.

God only knows what the little pukes were looking for, couldn't have been stars. Some elder stirred them up. Roused them from their tents. Convinced them, possibly, that the willing lips of area trout were puckering for their dangling worms. Rod and reel stuff. I don't have specifics.

What I do know is this: the Admiral had been at McGivern's cottage. Pounding whatever was wet and piney. McGivern's an attorney. The Admiral, something less. The story went he was uninvited. Sweat beading on his forehead. Half the wives repulsed, the other half goading him on. Tiki torches. A punch bowl. The party disbanded. The Admiral pontooning toward a lakeside hamburger stand (closed), or at least attempting to.

Back in the city, before the trial, in one of the Admiral's haunts, a chorus of comrade drunks began cobbling together a defense.

"Why were Cub Scouts on a dock in the first place?"

"That's not scouting. That's fishing."

"On a dock, after dark."

"Doesn't make sense."

"'Course you've heard about the Scouts."

"It's for queers, nowadays."

"I apologize, but *any*thing I've ever done on a dock after dark has not been morally sound."

"A dark dock's where you'd go to, you know, have a kiss, get your penis tugged on or something."

"Or where, if you were a sickening individual, you'd take a group of kids. Who are green about sexual matters. Then you'd talk them. Into letting you. Tug on *their* penises."

"Under the auspices of scouting."

"Or fishing."

"At their age, it doesn't even bring them joy. The Scouts. It brings the penis-tugger. Who is sick in the head. The joy."

"Christ, you're grossing me out."

"It was just probably one big tug session, led by a gay."

"Who lied his way into the scouting game. Moved up the hierarchy. To take overnight field trips. With children."

"And what the *Admiral* did, if we can even call it a crime at this point—"

"Was an intervention. Most likely by a higher figure. A god figure. Along with a pontoon as the vessel. Careening into a dock."

Truth be told, nothing much happened to those Cub Scouts, anyway. Nothing that casts and internal surgical plates couldn't fix. The Admiral got probation. Did the steps. Made the pledges. Raked the library lawn. Proceeded, in due time, to get shithouse drunk again, whenever the impulse struck him. He wound up catching a few more DUIs, sitting in the cooler, walking, eventually, with a few provisions.

We're friends now, sort of. I'll see him out, chugging Windsors and 7-Up. Like none of it ever happened. We all pretend it never happened, even McGivern, sometimes. And when the Admiral's wife calls, he turns to me, and I'll walk out into the parking lot and dutifully blow into the ignition-based sobriety device that will let him start his car, take a stab at driving home. This is what I do. I am a breather.

When my story gets to this point, people have a tendency to grind it right to a halt. Ask if it wouldn't be easier to just call a cab. What I am fairly certain of is, "No." Not with the Admiral, or any of these fuckers. Don't ask me why. They *need* to get in their vehicles. My father was this way, too. Santa Claus could arrive with a sack of authentic moon rocks, and he'd wave him off, throw the car in reverse, and back over a snow hill at the end of the driveway.

Their urge to drive is nothing they can control. Here's an exercise: set a bowl of chocolate pudding down in the middle of a sprawling hardwood floor. Now, set a morbidly obese glutton or a toddler down on that self-same floor. Imagine, momentarily, something else will captivate them beyond that pudding. If you chose Fatty, point to a sack of carrot sticks. If it's Junior—never mind—his face is already in that pudding dish.

That's how bad these people want to drive. Especially when they're wasted.

Now look at me. As much as they want to drive, I want them to drive. Don't tell me what I already know, that I'm just as bad, if not worse. I don't know why I do it. I haven't drank in forever. I have no sympathy for these fellows and their legal woes, nor their health. And no tears, either, for the family in the slow-moving Dodge Caravan that might eventually get sideswiped, and the passengers paralyzed.

Yet something gets me up off my barstool and out into their cars, dome light on, face lowered to my right knee, drunk guy impatiently attempting to balance against the car door as his state-sanctioned sobriety straw finds its way into my mouth. I blow, hop out, watch them make their way out into traffic.

And okay, sometimes I follow.

It's not a sexual fetish. I'm not steering with one hand, pumping my shlong with the other, watching them drift across the yellow line, scuff curbs, decapitate mail boxes. I'm actually seen as a hero to some. To many, in fact. I've had drunks tear up. Do that "We're not worthy" genuflection before sitting down in a bucket seat with a to-go-cup of Myers Rum and Dr. Pepper cradled between their thighs.

The inevitable: at a certain point, a drunk will plow into something substantial and I'll get a phone call. Have to put on a suit, take the stand, get admonished. Or worse.

2.

I live on what was enthusiastically referred to by my real estate agent as a bluff. The house is actually on a slight incline overlooking a service road that runs parallel to one of the major thoroughfares in my city. There are three public high schools in the area, and my home is in the district of the self-consciously second-rate one. Union families. Speedboats, lawn ornaments, driveway hockey nets, frozen hamburger patties.

I moved here after living across town in a similar home with my wife until one day in the summer of 1989, when she told me that I liked cold cuts. This was meant as an insult. We'd long exhausted everything real to fight about and now our battles consisted of reciting benign facts about one another, issued, of course, with pinch-faced repulsion.

Cold cuts signified bad breath, greasy fingers, clogged veins. Who in their right mind would consume them? I couldn't be bothered to formulate a defense, but I didn't shy away from it, either. After all, if we were bickering about snacks, there was an occasion where I discovered Chex Mix in her pubic hair. I didn't get all sanctimonious about that.

There are worse problems in the world. The Chex Mix could have had tiny legs. Could have only been eradicated via medicated shampoo and a special comb. May have arrived courtesy of a salesman named Reynolds who drifted into town from the Pacific Northwest. But, no, there was no evidence of infidelity. Needless to say, however, we packed it in. I treaded in tidal pools of nurse porn and audio books, Westerns mainly.

She taught aspiring lesbians how to garden (better), be less disappointed. We terrorized no children in custody wars. We liquidated our common assets and ceased all communication, save for death notices in the form of voice mails, left when we're certain the other person will not answer the telephone.

"Aunt Phyllis died. In Pensacola. The bird was eighty-seven."

That was the last one. I'd already left it two months prior. But I was lonely. My ex-wife never called back.

I see her sometimes at stoplights. Her glasses have now grown a necklace, that's how old we've gotten. The chain lets them rest near her bosom, which would sag if it were bigger, but it is delicate and small underneath her immaculate cable-knit sweaters. Sometimes she'll wave and when the light changes, accelerate slowly and drive away.

She's not the reason I do this.

I hear from our friends whose kids are finishing college. I dream momentarily, though not frequently anymore, of the family we never started. Thing is, there's a ceiling on the highs in this community, but I've discovered there's no bottom on lows. Why bring a kid into a city like that?

This was fine when we were young newlyweds having fled Chicago, convinced that all we really needed was each other. Nothing would get us. Not even boredom. For many years, I sat at a desk and said "Jerry Sandini" into the telephone when it rang. I provided answers about the most efficient uses of residential energy, according to customers' bills, as well as their location. Once a month I prepared a report for a large corporate meeting. I rarely got to elaborate on my results and my report was part of a larger file that got boiled into a tiny boxed stat on a newsletter.

This was fine until it led to cold cuts and Chex Mix. And blowing into cars.

Last summer I assisted a someone named Kevin. To many, he was known as Sgt. Sucrets—a stocky fellow, late thirties, with an over-grown bleach-blond crew cut. He returned from National Guard duty in Tikrit with an illness that could only be cured by eating cheese curls and washing them down with bar-rail brandy. Sometimes he had visions, sand-blown mind fucks where everyone within earshot could only imagine the original horror that birthed them into existence. Still, despite it all, he had enough sense not to tamper with his Intoxalock. If he did, he'd get jail time.

One night I blow-started his Cressida and crept behind as he ran it along a curb, gently at first, then quickly gaining steam, tires on the passenger side squealing like a duffel bag full of scalded kittens. I tapped my brakes and eased back as he over-corrected and wound up rolling quietly onto a lawn on a sleepy residential street, the car safely bumping up against a tree.

I threw my Civic into park and killed the lights. I left the engine running. I was maybe twenty yards back. I exhaled, mildly relieved for a second. I almost got out of the car, told the sergeant to get the hell out of there. Before we left, I'd made sure he had his seat belt on. He couldn't have been hurt.

I drummed my fingers on the steering wheel for a moment, then decided to go inspect. As I reached to open my door, a light went on inside the house. A figure moved behind a curtain in the kitchen.

Okay, I thought, well, shit.

I waited for the sound of sirens to fill the sky. I shifted into reverse. Sgt. Sucrets's dome light went on. He looked toward the light in the house, then wriggled from his seat belt. Before he could get out, I heard a loud whine. Must be some new cop vehicle, I thought. Then the tree, an ancient elm, toppled onto his car. The windows blew out and rained onto the lawn.

Here was my first real encounter with disaster. I did a Y-turn and floored it.

The cops, at some point, were going to be asking themselves "How?" Not in any broad, philosophical, self-questioning sense. More in terms of specifics. Like, "Who helped this shithead start his car?" Which led to this accident, which led to doctors, expensive stays in a hospital, property damage, calling a guy who drives a pick-up truck to haul in a stump-cutter, wood chippings landing all over sidewalks and lawns.

I made it safely to my garage, tapped the Sears garage door opener twice, listened to the machinery kick into action. I pulled in, killed the engine and literally crawled into the basement, holding my breath.

Day One

Nothing in the papers. No phone calls. Needless to say, I didn't sleep. I'd considered faking abdominal cramps and driving to the emergency room, just to see if Sucrets was there. But the city has two hospitals and if I went to the wrong one, sitting through the paperwork would kill me. If I got it right, and Sucrets was conscious, I feared when he saw me he'd most likely blab. So I stayed home. I was also afraid, truthfully, to see Sucrets toe-tagged, with the figure from the kitchen hovering over his body.

Day Two

Newspaper: Sucrets, war hero, in coma. No mention of his sobriety or lack thereof. No mention of his ignition-breathing device being hotwired. Just a Gulf Vet, tough times.

Day Six

Sucrets=coma.

In my home, in the dark, I began imbibing again. I hadn't for over a decade. I found a bottle of gin on a shelf in the garage next to some 10w30 motor oil, a thin layer of soot collecting around the neck. A few years earlier, I'd held a high school graduation party for the daughter of a coworker on whom I believed I could sustain a crush, if only as a distraction from conspiring with drunks. After the party, I found a few stray bottles tucked in some bushes on the perimeter of my lawn. Turned out the woman's son stashed them there, hoping to retrieve them later. I got to them first and for whatever reason, kept them.

I mixed the gin with crushed frozen raspberries I'd thawed out, feebly, in the microwave. I poured the whole mess into a plastic mug, adorned with the logo of the local college football team.

And waited for my phone to ring.

Day Nine

Gin and oranges. Would they come for me tonight? No. Guests on Jay Leno: Jerry Cantrell. Jenna Elfman. Light sleep.

Day Eleven

Sucrets awake. No reported memory of accident. No mention of device, nor drunkenness. For days I frazzled myself, considering who, if anyone, at the bar that evening would rat me out. Who saw me walk out to the parking lot with Sucrets?

Day Fourteen

Sucrets released from hospital.

Could the tree have mangled the car so terribly that the device was obliterated? If so, surely there were court records indicating that it had at least been installed. I waited for my world to crumble.

Later

Sucrets would not return to the bars. He moved in with an aunt an hour or two south of town, and either cooled down or plagued that community. No one paid me a visit, but I got the suspicion that I was under surveillance. Not one of those paranoid, *I'm-Jesus*-things. Just a feeling.

I found myself sitting in the darkened living room, thatched away from the traffic by conifers of assorted sizes. The only noise? Me chewing pretzel sticks. Rold Golds. The crumbs and salt collecting in the binding of an old *Reader's Digest* I'd look at in an unsuccessful attempt to distract myself.

As headlights of passing cars filtered through the pines, I waited for the pair that would inevitably pull into my U-shaped driveway, carrying people who wanted answers. They never showed up, and I grew tired of resisting my urge to visit the taverns. I slipped on some corduroy loafers and went out to my car.

3.

Months later, I'm following one of my accounts, Mike Trighe, out to the Schooner's parking lot, which is wet with patches of hardened sand-ice. I call people "accounts" for the hell of it. Since the Sucrets incident, I've worked up a steely resolve, stopped drinking, and I'm currently handling three guys with interlock devices. Baby steps. I had to reintroduce myself, basically. Everyone in this city drinks and drives. There's got to be 150 people who have them installed in their cars as a last resort. But I don't keep a ledger. When I die, no one will find a journal of my Greatest Ignition Blows.

So here's Trighe: forty-ish, confident but hapless. Brown hair—what's left of it—blown dry. Booze count: eight Stoli and sodas. Two pony bottles of Rolling Rock. A little weed in the men's can. Has a wife (no fun) and a daughter named Becca, third grader, cheeks of a kid in a commercial for wintergreen anything. She goes around, cheers cancer patients up. This is, honest-to-God, what she considers a good time. Okay, I'm lying, but the thing is, Trighe will never corrupt her.

It's midnight, Tuesday. Trighe and I know each other, but we do this dance where he won't acknowledge me. He knows he's too drunk to drive. But somewhere underneath vodka's fog, he's aware that he eventually has to go home. This gnaws at him, so he tries to drown it with more booze. The clock keeps ticking. He sees that I'm at the bar, at the ready. He understands that I have a gnawing, too. And yet he eludes me, weaves into a crowd near the basketball game on the TV set, Billy Packer's voice.

People are watching this, pretending a Villanova win is a catalyst tangential to future success and happiness in their own lives. I am, seltzer in hand, one of these people. I forget about Trighe for a minute. I see Villanova, barely hovering above .500 for much of the season, taking on water, getting walloped here and there. Then I see a crack in the door. Villanova clawing through it. Creeping into the semi-finals.

So few of us claw anymore, when we see it we appreciate it. When I breathe into a drunk guy's interlock apparatus, I feel like I might be clawing. It feels like something, anyway.

"Now hoops," a sober short guy—a sycophant—yells, nodding toward Trighe, "is something he definitely knows about." Trighe lit up our area college league in the era of the white 6'5" power forward. Actually that describes all of the eras of our area college league. The Magician of Dunks, they called him. He dunked maybe eight times in four years. A local appliance store used his image, briefly, to hawk stereos when he graduated, and a Turkish league team sent him a plane ticket. It ended up round-trip.

The ball goes off a player's knee out of bounds. "They gonna hang on, Triggsy?" the short guy wants to know.

Trighe shrugs.

"He don't wanna talk about it," an older fan says, authoritatively. "Respect that."

"Aw, he doesn't know shit," adds a young bitter skinny drunk guy whose hair is spidering out the back of his baseball cap. He turns toward the TV, stabs an index finger at it.

"No!" the short guy shouts, spooked by the young guy's opinion.

Trighe opens his mouth, closes his eyes, as if fighting off pain. "People don't get what I went through. And I don't feel like bragging."

"Dude," the bitter TV finger-stabber says, "When you talk about your collegiate basketball career, it ain't bragging. It's, like, just listing prerequisites for selling insurance."

Someone laughs. Someone else shushes them all.

Besides rooting with everyone for Villanova, I am also one of the people who raises his hand when bar manager Rick asks, hypothetically, if daytime bartender Tina (absent), were providing oral tribute on the roof in subzero weather would we wait in line? I raise my hand for waiting in line thirty minutes, one hour, ninety minutes. At two hours, I stop raising my hand. Hypothetical or not, I'm done with it. I'm also done with Villanova. It's in Pennsylvania. I've never been.

They win anyway.

Trighe raises his hand for something else. Another drink. He wiggles his fingers at Rick, postponing the inevitable. I set down my seltzer and approach.

"Let's get moving, champ," I say, patting him gently on the back.

"Huh?" He looks at me crazy eyed. I nod toward the door. Do a steering wheel motion with my hands. People laugh.

Trighe's embarrassed, so he takes it out on me.

"No, I won't French kiss you in the men's can!" He yells, lamely. When he says, "kiss" he turns to face the other patrons, letting them in on his disgust.

"I'm not here to kiss you, Trighe."

"Oh, okay," he says sarcastically, scans the room for a response.

"Come on, asshole."

"Oh really?" He says, raising an eyebrow. Hamming it up. "You're into women nowadays, eh? What do you go for? The tits? Or the ass?"

"Listen," I say. "Why choose? I'm not a city planner. It's all in the budget."

Over our shoulder is the Norwegian. He's Russian. But we're all descendents of Scandinavia, so somehow he's become the Norwegian. The way most of us see it, he got roped into marriage. Sure he probably wanted the Green Card. But that meant marrying his Internet ingénue, Kathy Tenchy, local porker. Does receptionry at one of the local siding outfits. Wears pocketless purple pants that stretch to accommodate her flan binges. She used to join him, booze it up. She went from hermit to sex goddess and now she's a hermit again. He comes out and drinks, and plots, presumably, his escape.

We rallied around the Norwegian at first. He was unique. A novelty. No one called him a Commie. They asked him about the Russian mob. Breshnev's eyebrows. Boris and Natasha. Then he started reveling in it, insulting our well vodkas. Our bar snacks. So now he gets abused. Titty twisters. He goes to the bathroom, people drink his drink. Make him buy them a drink and then leave before the favor is returned. In the old country, he was a professor. Did elaborate poeming. Captivated an audience dissecting Solzhenitsyn texts. Here he works in a lumber yard, fucks a fat, mediocre American, and finds no relief at the tavern.

Right now, a couple of guys are playing keep away with his wallet. The Norwegian is well into his thirties and carries a Velcro wallet with a surfer on it. I wonder if that was his American dream. Surfing. Seems sort of cliché, or off, maybe, for a man of his intellect to get worked up about Jan and Dean. Besides, there's snow on the ground here about seven months of the year. The only waves are made by the Admiral's pontoon boat. Maybe Kathy Tenchy bought it for him.

"Faggot's ass," he yells, pawing hopelessly in the direction of the wallet. He slaps an empty palm on the Formica bar. We've coarsened him. Only his slang's wrong. "Give it back, Shit in Your Brains."

I join him as the pig in the middle. Do a two-inch leap at the right moment and intercept the wallet. Return it to him. Turn back toward Trighe.

"Oh, hey there," he says, smiles.

"We were talking business," I reply.

For the moment, he's done pretending he doesn't know me. Again. He's wearing a new sweater. Striped number. Christmas present, probably. He belches and some marijuana smoke escapes.

"Sorry."

"I don't care."

"I don't normally smoke pot," he explains, thumbs over his shoulder toward the bathrooms.

"I'm not judging."

"Well, I know you're in with the, like, the community and stuff."

"Trighe, I start your car when you're fucked up."

"Yeah," he agrees, "but you have clout around here."

Two guys jut past us, bickering.

"Don, they live in a house with an old sink," the craggy-faced one says. "No one wants to live in a house with an old sink."

"You live in a house with an old sink, Glen," his handsomer pal reminds him, punctuating the statement by waving his drink. They move on.

"Trighe," I say. "I only worked for the power company. Now I'm retired."

"Oh," he says, raises his eyebrows, like he doesn't already know this. "Cool, man. Sounds like a good job."

"It was okay," I say. "The pension's nice."

"Hmm," Trighe says. He then adds, "Well, it doesn't impair my driving," nodding toward the bathroom, meaning the weed. "It helps, almost." He takes a quick, unsure step toward the door, the parking lot. "Wanna go out there?"

"Sure," I say. "Let's get this over with."

I start his car, a white Chevrolet Caprice. Looks like a cop car. There's an ABA basketball in the backseat. I flip the heater on as a courtesy. Throw my legs out, steady myself to avoid the ice. Then stand up. Trighe looks in, one arm on the door, and one on the roof. He considers the dashboard, like a camper would a newly pitched tent.

"Trighe," I say. "I know it's cold, but maybe turn the heat down when you get going. I don't want you zonking out on the way home."

"Phaaaah," he shakes his head like I'm bonkers. He plops his ass down on the driver's seat. His feet still on the ground. He looks up at me.

"So what do you think," Trighe asks. "Should I be driving?"

"You're fine," I say.

4.

The Admiral had a daughter once upon a time. Moved to Chicago to get away from the guy and his booze-parenting. Had two kids. A husband that turned out to be the Admiral 2.0. She left the guy, dragged the kids back to her hometown when the Admiral's liver went south. Kids, no matter what you put them through, crawl back to you. I don't know from experience. Just the movies.

The daughter ends up waitressing at night. A childhood friend who never left town watches her kids for her. She drives home alone after midnight. Maybe picks up her boyfriend.

This is not my epiphany.

5.

I follow Trighe. The snow is swirling around our cars. Like little stars. Our own galaxy. He weaves a little. Brakes late at a stop sign. Misses another one completely, but there are miraculously no cops. We wind up in front of his house. Mission accomplished, I think. My heart does no palpitations. No butterflies in my stomach. But I see exhaust still pluming from his tailpipe.

A babysitter materializes at Trighe's front door. She mouths something to Trighe, waves her arms. No wife in sight. Maybe no wife anymore.

Trighe steps out of the car. Wobbles backward one step, corrects himself. He shakes his head at the sitter. She puts her hands on her hips. She goes back inside the house. He follows. Pretty soon she's walking out the front door. Stomping away from the house in the cold. Pouting.

I start to pull ahead. Does she need a ride? I'll be a good Samaritan. I was one in the old days. But wait. Am I a perv? Who's going to take a ride from me? Why would I even be here? I stop. Trighe exits the house with Becca wrapped in an afghan, sleeping. He deposits her in the back bench seat of his car. Now I get the palpitations. Trighe pulls away from the curb. I follow.

He lassos the babysitter. Pulls out again. A little head materializes in the back window. Trighe weaves onto a busier street. But it's not busier. It's dead. The babysitter looks back at the head, smiles. So does Trighe, the snow now audibly slushing up into our wheel wells. He looks back for far too long. I can see the babysitter pinching at his sleeve once, twice.

6.

Trighe is in shock, probably. He emerges from the cloud of his passenger side air bag, crawls out of the car. The freeze of the night air snaps at him. Maybe sobers him momentarily. He inspects the other car. He sees blood. Compound fractures. Some as yet unnamed instinct compels him to pull the plates off of the victim's vehicle. He takes the woman and her male passenger's IDs. Their cell phones.

The Magician of Dunks.

He throws them in his backseat. Then he takes their phones out and throws them toward the trees across the street. He takes Becca out, she doesn't appear to be in too bad of shape. He leaves her on the curb, wrapped in the blanket. He returns to his car. The sitter is crumpled. He struggles to get her out of the car. I hear the rumble of a snow plow off in the distance. It's the only real noise I can make out. He drags her to the curb. Takes her purse. Throws it in his front seat.

The guy from the car he hit rises, staggers in Trighe's direction. Begs him to stop. Falls over. Paws Trighe's legs. Trighe steps out of the man's arms, waves the guy off. Gets into what's left of his car. I hear

him turn the ignition over, but it won't start. I wonder if it's the damage, or if he needs a blow. I look at the man in the street, dissolving.
I hear the plow off in the distance. I look at Trighe inside of his car,
door hanging open. I think of being tucked behind those pine trees
in my front lawn last summer, waiting for whoever never showed up.
And then I throw my hazards on, and slowly get out of my car.

Loss Prevention

James Hannaham

LAMBERT'S WAS THE LESSER OF TWO ANCHOR STORES AT AN outdoor mall, a hulking postwar vision of prosperity graced with a sandstone façade. Big cracks traveled across the front like interstates. Even so, walking toward it that first day, as the walls threw off sparks of morning sun, Art felt Lambert's had the splendor of an Egyptian tomb—well, maybe one from a movie. Inside, the place smelled strongly of perfume and new suits.

As he made his way to the security office, he heard some clerks in makeup mumbling secretively, at the same volume as the Muzak. "Investigation," one whispered. "Another job," said someone else. But he couldn't hear enough to make sense of the conversation, not above the noise of his nervous pride. He'd joined a harm-reduction group, cut way down on alcohol for what he hoped was the last time, found employment, and—I'll be damned!—a family member got in touch out of the blue after what, thirty years? Virginia, his aunt, had left a phone message. It warmed him to know that they'd kept his number. All this was enough to make him think that maybe the Lord was really out there, really giving a crap.

That morning, he couldn't help weighing the Art of four months ago—penniless, passed out in the snow by his doorstep—against the Art of today, strolling into an actual job, hardly missing a step but for his bunion. What he couldn't bear to do was weigh today's Art against the one from back then, whose sister Angie was murdered the night he left her behind at a club and ran off—drunk, of course—with a strange woman. Or even the Art of ten years ago, cut dead by the family, drinking harder despite the guilt (or because of it), divorced, alone, a hollowed-out garbage man at a public middle school. At fifty-five, he could have wept at how much he'd been through to get nowhere. Sometimes he thought he was depressed, but black people didn't get depressed, they just carried on. Depression was a luxury.

Art expected some kind of orientation meeting, but the store's management had a laissez-faire attitude. Nathan—the big boss of the LP department—shoved a manual at him, really a few photocopies stuck in a plastic binder, showed him the closed-circuit TVs on each floor, and left him alone. "Today you'll be at the women's department monitors," he said. "Sometimes you'll be on the floor."

"I've spent plenty of time on the floor," Art said. Nathan frowned and let the joke droop.

He led Art to a door. Plastic letters on the frosted glass read, LOS PREVENTION OF ICE. The room, about ten feet square, was equipped with two office chairs and a console with nine smoke-blue screens. One of the nine displayed only sharp stripes. Another showed endless grayness, like a rebroadcast of the moon landing. The odor of synthetic carpet filled Art's head. He sat down in a torn office chair and it creaked.

The manual suggested watching for "fake yawns" and "bags from faraway stores." But Art was farsighted—he couldn't see details on the CCTVs. He frisked himself for his glasses, which were on his nightstand. For the whole day, whenever he suspected a customer of boosting, he'd have to memorize a pattern in their clothing, their walk, or haircut, then roam through the department trying to look inconspicuous. He kept stopping innocent shoppers. One woman's son cried.

Not long after that, Gunsel plopped himself down in women's. Gunsel was a 320-pound former cop and high school wrestler who swung his chest around like the cab of a crane. Before even asking Art's name, he summed up the job. "There are more klepto-junkies in this joint than regular customers," he said. It wasn't a total exaggeration. "He's gotta get out of here before things get putrid."

"Who's *he?*" Art asked.

"Fuck you," Gunsel spat back. No one explained it for a while, but Gunsel had a brain problem where he couldn't talk about himself in the first person.

That night Art got ahold of Aunt Virginia. She was actually a few months younger than Art, the love child of an affair their grandfather had with a nurse. The family accepted her by ignoring that history. Virginia was moving from Jacksonville with her husband, Pooka, and their three sons to be closer to Pooka's sick mom. It turned out the landlord had a unit available in another three-family house nearby. If you craned your head out Art's kitchen window, you could see it diagonally across the small parking lot out back.

"It's been too long, Artie," she said.

"I've *tried* to get back in touch," Art began, but the dark waters of guilt and rage rose in his blood, and he couldn't say more. Everything led back to the scene his mother made at Angie's funeral, pointing and bellowing at him, saying he was the Devil. Without a suspect, Art caught the leading edge of the blame.

"It's wonderful to see you. I almost wouldn't have recognized you." He helped haul her family's belongings up the stairs, while Virginia told him the basics about everyone down in Jacksonville— Carlene, his mom, was still alive, though it was tough going with the arthritis, Daddy Ray too, with his angioplasties, but Grandma Hudson had gone, of Alzheimer's and old age. They'd sold the hardware store, retired, cut down the mimosa tree, and painted the house sea green. So much time had been lost, more time than it even felt like, that once he and Pooka and his sons heaved the couch up the staircase, Art was breathless and heartbroken. Counting all of his regrets, it took him hours to fall asleep that night. Even the small ones seemed to weigh as much the big one. Angie, he hoped, had to have forgiven him, if forgiveness could leak from the grave. The dead did not seem to hold grudges. But she was the only one—until now.

Art got into the habit of leaving his glasses by the door so he wouldn't forget them on the way to work. One slow day the next week, he made four apps and recovered $512 in merch. But he also saw one of the checkout girls, Yolanda, bring four blouses to her sister Sandy's line. She flopped the shirts into a bag and the number .50 appeared in the display. Sandy saw him watching and sneered at him like he was dog shit. "Don't fraternize with coworkers," the manual warned. "One day you might have to turn them in."

Then Art began to spot countless acts of employee theft. Lipsticks discreetly slipped into pockets. Pants pulled on over pants. Boxes of denim shirts chucked into dumpsters and recovered after hours. Snacks unshelved and devoured. Tag-switchings and underchargings galore. Eleven compact discs given away for a penny by a cashier nicknamed "Columbia House." Multiple unauthorized security tag removals followed by loading-dock heists. Snack bar boys lifting mannequin parts into vans with tinted windows. Sneakers sneaked.

He thought he ought to rat, but if he turned in everyone he'd seen lifting, Lambert's would lose three-quarters of its staff. Maybe he'd have to pocket some merch just to fit in. Bonuses for busting co-workers were five dollars higher, but no one was fool enough to reach out for that poisoned carrot. Everyone hated a sellout.

Fall came, and the infestations started. Thieves would form small groups and enter the department store individually. A veteran who recognized all the LP agents would lift stuff out in the open, so they would trail him, a decoy. He'd stroll around the departments, loading his pockets with expensive items, while his minions nabbed larger amounts of less closely guarded merch. The ringleader would drop the loot in "blind spots" where security cameras didn't penetrate, or outfox whoever tailed him. He'd leave the store with several agents on his case. When they made the app, he would be clean. At that moment, the other four would leave the franchise. By then it wouldn't matter if they tripped the security gate. For some reason, Lambert's always stationed nervous Cora at the exit. She moonlighted as a kindergarten teacher's aide, and wouldn't run after one perp, let alone four offenders fanning out in all directions.

Gunsel detested group hits more than any other criminal activity. The notion of supersized shoplifting gnawed at the taproot of his belief system. He'd come up with the term infestation. Naturally, a perp from a group hit was called a roach. Infestations left Gunsel empty-handed and humiliated at the moment he lived for. But what steamed him most was that they always succeeded.

A disgruntled former employee returned one afternoon with a gang of schoolgirls and lifted almost a hundred pairs of jeans.

Afterward, Gunsel paced on the concrete curb between Lambert's front doors and the asphalt. He slapped his palms against his thighs and panted, his forehead rippling. "He swears to God he's gonna find a way to stop these damn roaches."

The infestation had taken place early enough in the day that instead of becoming discouraged, Art decided to make up for it. He set his two-month app record that afternoon—a whole lot of non-shoppers piled in for the holiday sales. With a twenty dollar bonus per stop, Art went home in high spirits. Instead of the usual wings and rice with hot sauce, he ordered moo shu pork from around the corner and slipped *Brown Sugar 5: Anal Angels* out of its tattered case.

The doorbell rang. Art slid the tape under the couch and readied a twenty to pay the deliveryman. But when he opened the door, his Aunt Virginia stood there, scraping her feet against the welcome mat. Lately, when Art saw Virginia taking out the trash or pinning clothes to her line, she'd say, "I'm gonna make dinner for you!" But she worked at a Tookie's restaurant now, so she never cooked, she just brought food home, and the dinner never happened. As he swung the door open it came to him that he needed her to tell him exactly what his parents said about him.

"How did you know what I was looking for?" Virginia said, tugging his twenty dollar bill.

She accepted a beer, sat, and arranged her housecoat to balance the bottle between her legs on the chair. For a while, she picked nervously at the strip of Formica hanging off the counter. Art whistled something like "Turkey in the Straw" while he searched for a bottle opener.

"You seem happy," she said, almost resentfully. "What's wrong, Artie?"

Art described his new job in enough detail to bore himself. He recounted how the group hit had inspired him to put extra effort into nabbing perps that afternoon. The best, he said, was stopping a Rastafarian who'd hid a box of apricot body scrub in her knit hat. Eleven apps meant a $220 bonus added to his paycheck, almost doubling it. "Notice I ain't having a beer," he announced. While he spoke, Virginia held out her hand and he dropped the twenty in her palm, as if by autosuggestion. "Congratulations," she said.

The food arrived. It turned out that moo shoo pork was Virginia's favorite, too, so Art offered to share. He pretended not to mind her smoking while they ate and let her ash in the green cut-glass bowl his ex-wife had left behind. As they rolled tubes of shredded vegetables, Art answered Virginia's questions about his job.

"They don't need more agents, do they?" she asked. "'Cause it's only been three months and I have took about all I can from Tookie's."

She regaled him with a true story about a home-care attendant jailed for poisoning her charge's salad, thanked Art for everything, and went upstairs. He promised her he'd ask Nathan whether they were hiring.

"Do you talk to Mama and Dad?" He asked.

"Uhh, sometimes-ish." She gave him a timid look that said, don't pry. "Why?"

"Do they know you're in touch with me?"

"Sort of, I guess."

"Did you tell them?"

By now Virginia was concentrating hard on arranging vegetables and sliced pork on the pancake and drizzling brown sauce on it. She said, "Mph," but to Art it sounded right between yes, no, and a bite of food.

He nodded anyway. "Give them my best, okay?"

She said, "Mph" again.

On Lincoln's Birthday, Milla, a coworker from Russia, came in from her break with a newspaper. She pointed to an item crushed into the corner of page twenty-three, announcing that Lambert's had gone bankrupt. Management made no internal announcement. Instead, apparently homosexual men from the display department appeared everywhere, unrolling yellow sale banners, including one readable from the highway.

"We're toast," Gunsel said. "They don't need LP for a liquidation. Shoplifters will be doing them a favor. He should have quit a long time ago."

Lincoln's Birthday was also the day that Virginia came in to apply. When Art spoke to HR on Tuesday, they assured him that Lambert's was "on the up-and-up." "By all means, have her come in," Sonia said.

Virginia found Art in electronics after the interview. In a business suit with a periwinkle ruffle at the neck, she looked like her dream of a future self, except for the fresh scab indenting her upper lip. Art thought someone had donated the dress; it wasn't her. The cherry lipstick said "fuck me" too strongly. To their right, fifty television sets showed fifty innovative feather dusters sweeping through Venetian blinds.

"It went real well," she said with a bashful smile, raising her crossed fingers. "So we'll see . . ." Behind her, Art watched two guys with a ladder unfurl a yellow banner. Virginia pointed to it and squinched her face as he showed her out. "Oh, don't take that serious," he said.

Immediately he stopped in at HR to ask why they'd led her on. Sonia said management had not given them any directive so they couldn't have warned her, and did he know she had a felony on her record anyway? How she had concealed that from him Sonia didn't know. Art could only argue, childishly, that it wasn't fair.

By the next week, everyone had heard. Clerks worked overtime marking items down and dollying stock onto shelves. Customers flocked like hungry buzzards. These were the same people, Milla pointed out, whose absence had put the store out of business. "Where they are at when we need them?" she asked. She let her hands fall to her skirt and shrugged. "At better department store."

Employees and thieves alike stepped up the crime. Someone ripped off a patio table. Wheelbarrows, lawnmowers, and home-entertainment centers disappeared. Shoplifters returned stolen items for store credit. Some cocky bastard walked off with a cash register.

Tacitly the clerks stopped arranging the shelves, and randomness set in. Whole clothing departments emptied out except for orange pants sized XXL and up. Naked mannequins toppled over as if to bless the decadence. You never knew when you would stumble over their disembodied torsos, their severed legs. The slackness gave boosters an incentive, and everyone's stops per day soared. Cora even made an app. Infestations raged. Management blocked off the upstairs exit after a boost involving eight perps and several departments. "Liquidation is like little war," Milla declared.

Gunsel decided to work double shifts so he'd have money while he looked for a job once the store closed, but he'd underestimated his tolerance for long hours and high perp volume. The deep rasp of his voice turned squawky from barking at boosters. Once, during a busy Saturday, Art saw Gunsel throttle a shoplifter in menswear with one of the ties he'd lifted, *before* the guy left the store. According to the manual, the LP agent had to "observe the suspect in the act of not paying."

It wouldn't do any good to report Gunsel's misconduct to Nathan. Nathan starched his shirts. He took pride in putting the guy to use, the way a trainer prizes a vicious dog. Nathan would have let you criticize his wife's looks before Gunsel's behavior. "He's a good egg," Nathan said. "I wonder why he quit the force."

"Gunsel," Art asked on a freezing, blank afternoon when they'd been assigned to menswear, "What's up? Why you on the warpath, brother?" Between them, two or three gray suits hung on the racks like sleeping pigeons.

"Some roach pulled a knife on him," Gunsel grunted. "Ain't no way he's gonna bite it in a second-rate, bankrupt outlet with pinheads picking skippies out the bins. Fuck that." Unlike Gunsel, Art didn't always cuff a booster during a stop. These people had to be desperate, so why humiliate them? Desperation was punishment enough. Art remembered being handcuffed four months ago, after passing out in front of his apartment with his pants at his ankles and his keys in his hands, and shook his head.

"Why you need to get like that? Can't no shoplifter I ever seen in this joint take you down." He touched Gunsel's massive shoulder but it immediately felt like a mistake. Gunsel stepped back and met his eyes.

"Is he gonna protect himself so they can't pull nothing? You know it. Is it inhumane to do that? No. Would it be stupid for him to do anything else? Damn right."

A few yards away, one of the problem lights in the drop ceiling finally flickered out. Due to cost cutting, it would stay broken.

Every evening she had off, Virginia would come over and ask Art if he had talked to Sonia and what she said. He would tell her he hadn't heard; that they'd get in touch with her first anyway. "We're two rents behind," she'd say. "Contractors won't hire Pooka. He did his time, why he gotta pay for it the rest of his life? Ain't no second chances in this damn world." No second chances put Art in mind of his ex-wife, and his sister, and he longed for the sweet burn of a straight Scotch.

Art would palm Virginia forty, then sixty. Three apps worth. He thought of her now when he made stops. He decided that she was obligated to tell him exactly how his parents spoke about him, no matter how bad. How could they have held on to their anger for so long? Didn't people get more merciful as they got older, knowing they could give the gift of closure?

When she came by, he'd say he was having a microwave fettuccine, did she want one? They were just like the Olive Garden. The laundry, Virginia would say, or the kids, or I brought Tookieburgers. "Wasn't it fun that time with the moo shoo?" he'd ask. "Yeah," she'd say, "We oughta do it again." Then she'd let the screen door slam. In a week or two, she must have figured out about Lambert's. She stopped dropping in.

Nathan put Art and Gunsel together in housewares on a Saturday afternoon two weeks before the official closing. Housewares was on three. On the second floor, juniors and kids had been completely cleaned out, their display racks packed up and overhead lighting turned off. Unofficially, management gave salesclerks the authority to haggle.

Gunsel protected even the dwindling, chintzy merch with the ferocity of a Marine. Watching him concentrate, Art couldn't help thinking that he was tuned to some wavelength on which LP wasn't a hopeless cause but an undercover battle for the soul of mankind. Gunsel only read comic books, so he probably thought of his job in terms of myths and superheroes. He claimed he could see the evil auras of future criminals clearly, of course, and he encouraged Art to try. The auras were supposed to be reddish.

During a long lull between shoplifters, Gunsel half-awoke from his meditative state and decided to quiz Art. "Come look at this, Artie," he commanded, a researcher's chill in his voice. He pointed to a bat-like shape moving diagonally through the lower right hand corner of the second CCTV from the bottom right. "Can you see a halo? What color is it?" The security cameras on three were in notoriously bad focus, and he'd forgotten his glasses that day.

Art couldn't tell if his bad eyesight was tricking him. He replied that he could make out a pale pink corona surrounding the figure. He only said it to humor Gunsel. Nothing on those monitors had ever looked pink.

"The TV distorts it," he said, rising from his chair. "Let's go out on the floor. Bet it's red." Maybe the video camera was broken. Maybe Art was getting cataracts. He decided to keep his mouth shut.

As they headed onto the floor, Gunsel reached toward the small of his back, under his shirt, and adjusted his belt. He stopped at the door, waiting for Art to catch up. Art passed and Gunsel sneered at his shoes. "The fuck you thinking, old man? The only thing you'll catch wearing loafers is a cold. Knucklehead."

A crescendo of soft rock music hit them as they reached the department. A treacly oldie, vetoed as a wedding song by Art's ex, hit its chorus. Ahead now, Art heard a clinking sound accompanying Gunsel's gait. He'd brought hardware from home. Art turned when he noticed the sound and Gunsel somehow knew why. "No more Mr. Nice Guy with the namby-pamby plastic bracelets," he said. "And if Lambert's doesn't agree, he'll go it alone. He do not care." Art wanted to point out that it might make him conspicuous, but Gunsel had fastened the cuffs inside his pockets and concealed them with a jacket so that the average shopper would confuse their jingling for an overloaded keychain.

"You got any extra?" Art asked, joking that Gunsel's way might make more sense in the long run. Gunsel raised a corner of his mouth and let out a breath.

Art and Gunsel headed toward the baking supplies, where the potential criminal had been lingering near a stack of Pyrex casserole dishes.

Before they discovered their mark, they spent a few minutes walking separately up and down the aisles. As he passed through the vacuum cleaner section, Art brushed past a teenager and paused to watch him fumble with hose attachments.

"Moke?" he said, just loud enough to be heard, hoping he was mistaken. Instead, the kid raised his chin toward him and smiled. Moke was Virginia's youngest, not quite fourteen. The two made vacuum cleaner chit-chat while Art continued to search for the suspects over his shoulder. Art excused himself to find Virginia and apologize about the job interview. Moke told him that she'd gone to look at doormats, so Art moved backward in that direction.

Art didn't see Virginia anywhere near the stack of "Home Sweet Home" and "Welcome" mats. He couldn't find her or Gunsel in housewares, though he combed the aisles twice. He didn't bother with the deserted second floor.

As he rode the jerky escalator to one, he spotted Virginia in women's. She moved toward the exit, following the wall closely, plucking swimsuits from hangers like tropical fruit and dropping them into a Henri Bendel bag. She paid no attention to what she lifted, watching instead to make sure that no one saw. Behind her, a transparent mannequin wearing only a bikini top stared apathetically into the distance. Oh no, he thought. "To establish probable cause," said the manual, "You must see the shoplifter conceal, carry away, or convert the merchandise."

Gunsel had positioned himself at her rear left, about thirty yards away, by one of the clearance racks still stocked with a few pairs of no-name jeans. Art paced down the escalator stairs without breaking into a run. If he could get to her before Gunsel, he might be able to avert a disaster.

Virginia glanced at her wristwatch. Her slink toward the exit accelerated. Gunsel's pretend shopping became more agitated, less believable. He moved low and sideways to keep up with her, remaining hidden, then crossed the walkway into perfume.

Art reached the ground floor and stepped toward ladies' swimwear. He negotiated around a pile of plastic hangers and found Virginia, her features now blurred in his irises. She had unwittingly avoided Gunsel by walking in front of a high shelf that had once held dozens of boxes containing powder-blue sport bras.

"Hey Artie," she said. "I saw you over there but I know I'm not supposed to bother you while you're working." He leaned back so that her face came into focus. He squinted into her bag and spotted a colorful blur there. She smiled and flipped through the near-empty sale racks.

"What are you doing, Virginia?"

"Shopping. What do it look like?"

"Something else." He attempted to grab the handle from her but his reflexes failed him and she yanked it out of the way.

"That ain't from here," she protested.

"The nearest Henri Bendel is in Manhattan."

"So? I just been downtown."

"Put them back," he said firmly.

"Artie, has you lost your mind? I'm about to get insulted."

At that moment, Art saw Nathan strolling down the strip of terrazzo that led to the escalator and remembered that he and Gunsel had left their posts at the Housewares monitors. He tried to angle himself so that Nathan would not notice him, but the boss took a detour around a display case of scarves and sidled up behind Art, back-to-back, to question him. On the floor Nathan always took care to maintain the illusion that LP agents were regular shoppers.

"Where are you supposed to be, Art? It's not women's, is it? You always say you're embarrassed to patrol in women's."

Art didn't answer.

"We caught some clown downstairs trying to walk out with a spoon holder down his pants. So I'm thinking someone is sleeping up in housewares. I get to the monitors and where is everybody?"

Art continued to not answer. He couldn't let Virginia out of his sight. As the manual said, "The agent must observe the shoplifter continually."

"I'll talk to you later, Artie," Virginia said. "Sound like you got to go."

Nathan stood and waited for Art to start the journey upstairs to the monitor room before going in search of Gunsel.

Back in the tiny room, Art had to stand back from the monitor to make out what was happening. As the CCTVs flipped through various angles, he thought he could see Gunsel disappear among the mirrors, bright lights, and angular paths in cosmetics. A blurry Virginia seemed to move toward the wall. She lowered her center of gravity slightly, hoping to avoid detection by the cameras. She paused and disappeared behind a pile of leftover Christmas sweaters.

It didn't take him long to decide that his job was not worth rescuing. Soon it would not exist. He could fudge the reason for leaving on the next round of applications. No one called references. If I really think I'm useless, he thought, why did I get sober? He stood up, left the room, and tripped down the escalator, watching for Nathan. He arrived by the door in time to see Virginia leave the building and break into a trot.

Cora hadn't noticed. Without tripping the alarm, Art's aunt made it through the vestibule and tore off across the parking lot, dodging a van as it backed out. Gunsel leapt after her, not so much running as pushing the world behind him with his feet. Catching daylight, the reflective patches on his heels flashed in Art's eyes as he pursued.

Gunsel pounced on Virginia with both hands. She writhed like a caught marlin and hollered her innocence to the shopping public. Gunsel reached for his handcuffs while grasping her wrist, but Virginia wriggled away from him. He grabbed her shirt and pulled her back, then hooked his elbow around her neck. Art caught up to them, yelling, "Hold up! Hold up!" Gunsel fumbled with the cuffs, but the clasps kept slipping. It had been a long time since his days as a Detroit cop.

A suspension bridge of tendons appeared in Gunsel's neck, and his color changed to brick. "Artie, you dumbass," he rasped, "You're supposed to be looking behind you!"

Art turned to see two of Virginia's sons, each carrying a large bag, bolt from the front entrance. They set off in opposite directions. Cora toddled out after them. "Boys, don't do this!" she called. "Think about your education!"

Confused by the melee, Art stepped forward to start running after Moke, then took a step back, thinking that chubby Roland couldn't run as fast. But that gave Roland a head start. He called after them to stop, reassuring them that he wouldn't press charges if they just returned the merchandise. He chased Roland, but Pooka and Calvin had a van idling. One of Art's loafers fell off. The asphalt dug into the tender parts of his foot and slowed him down. Roland leapt into the van and it sped off.

Art turned back to help Gunsel in time to see Virginia bite his forearm. The gargantuan LP agent dropped the handcuffs and loosened his grip, growling curses. In his wounded moment, Virginia pulled away. Gunsel bent down, snatched up the cuffs, and after a short pursuit, caught her again by the waist. Gunsel attached one cuff to his wrist. He took hold of her arm, pulling it toward the ring. Virginia turned and slashed him across the eyes with her house keys. She squirmed out from under his grip and sidestepped between the cars. Art circled around a car and tried to get hold of her, but Virginia lifted a knee. He turned sideways to avoid her. She stuck her hands in his face, pushed him off balance, and ran. "Sorry, Artie!" she yelled, without looking back. Virginia ducked around an SUV and scrambled up an embankment at the edge of the parking lot.

The perp had dropped her bag. Crumpled sheets of wrapping paper wafted out, but otherwise it was empty.

In the scuffle, Gunsel's shirt had come untucked, revealing the glock behind his belt.

"How is it you carrying a piece?" Art exclaimed.

"How is it she know your name?" Gunsel asked. He shoved his shirt into his pants and dabbed the bloody toothmarks on his arm with a napkin. "She your bitch?"

"That wasn't my name," Art said.

Gunsel leaned into his face. "That's bullshit, Artie. You're a fucking roach!"

Stepping back became more important than explaining. Art kept stepping back until he felt safe, and by then he was inside the store.

Three days before Lambert's would close its doors forever, Nathan called a meeting before opening. Everyone staked out a bit of territory in the conference room, clutching a cup of tepid snack bar coffee. With so few chairs, most agents had to stand against the pink drywall. A few had arrived on time, including Milla and Art, so they waited for the rest to show up.

Milla drank tea and pored over the *Novaya Russkaya Slovo*. When a new person arrived, she would say, "They're going to fire us," with a dry certainty that surprised some of them. A hushed debate began among the LP agents.

Nathan took his place at the head of the table and skimmed his hands across the wood sheen of the table. From his unusually sad expression and inability to make eye contact with anyone, the whole room believed that Milla had guessed right.

"Recently it came to my attention that one of our agents was carrying a firearm," he said. "As you should all know, the use or possession of weapons is against company policy. The manual states this very clearly." He scanned the attendees as if to make eye contact with all present. "Now, that situation has been dealt with, but I wish to remind you. We are not policemen."

The group around Art, identical to a regular assortment of shoppers, immediately took inventory to determine who was missing. "If you violate this policy you will be terminated immediately, without severance. It's going to put a black mark on your record and you won't work in this field again." Everyone waited for the specifics, but Nathan had no more to say. He hurried out of the room, a legal pad clenched under his arm.

Those who lingered in the conference room had to arrive at their own conclusions. Other agents noted having seen the gun, but denied squealing. Milla concluded that one of the higher-ups had spotted the glock. "Nathan doesn't get rid of his pet unless to save his own skin," she said. Everyone filed out and manned their posts as the store filled with last-minute bargain hunters, but none of the LP agents could find enthusiasm for the job. The atmosphere of indifference became festive.

Art spent most of his shift on the floor, wandering through automotive, picking through the leftovers. He compared motor oils by price and volume and acquainted himself with the varied textures of car mats and beaded seat cushions. Then he noticed a woman coming down the aisle, carrying a pair of shopping bags. She wore a silk scarf and a pair of round sunglasses. The woman set the bulging bags down as soon as she reached him, out of breath. It was Virginia. Art peered into the bags and recognized the same kind of yo-yos and videotapes that were strewn around Lambert's basement, a few pairs of workboots, and a set of flannel sheets.

"This probably everything," she said. "The boys opened a few of the packages but I taped them all back together this morning. Pooka loved them boots so I waited 'til he left on out the house."

"What are you doing?"

"You tried to do right by me, Artie, and I know why you done it. And I got mad at myself and screwed up. This my way of saying sorry. It don't matter what Carlene and Daddy Ray think. You a good man. I know." She laughed. "It take a bad woman to tell a good man."

"Did the police ever . . . ?" he asked timidly. He'd really wanted to know *this* about his parents, but hadn't admitted it, even to himself, until then. If the killer was found, would they refocus their hate and forgive Art?

Virginia shook her head no. "Cold case. It's a shame and a half."

Art searched Virginia's eyes for signs of dishonesty and found none. They talked about times they'd shared with Angie: summers spent leaping through fire-hydrant fountains, dunkings at the public pool, and more carefully, the nightclub nights that had come to such a harsh, sudden freeze.

"Whoever it was, I bet he paid for it somehow." Virginia sighed. Art swallowed the beginning of a sigh and touched her shoulder. The moment became heavy, as if they might embrace, and then passed. Art had a vision of himself nabbing perp after perp, never catching the right one.

He glanced through Virginia's bags, then picked them up and led his aunt to the stockroom, where merch sat in Plexiglas bins and pallets and orange metal shelves. The ceiling was double height, and the garage door open all the way, bringing a pale, warm light into the space. A number of agents and other employees on break sat or stood just outside, smoking and chatting.

Art hefted the bags into a plastic bin and wiped his dusty hands off on his thighs. They walked across the concrete, past the parking lot toward the sun. Art told Virginia how he'd recently burned a pot by boiling eggs for too long. In the middle of the story he admitted to himself that he simply wanted to prolong the conversation. Virginia asked if he had to go back to work, but he assured her it was okay, they couldn't fire him now. She tossed her head back and relaxed, removing the scarf and shades.

"I ought to leave Pooka, take the kids back to Jacksonville," she said. "But it's not just him, it's me against all them men, y'know?" Art thought she looked radiant despite her wistful mood when they moved outside. He walked her down the alley on the side of the building toward the parking lot out front. They were alone. He rested his arm on her shoulder.

A third of the way down, Art heard footsteps behind them and saw a heavy shadow in his peripheral vision. Before he could stop and turn, Virginia started. A hand wrapped around her elbow and she halted. In a black leather jacket and baggy pants, Gunsel had shed the studied plainclothes look of an LP agent. He looked like a real civilian.

"Stop," he commanded. On one side of them was a high fence with a loop of razorwire across the top. On the other, the high, stucco wall of Lambert's. It would take an excellent sprinter to get to the parking lot ahead of Gunsel.

"Okay roaches, ready to get squashed? Citizen's arrest."

As if he'd been practicing, Gunsel clipped a pair of handcuffs around Virginia's wrist and his own. He turned and yanked Virginia back toward the loading dock. She followed, stumbling on the rough asphalt. "I didn't take nothing," she protested. "Get it off me."

"You said that the other day, too."

Virginia stopped. "I didn't take nothing then, neither."

"Gunsel, she brought it back."

"Can't bring my job back though, can she?"

Gently but firmly, Art told Gunsel, "The rule is no guns. You knew that. And if she wasn't carrying last time, management ain't going to turn around."

Gunsel glared at him like a jackhammer meeting pavement. He flinched, planning to attack. His expression lightened. Gunsel threw Virginia against the white wall and called her a fucking bitch. Her skull made an ugly percussive sound when it hit. She shouted at him to leave her alone and cried out for help. Art tried to bodycheck Gunsel, but the larger man took no notice. Art searched the ground nearby for a weapon but saw nothing. Gunsel twisted Virginia's cuffed hand into an awkward position and struck her in the face with his left, near the place where her lip had almost healed. She spat and tried to bite Gunsel. His fury intensified.

A couple of employees soon heard the scuffle and came around the side of the building. A few of the heartier men ran over and jumped on Gunsel's back. Each worked to restrain a shoulder or an arm. One dark-haired guy hooked his elbow around Gunsel's neck. He kept yelling into the big man's ear at the top of his voice, "You don't hit a woman! You don't hit a woman!"

Art saw Virginia worm her right hand into her pocketbook. She swung at the giant's face and connected. Gunsel grabbed his head with one hand and let out a bloodcurdling holler. He leaned his weight across the wall and kneeled there, wailing about his eye. Virginia maneuvered out of the way to keep him from pinning her against the wall. She had a nail file in her right hand, bright red with blood. She screamed, and pulled the cuffs taut, straining to get free.

Art found Gunsel's key ring and unlatched Virginia. He held the other wrist as tightly as he could, but she slipped free and ran toward the front parking lot and the mall beyond it. Art tried to explain what had happened to the guys, but the words only came in fragments. His legs took up the slack and he ran after Virginia. No one had anything on her, he thought. She shouldn't have run. She could plead self-defense.

It was one of those warm spring days that somehow crop up in winter. Hills of grainy snow melted into dirty streams along the walk-ways. The shoppers seemed dazed as they licked soft pretzels and skewered fries in cardboard boats. Panting, Art reached the mall, where two rows of stores faced each other with a patch of grass and hedges between them, and stopped. He'd lost sight of Virginia. He tried to see everyplace she could have run at once. But she had dis-appeared. And in a way, the whole family with her. He didn't know where to turn.

Remind Me What the Light Is For

Kate Hall

Dear occupants of the match stick forest,
we are getting taller. I lit my friend's barbeque
by striking a simple idea against
my visible landscape. Occupants,
I know you are thinking
if we left the twigs with leaves
they could grow up to be big enough that
our buses could pass through them
but this would take time. Time we may
not have. Remember the world
is shrinking as the universe expands.
And remember, it is possible
to light all this on fire,
then have it seed itself in the ash.

Dear occupants of the moving boxes,
there are days when I forget
you have to live here too, in cardboard
cubes, tossed in with lamps
that do not work. The boxes are covered
with words but, because we've reused
them, the objects are not
what's inside. So, occupants, I am losing
faith. The movers are also in motion.
You've seen how the basement can flood.
I've looked to Saint Thomas as one would
a plumber. I am motion sick.

Remind me that I live here, even if
I do not. Let the architecture go.
If the moon must be a pendulum,
let the reflection be still.

Dear occupants of space and time
subject to causal laws, I am escaping
out through a shattered window,
out to where the stars are, looking in
on myself through myself. It's so cold.
These are strange gifts. I gave my friend
hypothermia. We were wearing moon-suits
and tied together on strings tied to
floating objects. I transferred the ice crystals
through this composition. You know there are
post-resuscitation complications. I'm starting
to understand what they are. Occupants, the soul
is asking too many questions. It wants
to know if it has a beautiful form. And I do not
know how to answer it.

The Elegant Rube

Malerie Willens

WALLETS, LADIES. NOW!

That's what the mugger said to Michael and Wade when he ambushed them. They had just come out of a late movie, and were rounding the corner onto a residential block when he emerged from some shrubs. The teenaged assailant with lippy peach fuzz and a confusing accent called the brothers *ladies*. He held the grip of some weapon, stuck into his pants at the waistband. Michael dropped his popcorn, which flew up and then scattered onto the pavement. He tossed his wallet to the skittish kid, and then his brother did the same.

Turn around or I'll shoot off your face!

Michael and Wade turned and stood with their arms at their sides until the boy's staccato footsteps grew faint. Because it was late at night in Los Angeles, nobody was there to see them. They looked like life-sized wooden soldiers who'd been positioned on the sidewalk and then abandoned. Michael, whose scarecrow body and tentative manner made some women think of poets, stood with his back straight and long. He maximized each distinct vertebra but he still felt delicate in the presence of his brother's much larger body, just inches away. He glanced over at the spiny orange birds-of-paradise that separated one duplex from the next. The flowers looked like plastic from the ninety-nine cent store—odorless probably, and coated in a fine layer of dust. He conjured up the kid's voice. *I'll shoot off your face* is what he'd said, as though he and Wade shared one face—the meshing, hapless visage of a single victim.

The night on which a crime occurs is always the wrong night—always incongruous, inappropriate, charged with meaning. This night was no exception. It was the brothers' first encounter in nearly a year. In the early days of their estrangement, Michael had been optimistic. Because he couldn't trace it back to a decisive insult, it seemed like an adult's rift—a barely perceptible accumulation of subtle wrongs—rather than a brawl, beef, or blow-up. He visualized it as an artery, occluded with the plaque of misunderstanding, until, after too many awkward phone calls and canceled breakfasts, the blood barely pumped.

He could still see the two of them as boys, falling back onto the couch with the loose-limbed ease of brothers. He saw Yoo-Hoo spewing out of each other's noses, he saw Wade spinning Nina Marsak's tiny, mysteriously obtained underpants around his forefinger, and he heard the echo of handballs against the garage. Their parents had believed in the sanctity of the fraternal bond. "When we're gone," they would say, "it'll only be you two." And the boys would answer, "yeah-yeah" as they chased the dog past the TV, slammed bedroom doors papered with raunchy bumper stickers, and slouched sullenly around on Sundays in mismatched socks.

And then their parents were gone—run off the road three years earlier, on their way to San Francisco. It happened north of San Simeon but below Big Sur, the point at which the viscous, coastal fog wraps itself around the road like a big gray cat. On childhood car trips, Michael likened this misty stretch of Highway One to the Middle Earth in his books, where white cliffs arched and preened, like women getting dressed. It was their parents' favorite strip of the coast, which made Michael feel simultaneously better and worse that they had died there.

Attempts to stay in touch had been sporadic since then. After the accident, the brothers collaborated in the work of death, meeting in corner booths over french fries, cloaking their grief in logistics. Finally, after what felt like months but were in fact only weeks, the affairs of their short, round, easygoing parents had been streamlined into paper statements and reduced to receipts.

The brothers would make casual plans and then break them each time. It had been gnawing at Michael for a year. At home in his bed, after mixing sound for cartoons all day, he wondered about his brother. He'd allow himself one beer for two that were non-alcoholic, and then two reals for one fake and so on. He felt bloated and muzzy-headed, but he rarely got drunk. He spent his days wedged tightly between headphones and in front of screens—rising and falling to the manic, high-speed rhythms of big color and voice. This did sinister things to his nights, when the silence sounded loud and the stillness dizzied him—like sitting in front of a television that had just been turned off, the click and the blackness piercing the center of his forehead: a bindi of sudden quiet.

Michael doubted that Wade was as preoccupied with their estrangement as he was, not because Wade was a bad or callous person, but because his superpower was the ability to make himself slippery, so that nothing ever touched him. Michael assumed he was busy with his own life, which had always been somewhat mysterious. Wade had dropped out of law school and gone into "investments." Michael assumed he earned money making rich people richer. He was defensive and noncommittal when Michael asked.

Had one brother bullied the other or stolen a girlfriend, the situation would have been clearer. But Michael began to understand, during his bedtime alchemy of drinking, and not-drinking, and then drinking, that his problems with Wade were not fixable, and that Wade was a person he wouldn't have known had they not been related. They'd always been comfortable at home with their parents and on holidays in restaurants. They were good at being brothers. Boys. But the family made sense only as a foursome, and now the surviving two were thrust back into the world, maladroit on the skinny legs they'd inherited from their father. There were memories to unearth and stories to tell and retell, but without the parental glue, the brothers had come apart.

Michael called Wade on a Monday night. He made himself sound casual because Wade responded well to lightness. The ease of the call surprised him; they decided on Vincenzi's remastered 1948 triumph of Leftist desolation, *The Elegant Rube*. A movie date might have been a strange choice for a potentially tense reunion, but for Michael and Wade it made sense.

Fifteen minutes before the show, Michael arrived to find Wade in his usual seat: middle section, five rows from the front, on the left aisle. It was just the two of them, save for a woman in the front row, with long, wild gray hair and a complicated scarf. The deco sconces that lined the walls were the same ones that stood watch over Michael and Wade's childhood matinees and teenage late shows. Their parents had never understood the boys' interest in revival house fare—often the same movies they'd watched when they were kids—but they were relieved that their very different sons had this in common. Michael's magic lessons and Wade's soccer practice began dwindling in exchange for Westerns and war films at age ten. During teenage weekends, when Michael painted naked women (although he'd never seen one) and Wade played Atari, they'd line up together late at night for the culty, bloody, and bawdy. They'd sit together in that blue-lit space—that timeless, placeless fish tank of shadow and sound. At sixteen, Michael wrote an essay entitled "Breathing Underwater: Ode to the Cinema," in which the viewer watches a movie while pleasantly submerged in the indeterminate space of the theater: a warm, undulating zone of contrast, a fusion of land and sea.

Michael didn't want to creep up on Wade and scare him, so he weighted his gait enough to make it audible as he walked down the aisle.

Wade turned and smiled. He'd gotten fatter.

There was a simian brushing of hands and bumping of limbs against shoulder and knee. Michael sat down.

Wade handed him a half-eaten bar of expensive-looking chocolate.

"So?"

"So?" said Michael, who broke off three squares, already wondering where they'd go when the movie ended.

They finished the chocolate too fast. Michael wanted to slow everything down. He wanted them to take their time but he didn't know how to pause and linger in a way that wouldn't alarm Wade.

"You got fat," Michael said.

"I know. All I eat is meat and candy. Mirabelle's putting me on a diet."

Wade had always dated rich girls, who'd been carefully named: Mirabelle, Tatiana, Tallulah. Whenever Wade mentioned a girlfriend, Michael sensed he'd never be allowed to meet her. He knew little about Mirabelle, even though she and Wade had been dating for some time. She was a rock critic whose not unimpressive trust-fund allowed her to work on an extremely part-time basis. There was always a story about Mirabelle's disappointment when some rock legend turned out to be shockingly dull in person.

Michael tried to formulate a question about Mirabelle that would shepherd them past the small talk but Wade maneuvered the discussion back to familiar territory.

"Remember when we tried to freeze our nose hairs, like dad?" he asked. He was referring to a story their father had told repeatedly: an army story. He was stationed at Fort Devins in the middle of a bad Massachusetts winter. While marching back and forth on the parade ground one frigid, windy morning, he felt his nose dripping. He reached up with a gloved hand and squeezed it, wincing at the sharp pain inside his nostrils: his nose hairs had frozen into glasslike shards. He began to bleed as he marched. It was a morning of bleeding and marching, bleeding and marching: a wretched moment in a relatively comfortable life. He thought the story might ensure that his boys chose college over the service, although there was never any real danger that they wouldn't. What the story did do was encourage the boys to freeze their own nose hairs by shoving crushed ice from the refrigerator up their nostrils.

"Popcorn?" Michael asked, and with Wade's mildly irritating double thumbs-up, he left for the concession stand.

In line in the lobby, Michael studied the posters for the Vincenzi retrospective. They were all pop art and primary colors, as if to dupe today's moviegoers into thinking that the bleak neo-realist world of Vincenzi might be kitschy and mod. And the films' English titles had all been changed. *Crime Tale* was now *Riotous Corpse*, and *God Is Here* became *The Boss of Us*. The strangest of all was the movie they were about to see; the gently wrenching *The Elegant Rube* had been renamed *Uncle Paolo Is No Criminal*. Michael paid for the popcorn, pumped it full of liquid butter, and told himself to tell Wade about the title.

There was no one new in the theater, still just the wild-haired woman. Her ragged attractiveness, coupled with the fact that she sat alone and in front, made her seem self-possessed, European, and a little morose. She had begun to read a book.

"But Uncle Paolo's a minor character," said Wade with a mouth full of popcorn.

"What I don't understand," said Michael "is why *Uncle Paolo Is No Criminal* is a better title than *The Elegant Rube*."

"It's his best film," said Wade.

"I like the later ones, after the stroke."

"But he was paralyzed. Dude couldn't even talk!"

"He said those were the movies he'd always wanted to make, that he wasn't a genius until he had the stroke."

The European woman whipped her head around as though startled by a loud noise, and surveyed the brothers before returning to her book. Michael had mentally named the woman "Veronique," but then he changed it to "Simone."

The lights faded, which meant that in two minutes it would be dark. Michael stuffed a fistful of popcorn into his mouth and then rubbed his palms together so that the butter and salt stung the chapped grooves. He felt a fluid surge of trust in the next two and a half hours, as though he'd just taken a Valium on an empty stomach. He and Wade would sit there like they always had, snug in each other's idiosyncratic breathing and the periodic shifting of weight. They'd swell and break in tandem, like wrestling on the kitchen floor or kneeling over Tinkertoys, the stove popping with the first sounds of dinner. And after the movie they'd sit in silence for as long as they could stand it. They'd wait for the theater to empty and then they'd look at each other and smile—exhaling—slightly embarrassed at having just seen something great. They'd walk their identical hunched-over walk up the aisle, through the ancient lobby with its flocked wallpaper and whorehouse candelabras, and they'd rejoin the night. And before they began their postmortem, they'd look at each other again and just say, "Wow."

Wallets, ladies. Now!

Turn around or I'll shoot off your face.

They stood there until they believed the kid was really gone. Then they turned around and walked ten feet to the tub of popcorn and its splayed contents. The pieces of popcorn looked violated, as if they'd been alive before and now they were not.

"Great," said Michael, hands in his pockets.

Wade reached up and fingered the cartilage of his upper ear, a habit he'd had since he was a kid. "I think he was Latvian," he said. They weren't far from the Baltic section of town. "Lucky I only had a few bucks. Did you have cash?"

"None in my wallet. Five bucks in my pocket, which I kept," said Michael, kicking the tub of popcorn toward the gutter.

"He called us 'ladies.'"

"Ladies with no money," said Michael. "Little douche bag chose the wrong ladies."

They circled slowly around the pieces of popcorn, as though it might provide some insight into the situation.

"Now we have to cancel everything," said Wade. "I hate that."

"Like credit cards?"

"Credit cards, gas card, driver's license . . . my whole life was in there."

"If that's your whole life, Wade, I don't know. Not a good sign."

"Very funny."

"It takes five minutes to replace everything. You do it on the computer now. You'll have all your cards by next week."

"Okay. Relax."

"I am relaxed. You're the one who's worrying. Why do you care so much about your cards?"

"Jesus, Mike, calm down. If I irritate you so much, why'd you arrange this? Why'd you invite me out?"

"Because we're strangers, Wade. Because I don't know shit about your life after the age of eighteen."

"What do you want to know?"

"Come on."

"I'm serious. You've never asked about my life. When did you suddenly get interested in anyone besides yourself?"

"You have no idea what I'm interested in," said Michael, stunned at how suddenly their politeness had turned.

"Because you keep everything a secret. Your delicate little life, so sensitive. You think I'm some big dumb jock."

"You think I'm a depressed drunk."

"You are."

Michael began speed-walking up the middle of the street.

"Aren't you?" Wade yelled. He was a few paces behind Michael. Their loping gait was synchronized, their father's, something to do with those skinny legs and bad knees.

Michael stopped short and turned around. They were standing in the middle of the street, face to face, a foot apart. "At least I feel things, you bloated fucking robot."

They walked fast, heading toward the horizontal ribbons of light at the next big avenue. Tears crept down Michael's long face and Wade's broad one.

"If I'm a bloated robot, then you're a sullen teenager. If you're so unhappy, do something about it. You want to know who I am? Ask! You wait for the world to approach you, and when it doesn't, you pout. You're too old to feel so misunderstood, Mike. Unless you plan to die alone."

They passed a water-damaged apartment building with subtle metallic specks in its stucco façade, probably from the early sixties. On the grass in front, a young Filipino man was giving another young Filipino man—seated on a lawn chair and wearing a white smock— a haircut. It was jarring to see this after midnight, but the men on the lawn behaved as though it was the most natural thing in the world.

"You say I don't feel anything," Wade continued shrilly, wiping the tears from his face with the back of his hand. "You know *why* I'm pissed about my wallet? It's not the damn gas card. I had a picture of mom and dad in there. My favorite picture."

"Which one?" asked Michael, who felt all of a sudden responsible for what had happened, as if by orchestrating their reunion, he himself had taken the wallet from Wade's baggy, faded jeans.

The brothers stopped walking. They were in the middle of the street.

"A picture—from a long time ago. I just liked it."

"What were they doing? Where were they?"

"I think it was in the old backyard. You can't really tell. They're in bathing suits and they look like they're laughing at a dirty joke."

Michael saw Wade just then as a six year-old wearing Mickey Mouse ears. The guy at Disneyland had mistakenly embroidered "Wayne" onto the hat, but Wade didn't mind. He was a happy child, easygoing even then. He wore his "Wayne" hat for an entire summer.

"What are we doing, Mike? Where are we going?" There was a pleading tone to Wade's questions.

"We're walking it off. I can't go home yet."

"Don't you feel like a target?

"We're not going to get mugged twice in one night," Michael said. "Oh man, can you imagine?"

"Jesus," said Wade, and they both laughed a little.

At that instant, Michael knew that the mugging had earned the stamp of official memory. He imagined the story they would tell, the pithy paragraph, the recounting. He didn't hear the words but he could feel the shape of them. The moment of the shared chuckle was the moment the mugging had become mutual, an event, another installment in the brothers' soft mythology. This incident, Michael knew with a prescient pang, would assume an unearned weight strictly because it was a memory—a memory for two people who existed for each other only in the world of memory.

They arrived at the honking bustle of a major east-west artery with the four usual corners: giant supermarket, giant bank, giant parking structure, giant hamburger drive-thru. Everything in Los Angeles had grown giant, mom and pop shops bulldozed away from high-profile intersections like this one. The garish display blew at the brothers like a gust of wind, stopping them abruptly at the corner.

"I should go," said Wade.

"What?"

"I should go," he said. "Mirabelle's waiting up."

"Are you serious?"

"Yeah," he said, reaching up to finger his ear. "It's just starting to hit me. I don't want to be out in all this," he said, looking up and around at the lights and billboards and then down at the sidewalks and the pedestrians that weren't there. "If you want to spend your five dollars on a piece of pie, I'd split it, but I can't just traipse around."

Wade had always been an abrupt leaver, a fact that Michael only remembered during the mildly shocking moment of Wade's good-bye. His goodbyes seemed surprising and inevitable at the same time. Michael felt a twitching guilt about the night, but he didn't want to eat pie and he didn't want to reminisce. Memories offered little succor for him, perhaps because he and Wade always seemed to remember the same things. Didn't the power of memory lay in its ability to surprise and illuminate? Otherwise, wasn't it just an elaborate brand of small talk, starving the people in question while appearing, briefly, to feed them? Michael knew that a piece of pie with Wade would not feel like progress. Plus, there was nowhere to get pie after midnight, unless you were willing to drive, and what Michael needed was a beer.

"Okay," he said as he leaned in to his brother. They embraced like tin-men with unlubricated joints.

"I'll talk to you," said Wade. "Sorry." He walked back down the darkened street, toward the scene of the crime—or whatever it was—where his car was parked.

Michael sprinted through the blinking intersection and into the supermarket. It was painfully bright and operating-room-cold, but it was a familiar shock, and not unpleasant. He yanked a shopping cart out of the corral and began wheeling it through the meat aisle, which was far more populated than the street outside. The bustling aisle gave Michael the sensation of an approaching storm, of citizens stocking up on canned goods and butane, going about their business with the methodical American dread he'd seen on the news. He pushed his empty cart past the various meats. He passed at least three young women ogling lamb chops or pausing to consider a fillet or some other lonely cut. He wheeled past the breakfast meats and into the bread aisle, feeling well-adjusted because, surely, he was the only person there who'd just been mugged and then immediately resumed his quotidian duties. But as he gained momentum down the pillowy aisle of muffins and pita and all the other starches, he felt in his stomach the possibility that he might be wrong. There was the chance, however slight, that others in the market had also just been mugged—or if not mugged, then accosted, attacked, held up, assaulted, shammed, scammed, humiliated, beaten up, shot at, or victimized in some way. It was possible. He checked his watch. It was 12:53 and they were all contained there in the bunker-like supermarket, wherever they'd been before.

He began filling up his cart. He took peanut butter and tomato soup and cans of tuna packed in oil, and he looked long at his late-night shopping companions, who maybe just didn't want to go home.

He pushed the cart, which now also contained a sports drink with electrolytes and some boxes of couscous, into the cereal aisle, where he saw the unmistakable gray rat's nest of a hairdo, simultaneously abject and sophisticated. Simone, still alone and wrapped up in her Euro-scarf, walked quickly down the aisle with a small red basket.

There was a furtive grace to her gait, a hurried worry not unlike Alice chasing the White Rabbit. Here was a middle-aged, possibly European woman in a West Coast supermarket at one in the morning, but Michael saw the dewy, distressed heroine of a fairytale. Maybe the night would end well. She—Simone—would be his reward for calling Wade and trying to repair things. This serendipitous detour could alter his life more profoundly than his well-meaning lump of a brother ever could. Maybe he was right to let Wade go, not agreeing to get pie but rather following his instincts.

He began trailing Simone, but he feared he'd make her nervous. He wanted to talk to her without seeming dangerous or desperate. He was too far away to make out the contents of her basket, but from a distance, her knee-length hem revealed a skinny ankle and a strong calf. They were at the edge now, near the verdant maze of produce, when she turned abruptly, a sudden jerk of impatience sending her to the express lane. She fished around in her well-worn leather bag, which looked like a baseball mitt. Michael got in line behind her. She leaned back against the metal railing, staring at something—or nothing—and maybe she sensed the jumbled intentions pulsing in him because she gazed out of her reverie and into his eyes, revealing, maybe, some tiny bit of recognition. And then she began placing her groceries onto the belt.

He grabbed a roll of mints from the display and tossed them into his cart when his stomach—which knew things before he did—turned a lumbering somersault as he remembered that his wallet had been stolen, and that he had no cards and no identification. His pockets were empty—save for the five dollar bill and his car keys—but his cart was full. With his five dollars, he could afford to buy two of the beers in the six-pack in his cart, but he hated that guy, the one who buys two beers and nothing else, after midnight, alone. He scanned an imaginary list, mentally crossing off the things he would not do: he would not meet this brave and mysterious woman; he would not buy provisions for the imaginary storm; he would not call Wade to rehash the details of the mugging. He would excuse himself from the express lane, which had already filled up behind him, and he would leave his cart in the middle of some aisle, which is exactly what he did, and then he slipped a candy bar into his jacket pocket and he went to find his car.

You are holding yourself and you are watching yourself holding yourself. You are thinking window, window, window. (Brown, page 99)

The Devanes

Ian Martin

THE SUMMER THE DEVANES ARRIVED ON OUR BLOCK I WAS
selling digital tape wholesale in a building made of glazed white
brick. It was located in my hometown's only office park. Richard, my
boss, was short and wiry; he had curly black hair and an intensity that
made me uncomfortable. He was a man who should have been born
taller and never forgave God for the mistake.

My sales were abominable, only slightly better than Ankur, an
immigrant from India who read motivational books on his lunch
break and longed to lose his accent. Richard had twice asked if I
planned to go to grad school though, the way he asked, it wasn't so
much a question as a suggestion. I didn't have much of a future there.

It was while walking home from work that I first became aware of
the Devanes. I saw Mrs. Allen out in her front yard with her two little girls whose names I had trouble remembering. One was Ashley,
the other was Gina, though I could never remember which was
which. They chased their dog, Needles, around the yard. Mrs. Allen
was in her third trimester and wore a maternity dress patterned with
tangled yellow flowers. She smiled and waddled over to me. She held
a tricycle in one hand like it was an extension of her arm.

"We've got new neighbors," she said, and pointed to a house down
the block. A BMW with racing decals was parked in front of the
house. A moving truck was backed into the driveway.

"What's with the car?" I asked.

She put her hand over her eyes to block the sun. The sun was so strong that day that when she shaded her eyes I couldn't see them anymore. Her dress fluttered in the breeze.

"I don't know," she said. "Maybe they're into stock-car racing."

Then she told me what Mr. Greene had told her. They were rich kids, or the husband was anyway, the son of a well-to-do financier of some sort. Mr. Greene had heard that from someone on the block but Mrs. Allen couldn't remember who from. She put her hand to her forehead as she tried to recall Mr. Greene's source. I checked my watch and told her I had a telephone appointment.

Mitchell, the youngest Kane boy, was mowing his family's lawn. He wore headphones and a gray warm-up T-shirt. As a boy he had been gangly, with a voice like a robot, but over the years he had developed an unappealing Irish beefcake quality. Somewhere between those two stages he had decided I was strange and tried to ignore my existence. There was a flicker of uncomfortable eye contact as I stepped past their lawn and toward my house.

I was in the front room later that evening when the birds started chirping in unison and the reverberant drone of the locusts was at its loudest. All the windows were open in our house. We hadn't got to the thick of the summer when we would shut all the windows, turn down the blinds, and start up the central air. The subtle sounds of the neighborhood shot through our house with remarkable clarity.

I was rubbing my finger on the outer-lip of the windowsill, curious how much dust had collected since the last cleaning, when I saw a black Passat pull up behind the BMW across the street. No other family on the block owned two luxury cars. A young man in a business suit stepped from the Passat and walked up the driveway. I could hear gravel popping under the soles of his dress shoes. He had a long stride. That was the first time I saw Philip Devane.

My stepfather was waging war on the skunks living under our house. He dropped rags soaked in ammonia down their burrow and blared AM radio broadcasts at full volume in our basement. He pushed the clock radio against the wall next to where they lived. He had a stony look on his face as he set these deterrents in place, as if he didn't enjoy treating the skunks like this but couldn't deny the necessity of doing so.

The first Saturday after the Devanes moved in, my parents left to do charity work at church. I was in my room lying supine in bed, a cigarette tucked between my lips, reading an essay on Freud from a reader I hadn't opened in college. There was a British woman in my basement talking about Lebanon. Her voice echoed through the vents and drifted into my room.

In my periphery, I noticed movement on the lawn across the street. I turned my attention to the Devane's house. Philip Devane walked about the front lawn wearing nothing but dark blue flip-flops and low-riding khaki shorts that ended a little past his knees. He was lean and tan and his belly stuck out some toward his diaphragm. A bottle of imported beer in one hand, he shrewdly surveyed his front lawn. He was turned away from our house and I couldn't see his face.

Behind Devane were two younger men, early twenties, waiting patiently for instruction. Unlike Devane, they wore dirty jeans and worker boots. The aging pick-up in the driveway belonged to them. Devane took his time contemplating the lawn; a thoughtful hand covered his mouth. It was the first really humid day of summer and I could see the shirts of the workers dampening with sweat as he deliberated. Finally, after three or four minutes, he moved to action, drawing an imaginary box in the grass on each side of the front steps, very explicit as to the parameters. As the workers dug the new flower beds, Devane stood a few feet away on the front walk, arms akimbo, watching their work with an exacting eye.

I watched for a while and then went downstairs. I sat at the living room table while my mother sifted through the mail. My mother's cheeks were flushed from the humidity. She had gained about twenty pounds over the last five years and her pedal pushers fit snugly. Though the pastel color scheme of her outfits suggested optimism, her mood rarely seemed to match.

"How was the soup kitchen?" I asked.

"I don't know." Charity work disappointed her.

"They're doing some yard work across the street." She looked toward the Devanes.

"That guy's a jerk," she said, and tossed the mail on the table. "He needs to use a leash on his dog."

Their dog was a Weimaraner; a silver purebreed with radiant blue eyes. Weimaraners were originally used for hunting by aristocracy. Devane would let his roam around the yard without any restraints.

I flipped through the mail. Behind a camping magazine was an invitation to the annual Fourth of July block party. This gathering was an institution on our block. For me, it brought to mind obesity and bucket-sized citronella candles.

"How old do you think they are?" I asked.

"A little older than you. Twenty-eight maybe." She poured herself a glass of iced tea. "The Parrishes said he pulled the grass off his lawn right up to the property line."

"It wasn't their grass if it was on his side of the property."

"It's not neighborly."

"He's making a garden. That's nice."

I always seemed to disagree with my mother.

On my way back upstairs, I noticed that Devane's wife was out on their lawn. She wore a beige tank top and long wrap skirt. She stood toward the back of the driveway behind the worker's pickup. Devane walked to her. He gave her his empty bottle and said something to her. She nodded, looked at the workers, then walked up the driveway and into the house.

Fuller's was a very narrow pub, and that somehow created the effect of it always seeming crowded, even when it wasn't. It was all dark wood and yellow lighting—not a dive, just bar-moody. I was there that night with Franklin, a friend from high school, who was studying special education at the local college. He wanted to be a writer but I suspect it was a rare occasion when he actually put pen to paper. Mike Flannigan came over to sit at the stand-up table with us. He and Franklin smoked weed together and had a strong friendship based on their mutual appreciation of the drug.

Mike and I lived on the same block and I had known him since I was a boy. We never would have been friends otherwise. Mike had a lean athletic build and a shaggy beard. He had gone to state on a baseball scholarship and majored in philosophy but during his sophomore year marijuana got the best of him. Now he lived at home, chain-smoked, and was at the bars almost every night. He still had an innately athletic quality.

"Greetings," he said as he approached.

I nodded.

"What's up?" asked Franklin. They dapped fists.

Franklin slipped off his stool and nearly pulled the table with him. We both had drank too much but I was better at concealing it.

"I've gotta pee," said Franklin, and he walked slowly toward the bathroom.

I leaned forward toward Mike. The table wobbled a little as I moved. It was missing one of the feet. Mike raised a curious eyebrow as he lit a cigarette.

"Their garden is looking good," I said.

It took a second, but he laughed when he put it together.

"Have you seen his wife?" he asked, exhaling smoke. "I hear they're digging a pond in their back yard. That's a first for the neighborhood." He leaned back and pulled a drag from his cigarette. He looked up at the yellow ceiling.

"A pond?"

I thought about a pond on a summer night.

"That sounds lovely."

The conversation shifted topic but I couldn't get the pond out of my head. I imagined Devane digging in the moonlight, sinking into the summer mud, wearing shorts and his blue flip-flops. The image was potent and, in my drunkenness, inescapable.

When Franklin and Mike went to smoke weed behind the bar, I excused myself and walked home. My footsteps echoed on the street. Several blocks from home, I broke into a sprint and ran until I was across the street from the Devanes. I dodged behind a knotty elm tree and tried to slow my breathing. The only sounds were my rhythmic breaths and a neighbor's condenser whirring to life.

I looked up the Devane's driveway, hoping to catch a glimpse of something. The front of their driveway was illuminated by an overhead floodlight. Airborne bugs looped in and out of the light, beyond which was a wall of darkness. I considered sneaking into Devane's backyard from the other side of the block but my interest suddenly struck me as immature. So I went home and fell asleep drunk.

＊＊＊＊

The next day, Richard called me into his office. I knew what was going to happen by the way he gestured for me to have a seat and then folded his hands in front of him.

He said several employees had witnessed me smoking pot in the warehouse and taking naps behind pallets of inventory.

"Are they telling the truth?" he asked.

I said it wasn't exactly the truth: I was just smoking cigarettes and I only tried to take a nap once, but the clarification didn't make much of a difference.

Richard talked about community and work, he talked about my sales, and then he said that he was going to fire me.

"I believe this is in your best interest," he said.

I was too embarrassed to really listen to what he was saying, so I nodded and agreed and stared at his tie.

As we exited his office, he put a fatherly hand on my shoulder and looked me in the eyes.

"Is everything all right with you?" he asked. "I mean, outside of work?"

I tried to smile.

"Everything's great," I said.

In lieu of a job, my mother had me performing chores around the house, like burying a baby skunk behind the garage. My stepfather accidentally drowned it while trying to flood its family out.

My mother also had me distribute flyers for her nascent real estate career. I objected to the cursive font she chose for the letter. She argued that it looked like handwriting, which personalized the mass mailing. I disagreed: I told her the reproduction of handwriting was transparent and only underlined the lack of humanity in the letter.

I went door-to-door with the flyers. On my way out, one of the Kane boys almost backed over me with his SUV. I decided to ignore his carelessness. As he pulled past me and into the street, I forced a smile and started to raise my arm in a friendly wave. He shifted from reverse to drive; he saw my arm on the upswing and, before I could finish the wave, he had taken off down the street.

That left a bad taste in my mouth. I no longer had any interest in speaking to the neighbors. I decided that I wouldn't talk to them in person, I would simply roll the up the letters and stick them in the screen doors.

But I wanted to make an exception for the Devanes, so I rang the bell when I got to their house.

Before the Devanes moved in, a family of redheads had lived there. The father was an alcoholic who had destroyed his liver with drink. The redheads moved away after his death. Under their care, the front garden had been an unimpressive blend of pale pink geraniums and droopy coleus. It was only given enough attention to pass muster with the rest of the block.

When the Devanes arrived, the faded wood siding was torn down and replaced with aluminum. The garden had been turned with first-rate topsoil, so rich and earthy it looked edible. There was now a bright pattering of annuals in place of the coleus and geraniums. And the new brick walkway was admirably precise.

I rang the bell twice but no answer.

I casually tried to look into the Devane's backyard as I walked to the next house, maybe to see the pond, but it was a bad angle and all I got was a glimpse of a dirty shovel resting against the garage.

That night I called my ex-girlfriend. We dated our junior and senior years of college but, after graduating, she went to New York to get her master's in architecture. She broke up with me a week and a half before graduation. My parents kept asking about her when they came to watch me walk. It wasn't until the drive back that I had the heart to tell them what they had already guessed.

I called her once a month; I allowed myself that. When we spoke there was a duty-like tone in her voice.

"I miss you," I'd say after a while.

She'd sigh, and then ask: "Yeah?"

I had started dating a twenty-five-year-old named Lee who had been in the navy but now appraised properties for a living. She had a daughter named Jordan whose picture she had shown me when we first met in a rundown hotel bar. I had been too drunk to care that she had a daughter and, laughing, I told her I had a kid too. I thought that line was really hilarious. She laughed, but also looked confused, and that set the tone for our relationship. She tried to start earnest conversations; I acted aloof and superior.

OPEN CITY

Lee and I had been dating for two and a half months and, though I kept intending to end the relationship, it had somehow managed to drag on. I hadn't seen her in a week. After speaking with my ex-girlfriend, I went to the bars and started drinking. I knew Lee would call. She did every Wednesday. She of course asked if she could join me at the bar. "Be my guest," I said.

We drank in the back of the lounge and she kissed me every opportunity she had and I made no effort to blow my cigarette smoke away from her.

Later that night, as I walked up my driveway, I heard music and laughter coming from the Kane's house. The boys were having another party. The last party they had was in spring when their parents visited Ireland.

There were voices coming from the Kane's backyard. I saw cigarette cherries but I couldn't make out any faces. As I quietly crept up the back stairs, the motion sensor triggered our backdoor light. The light was very strong. The conversations next door went dead. They watched as I fumbled with my keys.

I lost track of the number of weeks it had been since I worked. My sleep schedule was backwards. I awoke every day at 5:30 p.m. just as Devane's wife would take their Weimaraner for a walk. It was the jingling chain that roused me. I could hear it through my open window.

I liked how she walked. She tried to resist the dog's forward pull by leaning back on the taut leash. But the dog insisted on a quick pace. So she had a quick, bouncy, backward-leaning stride. This looked the best when she wore baggy sweatpant capris and put her hair in a ponytail. The ponytail would bounce as she walked. The capris would wave around her calves.

One day I woke fifteen minutes before the daily walk. I don't know why. Without thinking, I put on my gym shoes and ran to the end of the block. I hoped it looked as if I was going for a jog. I checked my pulse. My pajamas kind of passed as workout clothes. But I never exercised. Mrs. Allen pulled a dandelion from her walkway. She saw me and gave me a funny look. I waved.

I ran into the woods at the end of the block. I stopped halfway to the main path that ran parallel to the park. I hoped the trees were thick enough to hide me from view. Ten minutes later, I heard the jin-

54

gling chain and Devane's wife came up onto the park. The dog went to the edge where the trees began and walked along the perimeter of the woods, sniffing and snorting as he walked. I followed her with my eyes. The shirt I had on was black. The bottoms were red and blue flannel. The sniffing of the dog was very loud. When they lined up with me, the dog stopped. I held my breath. The dog raised it's gray head and looked into the woods. He started to growl deep in his belly. She looked at the dog and then she looked into the woods. I saw her. She looked at me. But she didn't see me.

"C'mon," she said. And pulled the dog farther down the path.

I woke up before noon on Independence Day. I felt rested. The sun was bright and slipped in through the slats of the blinds. The light made the dust in the air glow. I heard children playing games outside. I went to the window. There was a picnic table in the middle of the street. I had forgotten about the block party.

I went downstairs to eat breakfast. My stepfather came in from outside. He wore navy blue shorts and a short-sleeve button-down.

"Coming outside?" he asked. He pulled a black comb from his pocket and brushed his hair.

"I don't know. Maybe."

I went to the window. Mitchell Kane and his older brother, Jerry, carried a beanbag board into the street. It was painted to look like the face of a clown. They smiled as the younger children played with it. That pissed me off.

I watched as Mr. Greene stood on a step ladder to tie a volleyball net between two trees. He looked too old to be doing it. The step ladder wobbled. Mr. Allen walked forward and held the ladder steady.

I went upstairs to my computer and checked my e-mail. I didn't have any new messages but I found two pubic hairs in the keyboard between the keys. I pulled them out and threw them in the wastebasket.

I decided to take a shower. I shaved. It had been a number of days and the hairs were long; it hurt to pull the razor across them. When I was done, my skin felt smoother than it usually did after shaving.

The sun stung my eyes when I went outside. I hadn't been outside that day and I couldn't remember if I had been outside the day before. I walked to the picnic table and took a handful of pretzels from a bowl.

"Hello," said a woman of fifty-something with large glasses and a giant ass. She looked me in the eyes and didn't blink. I ate pretzels.

"Hello." I couldn't remember her name.

I sat in a lawn chair and looked at people. The conversations I had with neighbors were not good conversations. They were choppy and forced. Many of these conversations went on too long because no one wanted to be the person to end them. But everyone seemed to want to have good conversations and that was nice to know.

I tried not to look for the Devanes but I couldn't resist. I looked at their house. It didn't look like they were home. All the lights were off except for one on the second floor.

At dusk, children lit morning glories and sparklers. I went to the end of the block and watched them write their names in the air. A teenage boy set off a single bottle rocket before Mr. Allen and Mr. Greene told him not to light anymore. A little girl lit off snakes on the sidewalk. Serpentine ashes coiled up from the ground.

People moved to the park to watch the fireworks display. It was put on one town over. The neighbors were staying out later than I expected. It was approaching nine o'clock. I stood on the street corner with Mr. and Mrs. Allen. For some reason I felt comfortable around them.

As we watched the display, a silver Honda Civic drove up the street between the park and my block. The muffler on the car was broken and it made an awful racket. People turned to look at the car. A freckle-faced boy covered his ears and the rest of the kids giggled at him.

The car looked familiar. The engine abruptly cut out and Lee stepped from the driver side. She walked up the sidewalk in the direction of my house. She kept her head down, uncomfortable with the kids still staring at her.

"Nice car!" One of them called out. And they all laughed.

Lee wore thin gray coat. Her hair was brown but she tinted it red. She liked the color red. She wore red leather shoes with chunky heels. She carried a small red crocodile purse with a thin shoulder strap. Though she liked red, it usually punctuated a wardrobe of olive, gray, and brown.

She walked right past me.

"Lee," I said. She turned.

"Steven."

"What are you doing?" I asked. My voice had an accusatory tone and I regretted that.

Mrs. Allen glanced at us. Mr. Allen put his arm around Mrs. Allen's shoulder and watched the fireworks, but I knew where both of them were focusing their attention.

"Just stopping by. Wanted to see if you wanted to go out." She shrugged as she said this. Her purse strap started to slip from her shoulder and she adjusted it. She had never been to my house.

Her teeth had a purple tint and I could smell wine on her. She loved to drink wine. I hated that about her. I suspected she felt sophisticated when she drank wine. Maybe that wasn't how she felt but that's what I suspected.

I wondered who was taking care of her kid. I had never asked who watched Jordan while Lee was out with me. It was probably her mother. I felt guilty.

I looked above the tree line of the park as a firework ignited. It was a large green explosion with a white center. It was the largest I had seen in the display.

"That's a pretty one," I said.

"Yeah," said Lee. But she was distracted. I noticed my parents at the end of the block with the neighbors. My stepfather and mother wore matching windbreakers. They were turned toward me, saying something to one another. My mother squinted as she looked at us. When they saw me looking at them, they quickly turned back toward the fireworks.

"Come on," I said. "I'll show you my house."

"I'm sorry if I interrupted something," she said, looking at the ground as she walked. "I just wanted to see what you were doing."

"You've been drinking?" I asked.

"Just a little wine."

"You've never been to my house."

"You never let me drive you home."

I didn't even look at my house as I led Lee past it. We crossed the street diagonally and stopped in front of the Devanes.

"Here it is," I said, presenting their house with my hand.

The light on the second floor was still on. The rest of the house was dark.

Lee looked at the house and nodded.

"Nice garden."

"Thanks," I said.

There was a moment of silence.

"Can I see inside?" she asked.

When we reached the back of the driveway, I saw the garage door was open. Their BMW was parked inside but the Passat was gone. Lee noticed the BMW. I could see her registering the car with her eyes but she didn't say anything.

I looked at the hole in the backyard. It was dug out nicely. A giant muddy bomb hole in a chest of grass.

"My parents are building a pond."

"That's great." She smiled and tucked her hair behind her ears. Lee wasn't as impressed as I expected. Her family had less money than mine—I was almost certain of that—but the tiny luxuries of the Devane's house weren't so impressive to her.

Lee seemed to sense my disappointment at her reaction.

"This is a really nice house," she assured me.

"My folks usually lock the back door," I said. But the door swung open when I tried the handle. The first floor was completely dark. I felt around for a light switch. I tried to laugh.

"Always have trouble with that," I said. I hit the switch.

We stood in a brief hallway that led to the kitchen. There was a wooden accordion coat rack on the wall. A fall coat hung from it. The wallpaper was decorated with small autumn leaves. We walked forward. I didn't want to try to find the light switch for the kitchen so I let the light from the hallway illuminate the room.

"This is the kitchen," I said, looking around. There was an island in the center. The surface had a built-in cutting board. There was a basket of fruit on it. There was a pot rack above the island. The wallpaper was barely visible in the dim light, but it looked like the same pattern as the hallway.

I ran my hand across the cutting board.

"Cutting board."

"Mm-hm," said Lee. She crossed her arms over her chest.

We went into the living room. I swiped my hand along the wall and, amazingly, hit the switch for the overhead lights. When I turned on the light, I heard something in the house shift.

The room was reflected in the large bay window. I could see both the houses across the street and the translucent reflection of Lee and myself looking outside. I heard the fireworks in the distance.

"This is the living room," I said.

"I like this window."

The room was painted white. Above the fireplace was a painting of a landscape. On the mantel were photos. Whoever bought the furniture had good taste: it had a timeless feel. A mahogany breakfront with antique dishes stood opposite the window. The dish set was certainly an heirloom. There was a grandfather clock next to the front door. Immediately across from the front door were stairs that led to the second story. The room was tidy. That tidiness satisfied me.

"What do you think?" I asked.

"Nice," said Lee, nodding. But she didn't seem affected. She shrugged. She laughed a single laugh and then said: "I don't know. It seems a little empty."

"It does?" I asked.

I looked around at the cracked paisley tile near the front door and the brown carpeting on the stairs that led to the second floor. I looked at the long shadows cast by the overhead light and the jagged crack in the ceiling. The house did seem empty in a way.

I heard a floorboard creak above us. My heart quickened.

Lee looked at the photos on the fireplace. She furrowed her eyebrows. She pointed at the photos.

"Who are these people?" I barely heard her.

"I don't remember," I said. I walked to the base of the stairway and looked up to the second floor. A light went on.

"How come you're not in any of these photos?" A door shut upstairs. Lee turned to me.

"Is somebody home?" she asked. I looked at the ceiling.

"I think so," I said.

People are watching this, pretending a Villanova win is a catalyst tangential to future success and happiness in their own lives. I am, seltzer in hand, one of these people. (Johnson, page 1)

Photographs

Noelle Tan

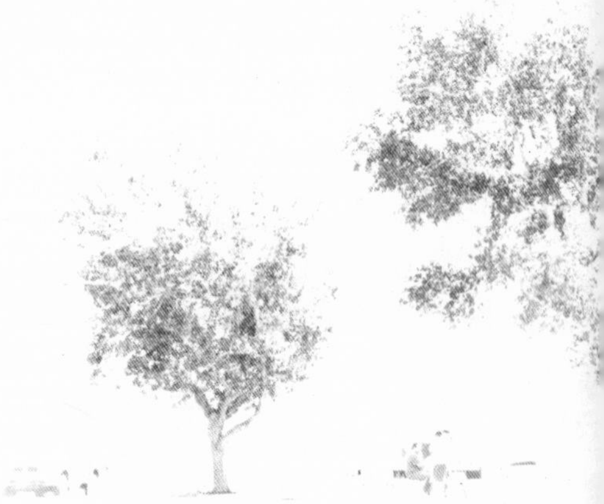

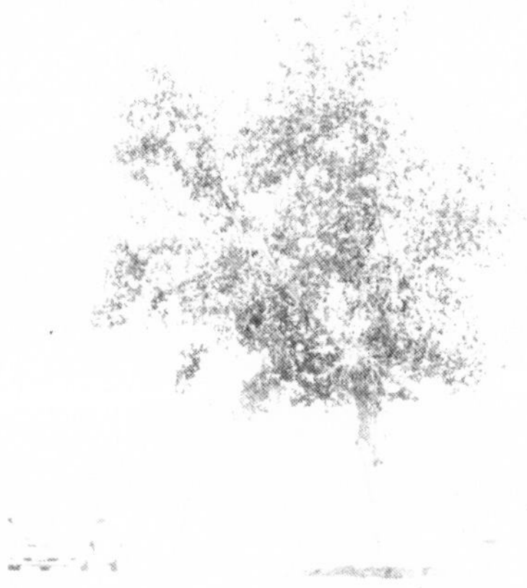

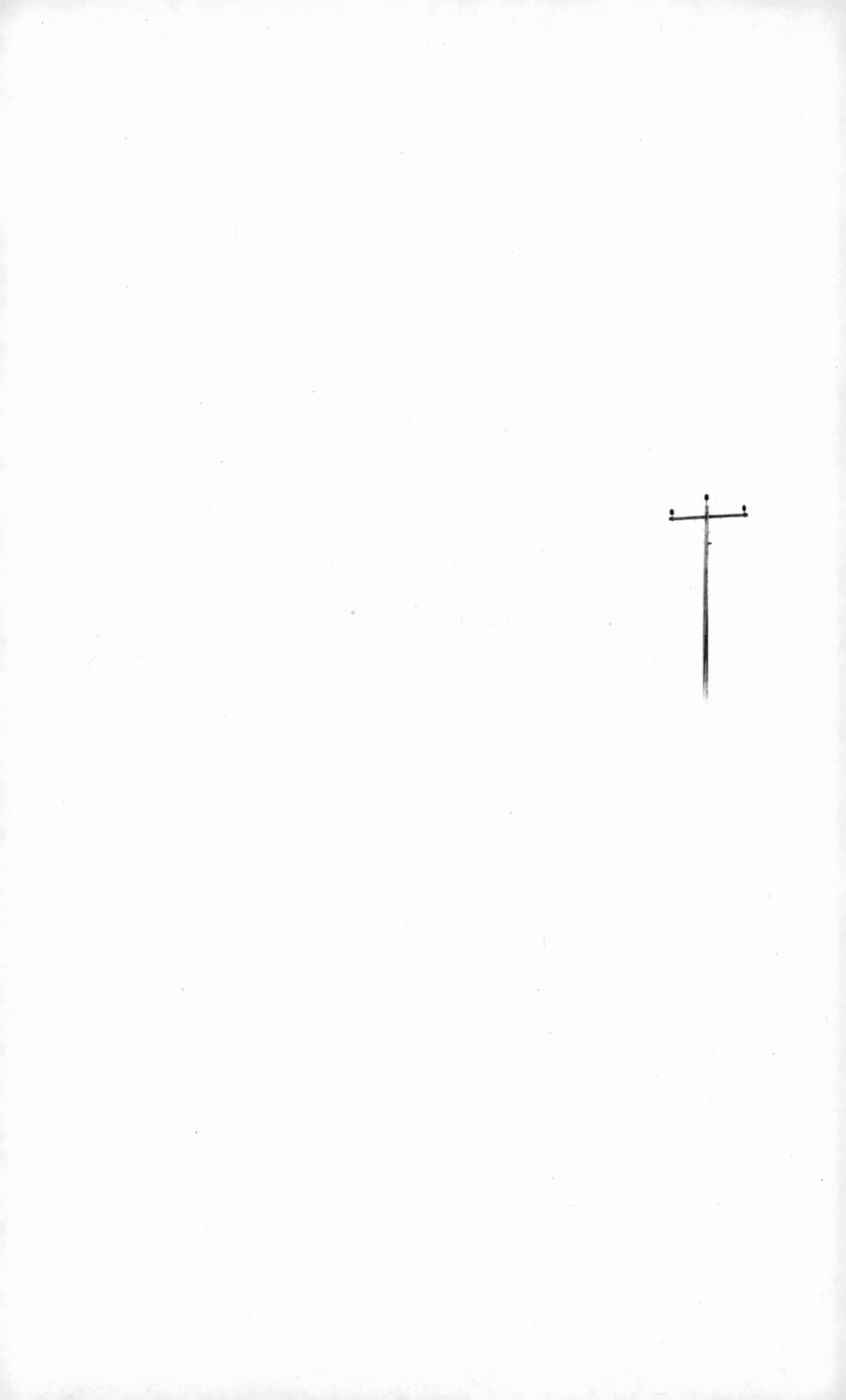

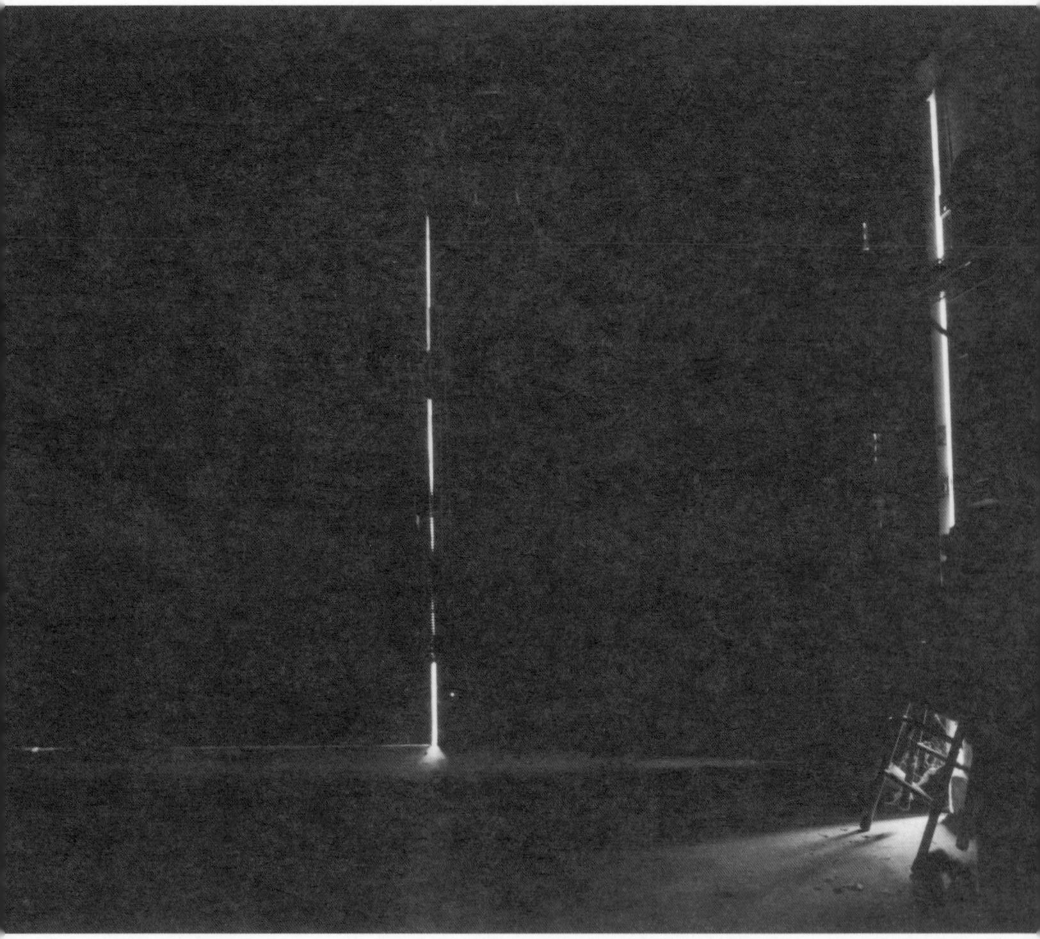

emotional triage in assorted shapes & colors

Mark Hartenbach

a false lead, a miscarriage, a wet book of matches
isn't it all about stopping the bleeding
any agenda at this point is a solitary endeavor
it doesn't matter how many signatures claim otherwise
a spray-painted non sequitur on a condemned building
an off-key rendition of irving berlin while on an amphetamine binge
where does one buy artistic license
& is the cost worth a more stable relationship
on the other hand, the security of a 75 watt porch light
can be an understanding that's never referred to as such
but there are so many other ways not to mention it
a ringing pay phone at the bottom of bradshaw avenue
that carries your imagination away like a love letter
or sets off paranoia despite three blue footballs
a half dozen stray metaphors are ripe for plucking
a world without end is a mind-blowing concept
until you shoo away the heavy smoke
& suddenly remember pages from a junior high science book
which was in it's fifteenth year
& despite marginal graffiti on every page
that distracted you from busy work
it pushed you to create your own scenarios
that had possibilities rather than probabilities
from stagnate whittling at adolescence
to full blown declarations of love

a two-toned oldsmobile going 85 mph

in black sheets of rain
is about to hit a concrete embankment
& flip a half dozen times
before winding upside down like a helpless insect
but i'm not driving.
i'm riding shotgun & fooling with the radio
being told—will you find something
& leave the damned thing alone
on one hand i know i'm not legally responsible
on the other hand i should stay sharp
in case of an emergency
at the moment, though distorted by hedonism
i'm convinced that whatever i imagine
will more than likely happen
but i also know the drugs are telling me this
but i can't be convinced
i'm too jacked for my own good
my figures are always incomplete
now i suspect that anything i do
will directly effect results
in the immediate future
i give it less than an hour

Mark Hartenbach

sodium nitrate

nothing can prepare one for implied convulsions
induced by a cleansing process of chemicals
swimming in your polluted bloodstream
in a cold room with no thermostat
& no curtains to cover 4x6 plexi-glass view at two a.m.
while yet another new roommate folds his clothes carefully
setting them in shelves next to yours
that are built into the walls without doors
except for the bottom drawer which has a lock on it
but you're not allowed to hold the key
instead a huge ball of punch lines are jingling
like uncomfortable applause
you wait for a position of authority to enter the well-lit room
because why waste your breath on a short, balding man
who seems to be more confused than you are
& sounds like a back-up singer & dresses like a gay librarian
but this tells you nothing really
so you'll be hard pressed
to come up with a revealing observation
at the next group meeting
you try stretching the boxes of a crossword puzzle
that has one answer, & one answer only
finally a stubble-faced man in sea green scrubs walks in
impatiently listens while you plead your case
your insanity defense, like it's just a minor complaint
& your arms & legs have mastered cell structure
without any assistance from your mind
so they don't need you around anymore
they have their own explanations now

Surrender
(after McGahern)

Claire Keegan

FOR FIVE DAYS THE SERGEANT KEPT THE LETTER IN THE INSIDE pocket of his uniform. There was something hard in the letter but his desire to open it was matched by his fear of what it might contain. Her letters, in recent times, without ever changing course, had taken on a different tone and he had heard that another man, a schoolteacher, was grazing a pony on her father's land. Her father's fields were on the mountain. What grazing would be there was poor and daubed with rushes. If the sergeant was to do as he had intended, there was but little time. Life, he felt, was pushing him into a corner.

All that day, he went about his duties. If Doherty, the guard in the dayroom, found him short, he did not pass any remarks, for the length of the sergeant's fuse was never disputed. It was a wet December day and there was nothing to be done. Doherty kept his head down and went over the minute particulars of the permit once again. Turning a page, he felt the paper cold against his skin. He looked up and stared, with a degree of longing, at the hearth. The fire was so low it was almost out. The sergeant insisted always on a fire but never a fire that would throw out any decent heat. The guard rose from the desk and went slowly out into the rain.

The sergeant watched him as he came back and positioned two lumps of timber at either side of the flame.

"Is it cold where you are?" said the sergeant, smiling.

"No more than usual," answered Doherty.

"Pull up tight to her there, why don't you?"

"It's December," said the guard, reasonably.

"It's December," mimicked the Sergeant. "Don't you know there's a war on?"

"What does that have to do with anything?"

"The people of this country love sitting in at the fire. At the rate we're going, we may go back to Westminster to warm our hands."

Doherty sighed. "Should I go out and see what's happening on the roads?"

"You'll go nowhere."

The sergeant stood up and put his cap on. It was a new cap, stiff, with a shining peak. When he reached out for the big black cape at the back of the door, he threw it dramatically over his shoulders. Never once had the guard seen him rush. Every move he made was deliberate and enhanced by his good looks. It was hard not to look at him but he was not, in any case, the type of man you'd turn your back on. If his moods often changed, the expression in his eyes was always the same, intemperate blue. The men who had fought with him said they couldn't ever predict his moves. They said also that his own were always the last to know. He had taken risks but had shown a strange gift for reading the enemy.

The timber spluttered into flame and its light momentarily struck the steel buttons of the sergeant's tunic. He bent over, folded the trouser legs and secured the bicycle clips. When he opened the door, the wind blew a hard, dappled rain over the flagstones. The sergeant went out and stood for a moment, looking at the day. Always, he liked to stand for a moment. When he turned back to Doherty, the guard felt sure he could read his mind.

"Don't scorch the tail of your skirt," he said, and went off without bothering to close the door.

Doherty got up and watched him cycling down the barracks road. There was something half comical about the sergeant and his bike going off down the road but the remark lingered.

It was the easiest thing in the world to humiliate somebody. He had said this aloud at his wife's side in bed one night, in the darkness, thinking she was asleep, but she had answered back, saying it was sometimes harder not to humiliate someone, that it was a weakness people had a Christian duty to resist. He had stayed awake pondering the statement long after her breathing changed. What did it mean? Women's minds were made of glass: so clear and yet their thoughts broke easily, yielding to other glassy thoughts that were even harder. It was enough to attract a man and frighten him all at once.

The barracks were quiet but there was no peace; never was there any peace in this place. Winter was here, with the rain belting down and the wind scratching the bare hills. Doherty felt the child's urge to go out for more timber, to build up the fire and make it blaze but at any moment the sergeant could come back and as little as that could mean the end. His post was nothing more than a fiction and could easily be dissolved. All it would take was the stroke of a pen. He pulled the chair up to the fire and thought of his wife and child. Another was on the way. He thought about his life and little else until he realized his thoughts were unlikely to reach any conclusion; then he looked at his hands, stretched out to the flame. What the sergeant wouldn't say if he came back and saw the firelight on his palms.

Down the road, the sergeant had dismounted and was standing still under the yews. The yews were planted in different times, and it gave him pleasure to stand and take their shelter. The same dark smoke was still battering down on the barracks roof. He'd stood there for close to an hour, on watch, but the quality of the smoke hadn't changed; neither was there any sign of Doherty going back out to the shed. *The way you rear your little pup, you'll have your little dog.* As soon as the rain eased, he moved out from the patch of sheltered ground and pushed on for town.

Further along the road, a couple had stopped and was talking. The youth, a MacManus off the hill, was leaning over the saddle of his bike with his cap pushed well back off his face. The girl was laughing but as soon as she laid eyes on the sergeant, she went still.

"A fine day it is for doing nothing," said the sergeant expansively. "Wouldn't I love to be out in the broad daylight sweet-talking girls?"

The girl blushed and turned her head away.

"I better be going on, Francie," she said.

The youth held his ground.

"Don't you know it's the wrong side of the road you're on?" demanded the sergeant. "Does the youth of this country not even know which end of ye is up?"

The young man turned his bicycle in the opposite direction.

"Does this suit you any better?" He was saying it for the girl's benefit but the girl had gone on.

"What would suit me is to see the youth of this country rolling up their sleeves," the sergeant said. "Men didn't risk their lives so the likes of ye could stand around idle."

If we can't be idle, what can we be? the young man wanted to say but his courage had gone, with the girl. He threw his leg over the crossbar and rode on, calling after her. The girl did not look back and kept her head down when the sergeant passed. The sergeant knew her mother, a widow who gave him butter and rhubarb in the summertime but all she had was a rough acre behind the house. As it turned out, there was hardly a woman in the entire district with land.

He rode on into the town and leaned his bicycle against Duignan's wall. The back door was on the latch. He pushed it open and entered a smoky kitchen whose walls were painted brown. Nobody was within but there was the smell of bread baking and someone had recently fried onions. A pang of hunger struck him; he'd gone without since morning. He went to the hearth and stared at the cast-iron pan on its heavy iron hook, the lid covered in embers. Close by, a cat was washing herself with a sput paw. Talk was filtering in from the front room that served as a shop. The sergeant could hear every word.

"But isn't he some man to cock his hat?"

"What do they see in him at all?"

"It's not as though he hasn't the looks," said another.

"Sure hasn't he the uniform?"

"A cold bloody thing it would be to lie up against in the middle of the night," and there was a cackle that was a woman's laughter.

The sergeant grew still. It was the old, still feeling of the upper hand that made lesser men freeze but the sergeant came alive. He felt himself back under the gorse with a Tommy in the sight of his gun; the old thrill of conspiracy, the raw nerve. He was about to stand closer to the shop door when suddenly it opened and the woman came in. She hardly paused when she saw him.

"Hello, Sergeant!" she called out, same as he was far away.

The banter in the shop drew to a sharp halt. There was a rough whisper and the clink of porter bottles. The woman came toward the pan with a cloth and swung the hook away from the fire. She removed the iron lid without letting an ember fall and took up the loaf. It was a white loaf with a cross cut deep into the surface of the dough. The sergeant had not seen a white loaf in months. Three times the woman rapped it with her knuckles and the sound it made was a hollow sound.

The sergeant had to hand it to her: her head was cool. There were few women in the country like her left. She went to the shop door and without looking beyond, shut it.

"I don't suppose those pigeons came in to roost?"

"They came in last night," she said.

"They didn't all come?"

"They're all there. The even dozen, fresh from the barrow."

"A fine price they must be."

When she told him what price they were, a fresh thrill ran down the entire length of his body. It was almost twice what he had anticipated and the extravagance was, in his experience, without comparison, but he hid his pleasure.

"I suppose I'll have to take them now," he grunted.

"It's as you please," the woman said.

The shop door flew open and a small boy, one of her troops, ran in from the shop.

"Slide the bolt there, Sean, good boy," the woman said.

The boy leaned against the door until the latch caught, then slid the bolt across. He drew up close to the woman and stared at the loaf.

"Is there bread?" the boy asked, tilting his head back. The boy's face was pale and there were dark circles under his eyes.

"You can have it when it cools," said the woman, propping the loaf against the window. She threw the bolt on the back door and opened the lower part of the dresser. The light wooden crate was covered by a cloth. When she pulled the cloth away, the sergeant got their scent. They lay on a bed of wood chippings, each wrapped in fine, pink tissue.

The boy leaned in over the table and stared.

"What are they, Mammy?"

"They're onions," she said.

"They're not!" he cried.

"They are," she said.

The boy reached out to stroke the tissue and stared up at the sergeant. The sergeant felt the boy's hungry gaze. He took the tissue off each one and lifted it to his nose before he pushed back his cape and reached into his pocket for the money. As he was reaching in, his fingers lingered unnecessarily over the envelope and he realized his hand was half covetous of the letter. The woman wrapped the crate in a flour sack while the sergeant stood waiting.

"Is it for Christmas you be wanting them, Sergeant?"

"Christmas," he said. "Ay."

She counted out the money on the kitchen table, and when he offered her something extra for the loaf, she looked at the boy. The boy's face was paler now. His skin was chalky. When he saw his mother wrapping the loaf in the brown paper, he began to cry.

"Mammy," he wailed. "My bread!"

"Hush, *a leanbh*. I'll make you another," she said. "I'll do it just as soon as the sergeant leaves."

The sergeant took the parcel out the back and tied it carefully on to the carrier of his bike. He was ready now for the barracks but he walked back through the kitchen, unlocked the door, and entered the shop. The talk that had seized up when his presence was made known had risen back to neutral speech. This, too, seized up on his entry. Walking in through the silence, he felt the same old distance and superiority he always felt. He was reared near here, they knew his people but he would never be one of them. He stood at the counter and looked at the stains on the dark wood.

"Isn't it a harsh day?"

Always, there was someone who could not stand the silence. This was the type of man who, in other circumstances, could get another killed.

"It's a day for the fire," said another.

The sergeant hoped one of them would open his gob and make an open strike but not one of them had the courage. To his face, their talk would stay in the shallow, furtive waters of idle banter; anything of significance they had to say would be said just after he was gone. He paused at the front door where a calendar was hanging from a nail. He studied it closely though he well knew the date. Standing there, looking at the month of December, a blade of conviction passed through him. He opened the front door and went out into the rain without having uttered a word.

"Well!" said Duignan, watching the sergeant pushing his bike eagerly up the road.

"Whoever would have thought it?"

"If you want to know me, come live with me!"

The porter bottles came back out. Duignan took a draught, straightened himself, and put his hands behind his back. In a perfect imitation, he slowly marched over to the wall and put his nose against the calendar.

"It isn't December?"

"Ay, Sergeant."

"Do you think oranges would be ripe at this time of the year?"

As soon as he mentioned the word, there was a ripple of laughter. Each man, in his own mind, had a vision of the sergeant, the big IRA man, sitting into the feed of oranges. Duignan went to the counter and sniffed the wood. Stiffly, he swung back toward the men.

"It isn't porter I smell?"

"It's on the stage you should be!"

"No, Sergeant!" cried another. "'Tis oranges!"

Duignan carried on. There were fresh waves of laughter but it did not come to a head until the woman, her hands covered in flour, came in from the kitchen asking what, in the name of God, it was that had them so entertained?

The sergeant saw all this in his mind as he pushed his bicycle back to the barracks in the rain. Let them laugh. The last laugh would be his. The rain was coming down, hopping off the handlebars, his cape, the mudguard. It was down for the evening. There had not been a dry day for over a week and the roads were rough and sloppy.

When he reached the dayroom, he softly pushed the door open and there was Doherty, fast asleep, in the chair. The sergeant stole over to the desk, lifted the box of papers, and let it fall. Doherty woke in a splash of fear.

"I think it's nearly time that you were gone out of this!" the sergeant cried.

"I didn't—"

"You didn't! You didn't what?"

"I didn't—"

"You didn't! You didn't! Get up off your arse and go home!" the sergeant cried. He looked at the ledger. "Did you not even bother your arse to record the rain?"

The guard stumbled out, half asleep, into the rain and read the gauge. All this was new to him. He came back and wrote a figure in the book and signed it.

"I hope you'll be in better form tomorrow," Doherty said, blotting the page.

"I'll be as I am," said the sergeant. "And don't think just because you're getting off early that you'll not have to make up for it some other day."

"Amn't I always here," sighed Doherty.

"Do you think I haven't noticed? Amn't I tripping over you?"

"I do whatever—"

"But are you ever useful? That's the question. If you're of no use, then mightn't you be as well off elsewhere?"

Doherty looked at him and put his coat on. "Is there anything more?"

"That'll be all," the sergeant clipped. "It's clearly as much if not more than you're able for. God help us, but I can't help but think sometimes that the force mightn't be better off with a clatter of women."

The guard put on his coat, went out, and softly closed the door. The sergeant went to the window and watched him, how eagerly he pedalled on home. Doherty could ill afford to lose his post, the sergeant knew. He watched him until he had turned the corner then he went out for the coal.

The coal was a turn from a Protestant for whom he'd done a favor. He pushed the poker deep into the fire and raked over all the old timber. He placed lumps of coal on the embers knowing, before long, that it would blaze. He wheeled the bike up close to the hearth and untied the parcel. Then he took off the clips and hung his cape on the back of the door and sat down. There was relief in sitting down, in being alone, finally.

He looked at the marks of the tires, of his feet, of the rain dripping off his cape onto the flagstones. He looked at these marks that he had made until the fire had warmed the room and the floor was dry. Then he took his tunic off and opened the letter. As soon as he opened the letter, the ring fell into his hand but his hand was expecting this. He looked at it briefly and went on to read:

December 9th

Dear Michael,

I have decided it is impossible for us to go on. I have waited long enough and this ring, which I took as a token of your affection, is now an ornament. Nothing is as I had expected. I had thought that we would be married by now and getting on with our lives. I don't know what it is you are doing up there or why you stay away. It must not be convenient for you to continue on with this engagement and it no longer suits me.

The time has come for us to be together or remain apart. I see no cause for any further delay. I hear you are throwing your hat at other women. You were seen outside McGuire's last week and the week before. If your heart has changed, it is your duty to let me know. I enclose your ring and pray God this finds you in good health as we are all down here.

Yours,

Susan

It was as he suspected: she was calling him in. He felt solace in the knowledge that he was right and yet it struck him sore that he had hoped it might be otherwise. Hope always was the last thing to die; he had learned this as a child and seen it, first hand, as a soldier. He held the ring up to the fire and looked at it. The stone was smaller than he had realized and the thin gold band was battered as though she hadn't bothered to take it off while laboring. He did not read over the letter again; the message was clear. He folded it back as it was, placed it in the heavy metal box and locked it. He placed the key and the ring on the desk and rolled up his sleeves.

The room was warm and the chain, at this stage, would be dry. The firelight was striking the rims, the handlebars, the spokes. He turned the bicycle upside down and, with one hand slowly turning the pedal, he placed the nozzle of the oil can against the chain. Oiling it, watching the chain going round, it struck him how perfectly the links engaged the sprocket, how the cogs were made for the chain. Somewhere, a man believed he could propel himself using his own weight. He had seen it in his mind and went on to make it happen. Oiling the bike stoked up the old pleasure he had felt in cleaning the guns: forcing the cloth down the length of the barrel, dull gleam of the metal, how snugly the bullet slid into the chamber. Everything was made for something else in whose presence things ran smoothly.

He had once, as a child, knocked the sugar bowl off the table. The sugar had spilled and was wasted, for it could not be sieved out from the glass. He could see it still, the bright shock of it on the flagstones. His mother had taken him out to the bicycle and spun the wheel, holding his fingers at an angle, tight to the spokes. It went on for an age and the pain he felt could not have been worse had she actually dismembered him. It was one of the first lessons he had learned and he would carry it all through life.

Now, he felt a childish pride in owning the bike. He turned it right side up and pumped the tires until he felt hot and satisfied. When he was sure the tires could take his weight for the distance, he propped the bike against the desk. Then he took the crate from the sack and positioned himself at the hearth.

In reaching out, he hesitated but the fruit he chose felt heavy. The rind did not come away easily and his thumbnail left an oily track over the flesh. When he tasted it, it tasted sweet and bitter all at once. There were a great many seeds. He took each seed from his mouth and threw it on the fire. Juice was staining his uniform but he would leave a note for Doherty to take it down to the Duignan woman and have it pressed. Before he had swallowed the last segment of the first orange his hand was reaching out for the next. This time he kept his thumbnail tight to the skin so as not to break to the flesh. The peelings singed for a while on the open coals but shrank and in time became part of the fire.

His knowledge of women swept across his mind. He tried to think of each one separately—of what she said or how, exactly, she was dressed—but they were not so much mixed up in his mind as all the one: the same bulge at the top of the stocking, the shallow gasp, the smell of malt vinegar in their hair. How quickly all of that was over. He ate the oranges and thought about these women, concluding that there was little difference between them. By the time the last seed was on the coals, he was glutted.

"Another casualty," he said aloud in the empty room.

The clock on the wall ticked on and the rain was beating strong and hard against the barracks door. He burned the crate and threw the coal dust on the embers. When he was sure no evidence of how he had spent the night remained, he lit the candle and climbed the stairs, feeling a shake in himself that made the light tremble. He did not take off his clothes. He got into the bed as he was and reached out for the clock. As he wound it and felt the spring tighten, the old desire to wind it until it seized came over him but he fought against it, as always, and blew the candle out. Then he rolled over into the middle of the cold bed. When he closed his eyes, the same old anxiety was there shining, like dark water at the back of his mind, but he soon fell asleep.

Before first light, he groped his way blindly to the outhouse and felt the oranges passing through his body. There was a satisfaction in this that renewed and deepened the extravagance, all at once. When he came inside, he lit the lamp, made tea, and buttered some of the white bread. He took the razor off the shelf, sharpened it on the leather strap, and shaved. There were unaccountable shadows in the mirror but they did not distract him. He washed, changed into his good brown suit, gathered up the ring and key and went outside to look at the day. No rain was falling but there were clouds stacked up on one side of the sky.

He wrote the note for Doherty, put on the clips, and threw the cape over his shoulders. When he got up on the saddle, he felt the springs give under his weight. He reassured himself that he had the ring, the key, and stood on the pedals, to get started. Soon he was laboring over the hills, knowing full well that the days of idling and making women blush were coming to a close. A cold feeling surged through him. It was new to him and like all new feelings it made him anxious, but he rode on, composing the speech. By the time he was pushing on for her part of the country, he grew conscious of the rain and the noise it made, the rattle of it like beads on the handlebars.

When he entered her townland he saw the rushes and knew the clay beneath them was shallow clay. With a bitter taste in his mouth, he faced up the mountain but before he was halfway up, his breath gave out and he had to dismount. Marching on, he could feel his future: the woman's bony hand striking a hollow sound in the loaf and the boy with the hungry gaze asking for bread.

Wade
had always
dated rich girls,
who'd been carefully
named:
Mirabelle,
Tatiana,
Tallulah.
(Willens, page 35)

The New Mode

Gerard Coletta

Watch this: the anchor slips
into a stupor, the harbor emerges
from its rest, ready for lunch.

Watch: mammoth wharfs cling
to the face of the shore, barnicles
cleave to other barnicles.

This is Friday, the bricks berry-stained
with late sun, with memory.

This is the new mode: the new swimmers
swimming the air, the swimmers
with beautiful frills—
                              the bones
of the great spirit, disarticulated,
scattered, hanging in the sky
like dozens of alien moons, placid,
farflung, sleeping—
                              the Roman soldier
lost in time, running through the plaza
and up the limestone stairs, up to the third floor
bathroom, smirking—what is he doing in there?—
leaving me here, alone, bound inside my skin,
my concurrent skins, like an elm, subsisting
on the medium but not its material.

OPEN CITY

This is the new mode, watchfulness
and all the dark suggestions,
the things we can and cannot say:
words like *listless* and *happy*.
I was supposed to be happy.

Are there parts of us now distributed
among the grids, across the squares of netting
that mark and divide this place?
Am I, in fact, happy?

In this city the streets are full of holes,
bottomless chasms as wide as nickels,
chasms harboring salamanders, joyous
in their brightness, brighter, tastier
than strawberries, than light, than light in water.

Let this be the new mode, this city
where the sun sweeps the Parcheesi pieces
from the street, the impediments, bow-legged
and menacing and fibrous midday, like limes
suspended in a dark oil—
                                  this world
where the leaves are always lit
by the night's secret face, the rain,
in whose orange phosphor the leaves
are as children in a floodlit baseball field,
transfixed, ever-attendant.

Let this be the place, the scent:
citrus and cloves, the simple wind,
so single-minded—
                              and watch: light
through the walls of peppers
as chords mature within.

Gerard Coletta

The Second Step

Under the icy sky, the bar-
headed geese, the griffon vultures,

the white disk of sun (that great
thing just hanging there), the phantasm
that was Betelgeuse, Sirius as it bores its hole

through the widening air—all fly
erratically, all wobble and fail—
they could be anywhere, now, they could be

going anywhere. Since you left
cold has settled here like an improbable dew,
a web of numerous and sovereign particles:

the inaccessible virtues, twisting like crystals
in the sky's blank world, its un-world—
they are not free, they are not free.

There is something radical about loneliness,
as if it in each of its moments holds
a false idea, a pulse, a bead,

the ghost of something not yet born.
I wait here in the afternoons and early evenings
beneath the curtain of your implacable faith,

the last thing you gave me.
Its heavy fabric warms
and comforts me, but all the while I feel

OPEN CITY

something approach, a bow shock,
some sort of wave, a fissure.
You always believed

it would spare us, charitably
disintegrate, as currents of water or air
part harmlessly around the birds. You believed

in the great metal ladder—and reached,
half-mad, for each succeeding rung,
cracked smile crackling over the glyphs
of your alchemies, the auxiliary sciences

of history—wound your sinews, that knotted tissue
barely concealed by skin, yew needles
bristling under cobweb, and climbed

the ladder where knowledge and observation end
and color and oxygen abrade and melt
in the high-altitude sun,

where flies flicker at either wrist; where
the ancient minutes, bloody with brass,
are in their vertiginous queue visible,

where all things are visible:
boats riding the world-curve, incident light,
light as miasmatic as light on a foil.

Brooklyn

Wayne Conti

"JENNY," SHE'D TOLD HERSELF WHEN SHE HAD HER DEGREE IN her hand. "Jenny, maybe you don't want to be in the working world, but think of each thing that's going to happen to you as just another part of an adventure." She'd felt she could get away with saying such a thing to herself since she was moving to New York City—well, Brooklyn—that she might not get away with if she'd stayed home in Connecticut. That had been then.

It was more than two years later. She was sitting on her French Provincial bed in her small apartment in Brooklyn. Outside her window the last light of a cold Saturday afternoon was falling. She was still in her pink silk pajamas. She hadn't been outside that day.

What *can* you tell yourself, she wondered, after you've joined a huge company, just after having convinced yourself that everything in life is an adventure, and you find out that your job is not?

She was in banking, which really meant that she calculated whether the bank would make more money by lending money or by just doing nothing. It was a strong message she'd hand to strangers—maybe she gave the clients what they'd asked for or maybe she just sat there and killed everything, then waited for someone else. She'd seen all that clearly the day before as she looked into the face of a big-time borrower, one Michael Gregory Taft, an independent real estate developer. She didn't have an answer for him about his loan.

He was handsome and confident, she thought. Older. He was telling her the details of his project. He'd smiled at her. She'd noticed a scar, which looked like a fencing wound, over his left eye. He'd paused. And right there, Jenny didn't know why, he looked like he'd just love to get it all over with and die. She'd felt it, she was sure she did.

"Why do you work in a bank?" he'd suddenly asked her. "You obviously have the intelligence, but you also seem to have an imagination. You don't appear to like loan approvals at all." She was shocked that he had said such a thing. He hadn't been smiling when he said it, either. She could feel how he wanted to die, right there; at that moment, so did she. And she was no less startled that *she* would be thinking of that, dying, during that interview, rather than just quitting and somehow getting married which, after all, could be an adventure, at least for a while.

When she'd started at the bank, she thought maybe she might kill herself, though it was only in the same way she'd thought of it years before, just after she'd fallen off a horse onto her back. Or once when she'd been sitting in a dentist's chair, her mouth open and bloody, the idea being that dying would get her out of that moment. Of course, the idea had always passed. Recently, nothing had really happened, but the idea was not passing.

Jenny had just sat looking at her client, Michael Taft, for a moment. He'd smiled a little, then said, "I suppose I should apologize for saying what I did. But, what are you doing tomorrow night? Could I take you somewhere?"

The next day, wandering around her apartment in Brooklyn, she had to tell herself again that he wasn't bad looking. With that scar over his eye she could actually have described him as "dashing." He was older. She'd said yes. She wasn't exactly looking forward to this date, but she wasn't exactly not either.

Jenny stood for a moment by her window. Late Saturday afternoon in Brooklyn, the winter sun just glowing over the rooftops, and she had time to kill. One second she was very aware of where she was, the next she felt she was flat on her back in the fine gravel of Connecticut, unable to breathe, looking up at the paddock fence, hearing the horse galloping away.

She supposed that if this Michael tried to take off her clothes, she'd let him, though she couldn't quite picture the scene. The idea wasn't too interesting, but she did have an evening to kill—and so did he.

"What dress should I wear?" she suddenly asked herself out loud. Then she answered, "Oh, I'll figure it out."

Whenever she'd buy a dress, she'd have her good thoughts and her bad thoughts, yet it all seemed to work out. But, as she had to admit, a little bit of that same deathly feeling was lurking there even in those stores, just as she was about to step in front of a mirror—pushing and slipping herself between circular racks of whatevers—the feeling that this is not going to work out, it's never going to work out, and it's better to just die. But then the saleslady would come up to her, or she'd think maybe she'd like it more in another color, and she'd forget about dying.

It was probably getting colder outside. Jenny wondered if she should wear something black or dark blue. Maybe light blue and sheer—that could be exciting, that might knock this Michael out. Emphasize the age difference! Perhaps she'd braid her hair. God knows how he might dress, good or bad, that could take the breath out of her. She might want to kill herself—even for a minute—just to get to the other side of that moment.

The clock on her dresser had hardly moved. It was the same as waiting to get up for work when she couldn't sleep, spending half the night thinking, I don't want to go to work, until finally she'd just get out of bed at 5:35 a.m., and slowly, so slowly, get ready. But she'd always found she could only dress just so deliberately—she would look at the little bottles of perfume on her dresser, or hear faint sounds outside her window, footsteps, or a truck passing, and in the stillness that followed she'd get that I-want-to-die feeling.

Would he want to peel her clothes off slowly? Or tear them to shreds? She wouldn't mind. She felt her heart accelerate. Who knew for sure if she'd like him—that would be something, to be wasting a Saturday afternoon all the way till seven, just to be back at nine-fifteen. Then what would she do? Stare at herself in the mirror? Count the stars in the sky? Can't see many in Brooklyn.

"You don't like anything, Jenny," her mother was always saying, "you're too critical." But then when she was with her friends from school, one of them, usually Hannah, would remark, "You know, you're too accepting. You just let people push you around."

She wondered how she could manage all that. Still, she never said a word when they would talk that way. She just went on, waiting for something to happen, though nothing ever really did, good or bad.

Since late Friday afternoon she'd known Michael wouldn't get the loan. The bank had moved on. But whatever he expected, he had to wait until the next business day, Monday, before he'd know—that left Saturday night, even all day Sunday.

She had heard that some women liken themselves to gladiators— they strap on their prettiest armor, pull back their hair, take their bra and thong with them and go off to the arena where everyone hacks at everyone else and who knows if they'll come home again?

"But here I go," she tells herself, "I can't wait any longer." She'll walk slowly. Wait in the cold. All those shadowy people passing, she can just picture them.

Withdrawn

Doug Shaeffer

oomph.

phew!

s920
cop. 1

LAVINE
Famous industrialists 3.00

NOV 19 1966

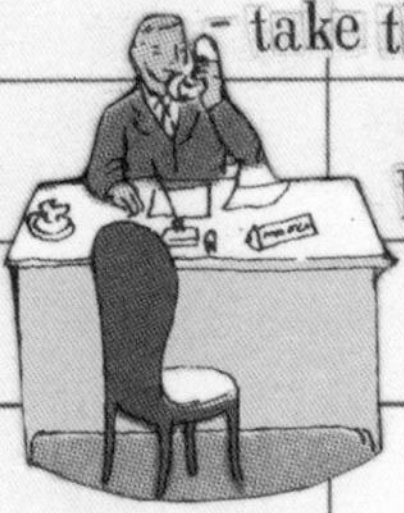

- take this flower
and
pluck it.

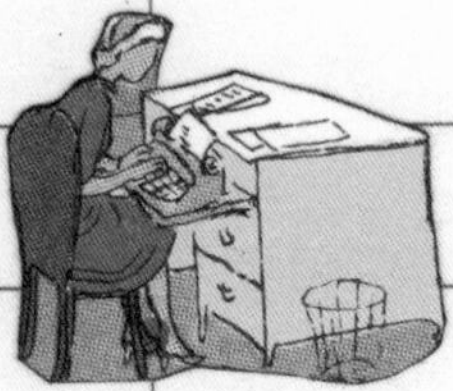

AUTHOR Feuchtwanger, Lion

TITLE Power

DATE	BORROWER'S NAME	ROOM NUMBER
	secret engines rise and shine.	

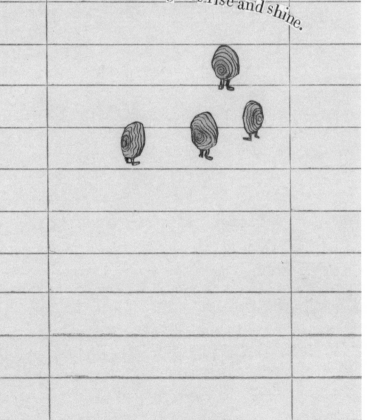

DATE DUE	BORROWER'S NAME	ROOM NUMBER
	't' is for terror.	

will we

ever

wake
up?

nah.

JUV
KF
9223
.Z9
J64
1985

Johnson, Joan (Joan
J.)

Justice PUDDING. 5̆ □ 0

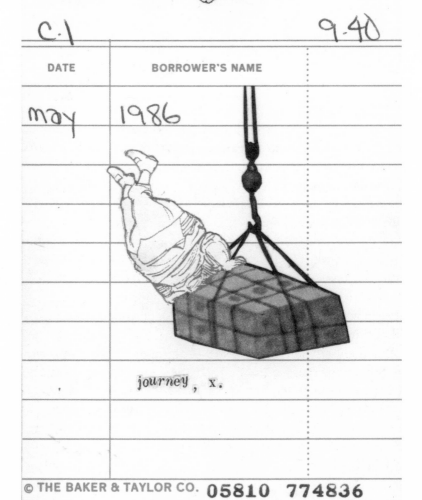

C.1   9.40

may 1986

journey, x.

Reckoning

Erin Brown

WHEN HE COMES INTO THE ROOM, YOU ARE HOLDING YOURSELF. You are a thin shape in the window; the flat, beckoning window. You are holding yourself and you are watching yourself holding yourself. You are thinking window, window, window.

It is dark. From where you stare, you can discern the apartments across the way; the backs of apartments. *Back*, you think. *Back*. There is an open space, a waiting space, a garbage and, perhaps, a *bodies* space between your building and the backs of the other buildings. You stare hard across that lot. You imagine all those eyes draped behind curtains and hands, boxed in, with shut lids—and something hard and precious falls inside of you, something that had been lodged between your shoulder and your throat. Open your mouth. Nothing, still nothing.

But there are sounds creeping in through the window's parted lips. Something slams. Something shatters. Tinny Indian music floats in, reassuring in its novelty. A cat cries—a strangled woman? You hear nothing in its entirety. Everything is dissected into hard vowels and exclamation points. They stab at you where you are sitting, and you hold yourself very still to keep from flinching.

Behind you, movement. A step. Or a shuffling. Or an advancing hand. Immediately, your back curves like a shell, and your shoulder blades pull together until you think they are going to hit and grate, a steel sound. You know he is watching you and you hope that he sees only your outline, your pitiful shell, and that this deters him. You try very, very hard to focus on the night, to stare it down, to pick at it like crumbling wallpaper until you can see the day behind it; the day *after*. Your breath sounds distant, distant but bearing down, and you stop breathing to make sure the breathing is yours. You don't want to have to turn and look.

It's yours: breathe in, breathe out.

You are searching for lights. Left to right, end line, quick reverse, left to right, end line, quick reverse. Your eyes are dizzied by the dark pocks of windows that are stamped across the other buildings. Blur your eyes. It's easier for the count. You are looking for something with form, imagined or otherwise. A point to dive into. You want to tear yourself out of this flat, beckoning window, and hurl, glide, swim into one of those other dark yawns. All you need is a point of reference.

Behind you a candle is lit. You know this is how he means to begin.

Intent now. Focus. There is a light in one of the windows. A hazy, gauzy light. Narrow your eyes. Try to bring it closer. Ignore the shuffling sounds and make your body a tight anchor, heavy and rusted, splintering to touch.

Across the lot, framed by a window's unforgiving lines, two lovers quarrel. You see only the dim shape of their arms as they pull and resist, pull and resist. *Resist*, you think. *Resist*.

He comes close, two steps. Too close. Don't turn. Imagine yourself iron. You are twenty-ton.

Across the lot, one arm cajoles, the other refuses. One arm insists. The other refuses. Back and forth, the leaning and the straightening, the force and withdrawal. You imagine a tightening wrist. You imagine the release.

Then, a hand on your shoulder. Fingers in your hair.

You are waiting, enduring. Your skin is separated from your body by so many hard layers of intent. Across the lot, you want only to see who wins and who gives in, who gives up. You are waiting to see one pull the other down; to see, at least, a reckoning. But they wave back and forth like weeds, rooted in one another, even if through struggle.

You decide there is nothing more to see—you turn back to *your* body, the hand on your thigh, the hand on your face. Turn, now. Turn away from the window. Turn toward the voice that is caressing your ear. Low and methodical. Try, try again. Try. Try. Again.

****

In the morning, you sit in the light. You hold your coffee with both hands, a careful pose. Look out the window and notice the lot, the weeds and the flowers, the truck tire and the vegetable garden. Cats walk with muted purpose, pawing the air for phantom birds. Somewhere close, a child's cry turns into laughter. Behind you, you can hear the rattle and crash of the kitchen. Breakfast sounds. Across the lot, tied to the fire escape and framed by a window, a hammock bends and swings lightly, like the arms of two lovers, pulling, resisting.

Dourine

Alex Lemon

Don't you think it'd be cool if we hung
        out? I mean, I once pulled

all of my fingernails off with my father's pliers,
        and still slivered the avocado perfectly—

you should have seen that salad. Grape
        tomatoes, red cabbage—I let the cold

water run over the cucumber in the colander
        until the tears on my face had dried.

The only thing I miss about those days
        was the morning light—how I could see

time countdown like a tiny digital clock
        on the necks of all the people I loved.

Everyone was trying to be the best
        animal they could be. Everyone wore

sundresses. Now, to be honest with you,
        I mostly stare blearily at mannequins

in the fancy stores downtown. One of these
        times I swear, with just the twitch

of an eye, a finger popped from inside
      my lip—I'll make one of those plastic

bastards come alive. I'll do anything you want
      me to do, anything at all for my sixty seconds

of pain. Look: red boots! And matching lipstick!
      I feel all of your love! And beneath this

ice-cream-cone-painted rain slicker—I just might
      not have a lick of anything on

Alex Lemon

Hallelujah Blackout

Backwards bending nothing rises
Out of me when I go to lose

       Myself on the river sinking
       Crunched cans & listening to rabbits

Swifting through the elmbrake   Stripped birches flung & floating away
     Gracenotes wickeding the latticed-lit trees

As they miraculously fill   The chirps   The chirps
     Shotgun shells & a bible stitched of leaves—
          The first psalm of which
          Sings of the contour
          A body makes in rivermud

     ***

O song of a shape that sings: honesties
     Of a body sleeping
Twisted in front of headlights
     White-sheeted—

Night beetles already eating
     Through the gluey-flesh
Bleating figures on the edge
     Of the charmed glow

OPEN CITY

All of it—black & white
      Photographs—
            Beautiful & still
                With hewing

      ***

Which held to the swinging bulb   are hollow open & always
         my ice-boxed insides
Swan-stitched   for whomever wants a tumble
         plumbers & strangers

With halos & wings   I beg   forever ecstasy   I beg
For more scars & moths fluttering a sill in the sunshine—a sad lone voice

Uttering breathily through morning   a cry   that starts beautifully
      A violin sawing in the head   of anything that hears it

             I beg & beg   for good blessings
                    & blackout the world

      ***

So up from my back in the yard I have to be
      Picked away from the stars

      That fine therapy—
      The thrashing roll
         Of an empty wheelchair cruising down the hushed street

             This pockmarked   Tongue

    Clucking blood when it grinds on by

Home at Last

Dinaw Mengestu

AT TWENTY-ONE I MOVED TO BROOKLYN HOPING THAT IT would be the last move I would ever make—that it would, with the gradual accumulation of time, memory, and possessions, become that place I instinctively reverted back to when asked, "So, where are you from?" I was born in Ethiopia like my parents and their parents before them, but it would be a lie to say I was from Ethiopia, having left the country when I was only two years old following a military coup and civil war, losing in the process the language and any direct memory of the family and culture I had been born into. I simply am Ethiopian, without the necessary "from" that serves as the final assurance of our identity and origin.

Since leaving Addis Ababa in 1980, I've lived in Peoria, Illinois; in a suburb of Chicago; and then finally, before moving to Brooklyn, in Washington, D.C., the de facto capital of the Ethiopian immigrant. Others, I know, have moved much more often and across much greater distances. I've only known a few people, however, that have grown up with the oddly permanent feeling of having lost and abandoned a home that you never, in fact, really knew, a feeling that has nothing to do with apartments, houses, or miles, but rather the sense that no matter how far you travel, or how long you stay still, there is no place that you can always return to, no place where you fully belong. My parents, for all that they had given up by leaving Ethiopia, at least had the certainty that they had come from some place. They knew the country's language and culture, had met outside of coffee shops along Addis's main boulevard in the early days of their relationship, and as a result, regardless of how mangled by violence Ethiopia later became, it was irrevocably and ultimately theirs. Growing up, one of my father's favorite sayings was, "Remember, you are Ethiopian," even though, of course, there was nothing for me to remember apart from the bits of nostalgia and culture my parents had imparted. What remained had less to do with the idea that I was from Ethiopia and more to do with the fact that I was not from America.

I can't say when exactly I first became aware of that feeling—that I was always going to and never from—but surely I must have felt it during those first years in Peoria, with my parents, sister, and me always sitting on the edge of whatever context we were now supposed to be a part of, whether it was the all-white southern Baptist church we went to every weekend, or the nearly all-white Catholic schools my sister and I attended first in Peoria and then again in Chicago at my parents' insistence. By that point my father, haunted by the death of his brother during the revolution and the ensuing loss of the country he had always assumed he would live and die in, had taken to long evening walks that he eventually let me accompany him on. Back then he had a habit of sometimes whispering his brother's name as he walked ("Shibrew," he would mutter) or whistling the tunes of Amharic songs that I had never known. He always walked with both hands firmly clasped behind his back, as if his grief, transformed into something real and physical, could be grasped and secured in the palms of his hands. That was where I first learned what it meant to lose and be alone. The lesson would be reinforced over the years whenever I caught sight of my mother sitting by herself on a Sunday afternoon, staring silently out of our living room's picture window, recalling, perhaps, her father who had died after she left, or her mother, four sisters, and one brother in Ethiopia—or else recalling nothing at all because there was no one to visit her, no one to call or see. We had been stripped bare here in America, our lives confined to small towns and urban suburbs. We had sacrificed precisely those things that can never be compensated for or repaid—parents, siblings, culture, a memory to a place that dates back more than half a generation. It's easy to see now how even as a family we were isolated from one another—my parents tied and lost to their past; my sister and I irrevocably assimilated. For years we were strangers even among ourselves.

****

By the time I arrived in Brooklyn I had little interest in where I actually landed. I had just graduated college and had had enough of the fights and arguments about not being "black" enough, as well as the earlier fights in high school hallways and street corners that were fought for simply being black. Now it was enough, I wanted to believe, to simply be, to say I was in Brooklyn and Brooklyn was home. It wasn't until after I had signed the lease on my apartment that I even learned the name of the neighborhood I had moved into: Kensington, a distinctly regal name at a price that I could afford; it was perfect, in other words, for an eager and poor writer with inflated ambitions and no sense of where he belonged.

After less than a month of living in Kensington I had covered almost all of the neighborhood's streets, deliberately committing their layouts and routines to memory in a first attempt at assimilation. There was an obvious and deliberate echo to my walks, a self-conscious reenactment of my father's routine that I adopted to stave off some of my own emptiness. It wasn't just that I didn't have any deep personal relationships here, it was that I had chosen this city as the place to redefine, to ground, to secure my place in the world. If I could bind myself to Kensington physically, if I could memorize and mentally reproduce in accurate detail the various shades of the houses on a particular block, then I could stake my own claim to it, and in doing so, no one could tell me who I was or that I didn't belong.

On my early-morning walks to the F train I passed in succession a Latin American restaurant and grocery store, a Chinese fish market, a Halal butcher shop, followed by a series of Pakistani and Bangladeshi takeout restaurants. This cluster of restaurants on the corner of Church and McDonald, I later learned, sold five-dollar plates of lamb and chicken biryani in portions large enough to hold me over for a day, and in more financially desperate times, two days. Similarly, I learned that the butcher and fish shop delivery trucks arrived on most days just as I was making my way to the train. If I had time, I found it hard not to stand and stare at the refrigerated trucks with their calf and sheep carcasses dangling from hooks, or at the tanks of newly arrived bass and catfish flapping around in a shallow pool of water just deep enough to keep them alive.

It didn't take long for me to develop a fierce loyalty to Kensington, to think of the neighborhood and my place in it as emblematic of a grander immigrant narrative. In response to that loyalty, I promised to host a "Kensington night" for the handful of new friends that I eventually made in the city, an evening that would have been comprised of five-dollar lamb biryani followed by two-dollar Budweisers at Denny's, the neighborhood's only full-fledged bar—a defunct Irish pub complete with terribly dim lighting and wooden booths. I never hosted a Kensington night, however, no doubt in part because I had established my own private relationship to the neighborhood, one that could never be shared with others in a single evening of cheap South Asian food and beer. I knew the hours of the call of the muezzin that rang from the mosque a block away from my apartment. I heard it in my bedroom every morning, afternoon, and evening, and if I was writing when it called out, I learned that it was better to simply stop and admire it. My landlord's father, an old gray-haired Chinese immigrant who spoke no English, gradually smiled at me as I came and went, just as I learned to say hello, as politely as possible, in Mandarin every time I saw him. The men behind the counters of the Bangladeshi takeout places now knew me by sight. A few, on occasion, slipped an extra dollop of vegetables or rice into my to-go container, perhaps because they worried that I wasn't eating enough. One in particular, who was roughly my age, spoke little English, and smiled wholeheartedly whenever I came in, gave me presweetened tea and free bread, a gesture that I took to be an acknowledgment that, at least for him, I had earned my own, albeit marginal, place here.

And so instead of sitting with friends in a brightly lit fluorescent restaurant with cafeteria-style service, I found myself night after night quietly walking around the neighborhood in between sporadic fits of writing. Kensington was no more beautiful by night than by day, and perhaps this very absence of grandeur allowed me to feel more at ease wandering its streets at night. The haphazard gathering of immigrants in Kensington had turned it into a place that even someone like me, haunted and conscious of race and identity at every turn, could slip and blend into.

Inevitably on my way home I returned to the corner of Church and McDonald with its glut of identical restaurants. On warm nights, I had found it was the perfect spot to stand and admire not only what

Kensington had become with the most recent wave of migration, but what any close-knit community—whether its people came here one hundred years ago from Europe or a decade ago from Africa, Asia, or the Caribbean—has provided throughout Brooklyn's history: a second home. There, on that corner, made up of five competing South Asian restaurants of roughly equal quality, dozens of Pakistani and Bangladeshi men gathered one night after another to drink chai out of paper cups. The men stood there talking for hours, huddled in factions built in part, I imagine, around restaurant loyalties. Some nights I sat in one of the restaurants and watched from a corner table with a book in hand as an artificial prop. A few of the men always stared, curious no doubt as to what I was doing there. Even though I lived in Kensington, when it came to evening gatherings like this, I was the foreigner and tourist. On other nights I ordered my own cup of tea and stood a few feet away on the edge of the sidewalk, near the subway entrance or at the bus stop, and silently stared. I had seen communal scenes like this before, especially while living in Washington, D.C., where there always seemed to be a cluster of Ethiopians, my age or older, gathered together outside coffee shops and bars all over the city, talking in Amharic with an ease and fluency that I admired and envied. They told jokes that didn't require explanation and debated arguments that were decades in the making. All of this was coupled with the familiarity and comfort of speaking in our native tongue. At any given moment, they could have told you without hesitancy where they were from. And so I had watched, hardly understanding a word, hoping somehow that the simple act of association and observation was enough to draw me into the fold.

Here, then, was a similar scene, this one played out on a Brooklyn corner with a culture and history different from the one I had been born into, but familiar to me nonetheless. The men on that corner in Kensington, just like the people I had known throughout my life, were immigrants in the most complete sense of the word—their loyalties still firmly attached to the countries they had left one, five, or twenty years earlier. If there was one thing I admired most about them, it was that they had succeeded, at least partly, in re-creating in Brooklyn some of what they had lost when they left their countries of origin. Unlike the solitary and private walks my father and I took, each of us buried deep in thoughts that had nowhere to go, this nightly gathering of

Pakistani and Bangladeshi men was a makeshift reenactment of home. Farther down the road from where they stood were the few remaining remnants of the neighborhood's older Jewish community—one synagogue, a kosher deli—proof, if one was ever needed, that Brooklyn is always reinventing itself, that there is room here for us all.

While the men stood outside on the corner, their numbers gradually increasing until they spilled out into the street as they talked loudly among themselves, I once again played my own familiar role of quiet, jealous observer and secret admirer. I have no idea what those men talked about, if they discussed politics, sex, or petty complaints about work. It never mattered anyway. The substance of the conversations belonged to them, and I couldn't have cared less. What I had wanted and found in them, what I admired and adored about Kensington, was the assertion that we can rebuild and remake ourselves and our communities over and over again, in no small part because there have always been corners in Brooklyn to do so on. I stood on that corner night after night for the most obvious of reasons—to be reminded of a way of life that persists regardless of context; to feel, however foolishly, that I too was attached to something.

Annals of Allegory #36

Baron Wormser

Pathos is what happens when Sorrow has to work a day job.
She patches a tear in her purple dress
And carefully scrapes some facial cream
That has congealed at the bottom of a plastic jar.

She does not look any better but her rouged fragility
Has the implausible pensiveness of an over-the-hill starlet.
She knows she has slipped a couple of notches.
Tragedians have no interest in her but since there are

No tragedies anymore, it doesn't matter. She has numerous admirers.
Screenplay writers swear by her. Poets protest but can't get enough
Of her as their lines trail off into the blue ether of disappointment.
Her shares sell briskly in the commerce of feelings.

Once she was embarrassed but Weariness has made her brazen.
She will tell you the story of her abandoned childhood.
She will tell you the story of her faithless husband.
She will tell you the story of her hopeless diet.

Look at the scale, she will almost sob. Look at the scale!
Then she will brighten up, sensing a camera in the vicinity.
She can smell an interview three blocks away.
Nothing is final, nothing is irrevocable, your desires

And wants are bound to curdle like old milk but so what?
She winks provocatively. She has the inside scoop that
Hamlet and Lear missed. Rosencrantz and Guildenstern
Were on a business vacation. Cordelia needed to take

A course in communications. It isn't Cynicism; it isn't
Love or Sympathy either. Pathos knows the sun will come up
And the farewells will be bearable.

Fantasia on Three Sentences from a Letter by Robert Lowell

Elizabeth is finishing her novel.
I'm teaching Homer.
My car won't start in the snow.

If I drank less, I'd turn
Into an amiable bore.
Take up golf, scan the *Times*
As if it meant something to me personally.

Achilles is the name of our
Neighbor's cocker spaniel.
He sits at the window and yaps
At Helen's fraught ghost.

Novels are the aspirin of
Diminished possibility;
Narrative is the condom
Of optimism. Don't I love

To make pronouncements!
Yesterday I bit down on a candy bar
And broke a tooth.
Not a bad scene with which
To start a novel:
"Not particularly out of sorts
For a permanently *louche* nincompoop
Arthur bit down on a Baby Ruth

And felt a molar on the left side
Of his mouth moan."

Why do people clean out their cars?
Mine is cozy with candy wrappers,
Library books and loose cigarettes.
I could nest there,
A zero at the end of a large number.

Lately, I've been lingering
In the polite precincts of the eighteenth century.
It isn't that things were
Better then or braver or smarter.
They were, however, articulate
In the smallest matters,
Veritable mice of precision.

I need to reside in an era where
No one sits on a cold seat
While snow sighs
And tries by turning a small key
To coax a heap of metal
Into petrol swigging life.

Dismal folly.

The snow rests on our car
Like a hopeless benediction,
Like the pope giving Kafka an audience,
Like God exhaling,
Like a cut-rate eternity.

Coughing like a minor character
With an endearing surname,

Time's rigor sputters to life,
A weary war horse,
A De Soto with a faulty muffler
Chauffeured by Hector who is wiping
The frosty windshield with a gloved hand
And looking for the corner of Eighth
And Continuity.

Naked mannequins toppled over as if to bless the decadence.
(Hannaham, page 15)

**People Like This
Hate People Like You**

Jay Batlle

8440 SUNSET BOULEVARD WEST HOLLYWOOD CA 90069 PHONE 323 650 8999 FAX 323 650 5215
IAN SCHRAGER HOTELS. NEW YORK MIAMI LOS ANGELES

THE GRAND HOTEL

Business Centre

"Where the future is decided today"

THE RITZ-CARLTON®
WASHINGTON, D.C.

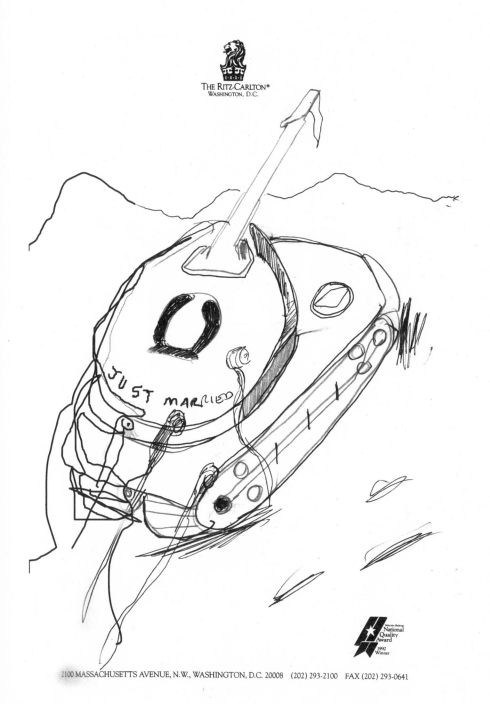

FOUR SEASONS HOTEL · WASHINGTON

2800 PENNSYLVANIA AVENUE N.W., WASHINGTON, DC 20007, USA, TELEPHONE: (202) 342-0444, TELEX: 42-904005 FOUR (202) 342-1673

Canada: Minaki (Minaki Lodge) · Montreal · Toronto · Toronto (Inn on the Park) · Vancouver · Caribbean: Nevis · West Indies · England: London · Indonesia: Bali · Italy: Milano · Japan: Tokyo
United States: Austin · Boston · Chicago · Chicago (The Ritz-Carlton) · Dallas at Las Colinas · Houston · Los Angeles · Maui at Wailea · New York · New York (The Pierre)
Newport Beach · Philadelphia · San Francisco (Clift) · Santa Barbara (Biltmore) · Seattle (The Olympic) · Washington, D.C.
UNDER DEVELOPMENT: Caribbean at Aviara · Hawaii at Kona · Mexico City · Singapore

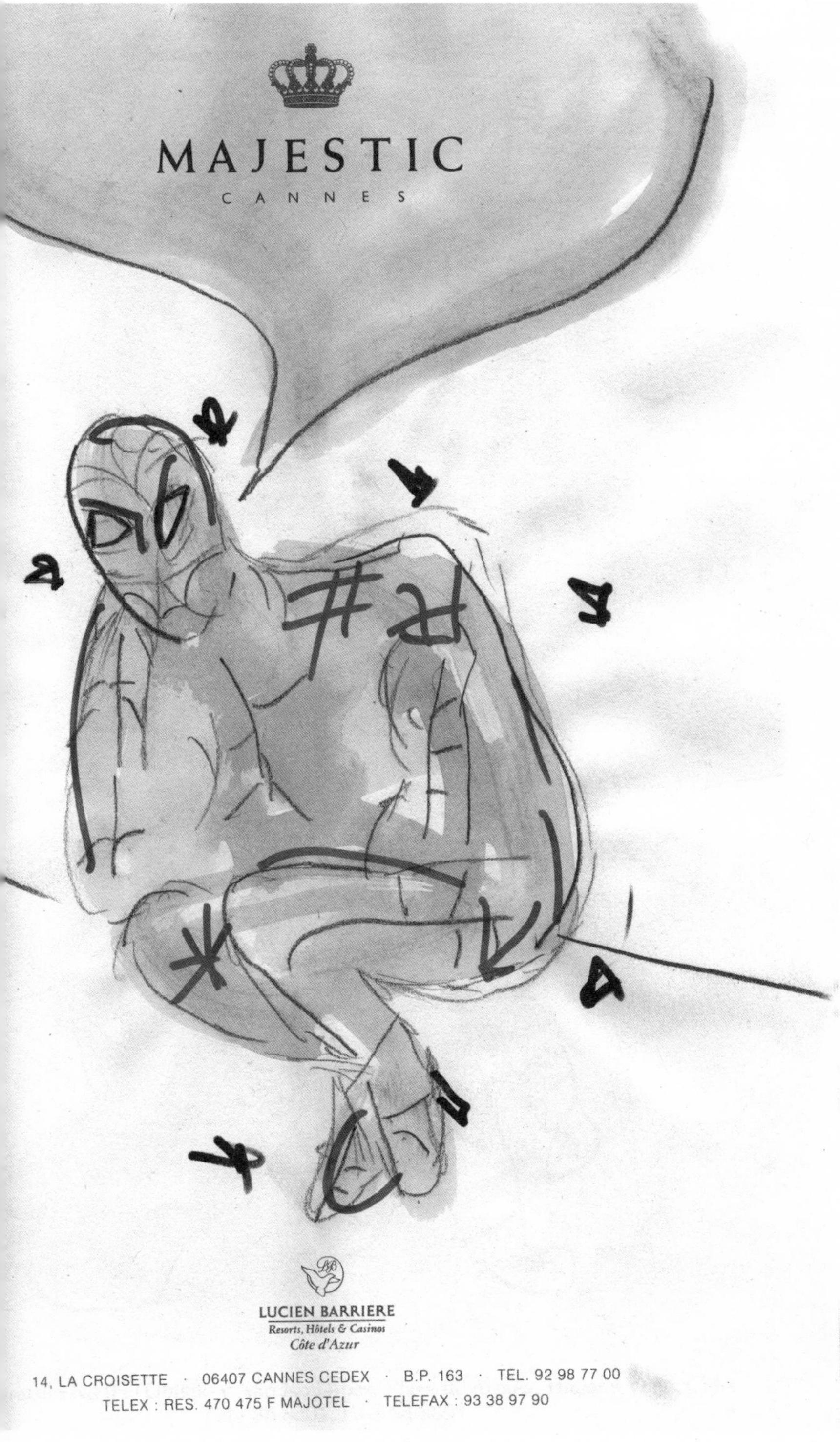
MAJESTIC
CANNES
LUCIEN BARRIERE
Resorts, Hôtels & Casinos
Côte d'Azur
14, LA CROISETTE · 06407 CANNES CEDEX · B.P. 163 · TEL. 92 98 77 00
TELEX : RES. 470 475 F MAJOTEL · TELEFAX : 93 38 97 90

Hotel Gravenbruch

FRANKFURT

FIANCÉE **In Residence**

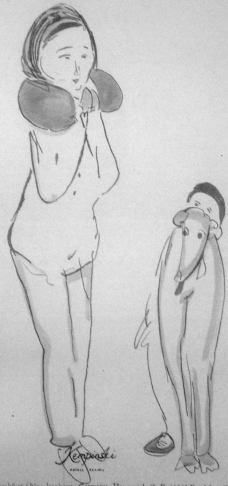

Postanschrift: Postfach 21 68 · D-63243 Frankfurt / Neu-Isenburg · Germany · Hausanschrift: D-63263 Frankfurt / Neu-Isenburg · Germany
Tel +49-6102-505-0 · Fax +49-6102-505-900 · e-mail: reservation.fra@kempinski.com

Travels with Wizard

Jonathan Baumbach

AFTER TURNING SIXTY IN THE THROES OF A DEBILITATING WINTER that had persisted long beyond expectation, after his latest live-in girlfriend had moved out in a cloud of dust, after renewed feelings of hopelessness had moved in to replace her, the biographer Leo Dimoff, sensing the need for radical change in his life, decided to get himself a dog.

Why a dog?

For one thing, living alone after a lifelong failed apprenticeship in the relationship trade, Leo felt deprived, wanted companionship though without the attendant complications. All the women in his life, or so he understood his history of failures, had burdened him with unanswerable demands.

"You want a dog because they don't talk back," Sarah, his most recent former live-in companion, told him over dinner at the very Japanese restaurant that had hosted their break-up. They had lived together for almost a year in the not so distant unremembered past and had remained contentious friends.

"Dog owners are never called chauvinists," he said. "And certainly not by their dogs."

"I love dogs," she said, "though I've never had one. What kind of dog are you thinking of, Leo?"

"I've been doing the research," he said. "I may have read every-thing about choosing the right dog the Written Word had in stock. I may, in fact, have acquired more information than I know what to do with. What I'm in the market for is a medium-sized, aesthetically pleasing, low maintenance puppy who is affectionate, intelligent, and, most importantly, faithful . . . I'd be grateful for suggestions."

"Whew!" she said, turning her face away to issue a brief secretive smile. "Well, I know it's not for everyone but I've always been partial to the Russell Terrier."

"I don't know," he said. "That's a kind of circus dog, isn't it? One of my dog texts—it may be *Puppies for Dummies*—says that Russells tend to be high strung."

"Too high strung, huh? You want a placid, doting, drooling dog, is that it? Mixed breeds are thought to be less high strung than full breeds, Leo. You could go to a shelter and pick out a puppy."

"I could," he said. "Would you accompany me?"

"I might," she said. "And then again I might not."

That the heart has its reasons and usually poor ones represented a good half of Leo's shaky acquired wisdom. On the other hand, as a biographer, he was generally esteemed for an empathic understanding of the wisdom and frailty of others.

Nevertheless, in careless love, he had come home one day with an odd-looking, long-legged, long-haired, big-nosed, tan-and-white puppy that had, said the shelter report, some lab, some poodle, and a soupçon of spaniel in its otherwise indecipherable makeup. The woman running the shelter, who reminded him of a former grade-school teacher whose name he sometimes remembered, said he could bring the puppy back in a week if it didn't work out. "It'll work out," he told her.

Leo stayed awake much of their first night together, concerned that the silent puppy, tentatively named Wizard after the subject of his latest biography, might suffocate without him there to monitor his sleep. The woman who ran the shelter had warned him that the infant dog, feeling displaced in new surroundings, might cry his first night away from the only home he knew. That Wizard's behavior defeated expectations gave the biographer, a worrier in the best of seasons, cause for concern. The puppy started the night in an over-sized crate, newly acquired, at the foot of Leo's bed. In the morning, when Leo opened his eyes, unaware of having slept, his charge was on the pillow next to him. In fact it was Wizard's cry, or perhaps it was only a high-pitched bark, that woke Leo from a dream in which the small dog he was caring for grew unacceptably large overnight.

At Sarah's advice and against his own predilections, Leo took Wizard to a local trainer, a friend of Sarah's also named Sara (without the h) for obedience lessons.

Rosy cheeked, slightly pudgy, the trainer, the other Sara, seemed barely out of her teens. When Leo asked her age, all she would tell him was that she was older than she looked. And that she was very good at her job.

In the following moment, they had their second misunderstanding. It came when she asked him the puppy's name. "Wizard," he said, not yet comfortable with the choice.

"Whizzer?" she asked.

"Wizard," he muttered.

"I understand," she said. "Whizzer."

From what he could tell, Wizard seemed to be failing his first lesson, which embarrassed the biographer, who offered excuses for his charge's slow-wittedness. "He tends to be shy with strangers," Leo said.

"Oh, he's doing just fine," Sara said. "And since we're already friends, aren't we, Whizzer? (chucking the puppy under the chin), we can no longer be considered strangers. I think we need to do this twice a week and you need to practice commands with him in the morning before breakfast and at night before he goes to sleep. If it will make it easier for you, I'll come to your house next time."

Leo reluctantly accepted her offer, having no reason—none he could find words for—not to.

For the next several weeks, on Tuesdays and Fridays, Sara appeared at his door promptly at 4:30 for Wizard's lesson. At their first session, Leo offered the trainer a cup of coffee, which she declined. Thereafter he made her herbal tea, specifically the ginseng-chai combination she favored, and more often than not the trainer stayed beyond the forty minutes set aside for the actual lesson. Though he was old enough to be her father and then some, Leo sometimes imagined that her extended stays had something to do with him.

"Whizzer's very bright," she told Leo who, although pleased by the compliment, remained skeptical. Not only was the dog not toilet-trained after three weeks in his care, but he tended to leave his shit just off the edge of the paper—usually the *New York Times* sports page—laid out to take its measure.

And then one day when least expected, Wizard stopped doing his "business"—that repellent dog-manual euphemism—in inappropriate places. Not one to believe in undeserved good fortune, Leo obsessively searched the three rooms available to his charge, sometimes on hands and knees, before acknowledging that the puppy was not as dim as previously suspected.

Whenever Sara arrived—at times her knock at the door would be sufficient—Wizard would do a pirouette in ecstatic expectation, which made Leo jealous despite the murmurs of his better judgment. It was important of course that the puppy be fond of his trainer. Still, the 360 degree turn, sometimes restated, seemed a little much. Although Leo fed the puppy, doted on him, walked him in good and bad weather, early and late, he sometimes imagined that Wizard, in his faithless heart, actually preferred Sara.

So after a while, after a particularly good training session, after herbal tea and cookies, Leo wondered aloud if Wizard (and owner) weren't sufficiently trained at this point to go it on their own.

"If that's what you want," she said, her stern cherubic face in unacknowledged collapse. "He still has a few things to learn, you know. You said he pulls on the leash when he sees another dog. We might do a few outdoor lessons. It's much harder to get him to obey when there are distractions around."

It struck Leo that Sara, though otherwise a bundle of positive qualities, had almost no sense of humor. Possibly her sense of humor was so subtle that his own crude radar failed to acknowledge it.

"You've done very well with him," Leo said, trying not to sound condescending. "We're both pleased, you know, with his considerable progress."

His compliment seemed to distress her. "If there's a financial burden," she said, "I'd be willing to cut my fee. Would that make a difference? I think Whizzer is on the verge of his next big breakthrough."

"Look, why don't we take next week off," Leo said, "as a kind of vacation for all of us. I'm doing a reading from my book on Nikola Tesla in Rochester and I'm thinking of taking Wizard with me to see how he handles the trip."

"I have a sister who lives in Rochester," Sara said.

"Do you?"

"Yes, and she's been having a hard time since her divorce. I've been planning to go up and see her but then something always comes up that gets in the way. I'll have to check my schedule but maybe I could go along for the ride and give you both a hand. Have you considered what you're going to do with the pup when you're reading whatever it is in front of an audience?"

Feeling trapped, Leo improvised a barely credible explanation as to why it wouldn't work for Sara to accompany him. "I appreciate your offer," he added.

"I'd better go," Sara said.

Leo awakes the next morning aware that it was a mistake to reject Sara's offer, a foolish and mean-spirited miscalculation. He'd have to be some kind of wizard himself to handle a puppy without help on an extended trip.

Perhaps the only way out for him is to phone the trainer, apologize for his abruptness, admit that he needs her on the trip and ask her, virtually plead with her, to join them.

He has allowed himself to imagine Sara's pleasure in getting this call from him.

"You're too late," she says. "I've already made other plans."

That is the not the answer he has anticipated, so he hangs on waiting hopelessly for better news.

"Is there something else?" she asks.

"That's about it," he says, noting out of the corner of his eye that Wizard has one of his shoes in his mouth, wagging his head ferociously from side to side as if it were a fearsome opponent.

"Stop that!" he calls to the dog.

"What are you saying?" Sara says. "What should I stop?"

"Not you. Wizard was chewing on one of my shoes."

"Whatever," she says. "You never shout at your dog. If he's well trained, a quiet command should be sufficient to deter him."

"It's only in the last few days that he's started these life-and-death battles with my shoes. He gets so much pleasure out of it, it seems churlish of me to deny him."

"I don't know that you want to encourage bad behavior, do you? If it were me, I wouldn't want him chewing on my shoes."

"Of course you're right," he says.

****

There are a few timid out of season snow flurries when they take off in the morning for Rochester, but several hours into the journey, Leo finds himself driving in blizzard conditions. Losing traction here and there despite his all-wheel drive Forester, he considers pulling over to the side of the road to wait out the worst of the storm. That the others seem oblivious to any danger makes it difficult for him to concede to the weather. Wizard, trussed into the passenger seat next to him, is staring out the window like a tourist. Sara, keeping company in the backseat with her cell phone, has been trying relentlessly to reach her sister in Rochester, the phone failing or the sister not available, Sara unnervingly patient.

After awhile Sara gets through to her sister and Leo learns that the reading has been postponed. Exhausted from his unrewarded efforts, he suggests they stop at the Wanderer's Motel in the near distance while waiting for the storm to abate. As they have no plans to stay the night, they agree for economy's sake to take a single cabin. So as not to set off any false alarms, Leo registers Sara as his wife.

"You must be exhausted," Sara says in wifely fashion as they move through the mix of sleet and rain to their cabin. Why don't you sack out and I'll get the pup from the car and give him his bathroom walk."

"That's okay," he says. "I appreciate the offer. It's just that walking Wizard is one of the unsung highlights of my day."

"Oh, go ahead, you look dead on your feet. I know how stressful it can be driving in treacherous weather, Leo. You don't have to prove anything to me."

So, feeling anything but grateful, carrying an overnight case in each hand, Leo lets himself into the motel room while Sara takes the puppy on the stretch lease, the two wandering into the distance like snow ghosts. The boxy cabin is furnished (along with a low-slung three-drawer dresser, a writing table with a Bible wrapped in plastic and two picture postcards on its otherwise virgin surface) with two three-quarter-size beds barely a foot apart . Not bothering to remove his shoes, Leo throws himself on the bed farthest from the door.

He dozes or imagines he has and wakes to find himself still alone in the room. Where are the others?

There is a heavy green curtain over what seems like a back window and, though it takes awhile, he finally locates a device that parts the brocaded cloth.

He is surprised to discover a back garden with tables under umbrellas—a place to picnic perhaps—overwhelmed by the blinding whiteness of the still falling sleet. He has no idea what he is looking for, but as his eyes adjust, he sees something that speaks to the worst of his expectations.

He closes his eyes as if to return to a dream from which he then might shake himself awake. When after a moment of inconsequential reverie, he allows his eyes to open, nothing has changed or nothing has changed sufficiently to put his original perception in doubt.

As near as he can make out, Sara is sitting under one of the umbrellas in the garden with her back to him. At first he assumes that she has returned Wizard to the car, but then he sees that she is not alone. Something—a head, Wizard's head most likely—is sticking out from the opening in her yellow down jacket and Sara's hooded head is tilted forward so that the two heads seem at some point to converge. It is only when she returns to her original position that Leo can tell that Sara and Wizard have been—there is no other word to describe it—kissing. Sara's head moves forward again and her mouth meets the dog's (a suspicion of tongue flashing), which is more than Leo can bear to watch.

Not wanting to eavesdrop any longer than he has, he closes the curtain and goes into the bathroom to wash his hands. For a moment, he has difficulty recognizing the face in the mirror over the sink that answers his troubled glance.

Perhaps ten minutes later, Sara enters the room alone, reporting that she has left the dog in the car because of the No Pets Allowed sign they hadn't noticed before.

"Did you get some sleep?" she asks, pulling off her boots. "I stayed out for awhile so as not to wake you."

Lying on her back, eyes flickering shut, the whisper of a snore in counterpoint to the indeterminate hum of the room, the trainer is apparently asleep before the biographer can frame an answer to her question.

A few hours later, the weather has quieted sufficiently for them to return to the road. Unaccompanied in front this time around—Sara and Wizard sit shoulder to shoulder in the backseat—Leo feels deserted. A sadness he hasn't acknowledged in months, perhaps since the dog entered his life, holds him in its sway.

Could they have missed a turn? They have been driving a while now—he has lost track of the time—and the passing scene, what he can make of it from the badly lit road he has been following slavishly, seems unfamiliar.

"Are we lost?" Sara asks him.

"I don't see how," he says. "We haven't left the route we started on."

"Whizzer is getting anxious," she says. "He senses something's wrong."

They are approaching a restaurant called The Helden Inn on their right and Leo announces as if he were some kind of tour guide that it might be a good idea to stop for a bite. "What do you think?" he says to no one in particular.

"If that's what you want to do," Sara says. "I can't speak for everyone but I suspect we're all a bit peckish."

There are an impressive number of vehicles, mostly high-end SUVs in the restaurant lot, which suggests, given the deterrence of the weather, a devoted local following. "I think we may have lucked out," he says to Sara.

Sara calls his attention to a sign on the parking lot side of the Inn rising out of the white ground, which offers the modest recommendation, "JUST GOOD FOOD," the remark in quotes, the speaker unattributed. Underneath the quote in smaller letters it says, PETS AND CHILDREN WELCOME.

Leo parks the Forester at the far end of the lot—he feels fortunate to find a space in the crowd of vehicles—and they have to wade, Wizard in Sara's arms, through several inches of slush to reach the Inn.

As they find their way inside, an elderly couple, oddly costumed (the old man in lederhosen, the woman in frilly blouse and apron), seem to be waiting for them (or someone) in the cavernous foyer. "Do you have reservations?" the woman asks, her broad smile welcoming them.

"We don't," Leo says. "Is that a problem?"

"There are only problems if we make them problems," the woman says, her accent vaguely foreign, the smile seemingly frozen on her face. "We'll do our best to take care of you. Please to follow."

She leads them into a spacious dining room—thirteen tables by Leo's quick count—in which surprisingly there is only one other diner, a fat man in a three-piece suit, at the far side of the room, working at what appears to be an elaborate cream-filled desert.

Leo dries Wizard off with his rumpled cloth napkin while Sara inspects her menu. "There isn't anything here I can eat," she says. "I don't eat meat."

"What about a salad?" Leo says. "They must have salads."

"The truth is," Sara says, "and I hope you won't mention this to anyone, though I don't eat meat, I don't really like salads."

Wizard, who seems to have grown during the difficult trip, barks from under the table at some unseen menace.

The proprietress, her perpetual smile a kind of rictus, returns with a basket of sliced rye bread and three glasses of water. She seems poised to take their order when someone or something whistles from the kitchen, and she hurries off.

Coming out from under the table, Wizard has taken residence on one of the padded chairs, accomplishing the feat with an impressive jump.

The fat man on the other side of the room lifts his head languorously from his dessert long enough to clap.

When Leo has a chance to go through the menu, which is several pages long, he has a greater appreciation of Sara's concern. The Helden Inn is celebrating something called Carnivore Days and all or virtually all of the dishes offered have some kind of animal meat as its base. Even under "Starters." Leo can find nothing that seems like a green salad. Under the Carnivore Days Specials, there is a quote in italics as a kind of epigraph.

"The carnivore loves his animals so much he is willing to eat them."—THE MANAGEMENT

"If you don't want to stay," he whispers to Sara, who has been negotiating a slice of stale bread, "I'm willing to leave."

His offer seems in equal measure to puzzle and please her. "Leo, wouldn't it be rude to just walk out after they've gone to all this trouble on our behalf? I was actually thinking of ordering my first burger in about six years. Did you notice that they have a puma burger on the menu?" She smiles self-deprecatingly, almost seductively. "I've been known to compromise in emergencies."

Out of the corner of his eye, he notices that the suited fat man has fallen asleep facedown in his dessert. Sara, intent on the menu's extended narrative, seems not to notice.

An odd muffled cry sounds from behind one of the walls.

Wondering, and not for the first time, where the people from the parked cars have gone, Leo takes a twenty-dollar bill from his wallet and leaves it under the white enamel matching salt-and-pepper shakers. "That should pay for the service," he says. "Did you notice that they actually have a Bow Wow Burger on the menu?"

"They don't!" she says, rising from her chair.

Sara is in the process of putting the puppy under her jacket when the proprietress, her smile unaltered, returns with a tray of unidentifiable appetizers. "I apologize for the delay," she says. "The chef has made something special for you."

Leo is about to offer an explanation for their abrupt departure, but instead takes Sara's hand and heads to the door that leads to the cavernous foyer.

The old man in the lederhosen is standing by the register as they hurry past him. "Come visit us again," he says in an uninflected voice. "And don't forget to drive safely."

Since almost all the vehicles in the lot are covered with some residue of the weather, it is hard to determine in the dark which car is theirs.

In his hurry to get going, Leo, using the sleeve of his coat, clears off the front window of the wrong Forester.

A Lexus SUV, pulling out from the row behind them, startles them with its horn. The driver, who could be the younger sister of the proprietress, rolls down a window and offers them a ride.

In the chaos of the moment, Leo is tempted to accept, but Sara, who is clearing off another car, says, "Wait a second. I think I found ours."

They pile into the Forester Sara has cleared, though Leo is not at all sure it is the one that had brought them there.

This time, Sara drives while Leo and Wizard sit next to each other in the back, a larger space between them than the one Leo observed between Sara and the puppy when he was at the wheel.

Still he is pleased to be alone with his charge without other responsibilities and he reaches out awkwardly to rub the puppy's head. Closing his eyes, Wizard accepts Leo's homage. When after a while Leo reclaims his hand, Wizard turns to look at him, the dog's wise face making unspoken judgments, seeing though to the very bottom of the biographer.

For an unguarded moment, Leo considers apologizing for his failings, promising to do his best to transcend his limitations in the future.

At some point, at Leo's request—the gauge registering empty—Sara pulls into a Mobil station to gas up and to find out where they might be in relation to where they are going. Apparently, they have been heading for the most part in the wrong direction and are farther away from home than ever. The source of their information, an overeager teenaged attendant, apparently taken with Sara, says he knows of a shortcut and he draws them a not-quite-decipherable map on a coffee-stained napkin.

"What do you want to do?" Sara asks Leo, showing him the makeshift map.

Instinctively, Leo turns to Wizard, but the shaggy dog, head pressed against his leg, eyes mostly shut, offers merely the example of his silence.

As Leo considers his options, he imagines them—Sara driving, himself in back with Wizard—moving on in whatever direction, letting the trip take them where it will, the hand-drawn map, the various maps, just an excuse to pursue space and distance. Without warning, Sara pulls the car off to the side of the road. "I'm getting tired," she says, moving into the backseat occupying Wizard's other side. "Would you take over?"

"Take over?" Leo has his arm around Wizard's shoulder.

"Yes, would you mind taking the next stretch?"

"I don't mind," he says, imagining himself getting out of the car and taking his place behind the wheel while in fact not moving at all.

"It's good that you don't mind," she says, putting an arm around Wizard from the other side, grazing Leo's fingers.

The trip continues a while without discernible movement—the Forester like a beached whale on the shoulder of the road—the passengers in the backseat each with an arm around Wizard, each taking possession of the one thing that matters, hugging each other through the surrogate in their midst.

It wasn't until after I had signed the lease on my apartment that I even learned the name of the neighborhood I had moved into: Kensington, a distinctly regal name at a price that I could afford; it was perfect, in other words, for an eager and poor writer with inflated ambitions and no sense of where he belonged. (Mengestu, page 107)

Satyr Song

Stanley Moss

When I was a child, I moved my pillow to a different part of the bed each night because I liked the feeling of not knowing where I was when I woke up. From the beginning I yearned for the nomadic life. I wandered, grazed like a goat on a hill—the move from grazing to exploring was just a leap over a fence. In my seventh year, I had a revelation. A teacher asked me a question. I knew the answer. Miss Green, a horse-faced redhead, asked the 3A class of P.S. 99, Kew Gardens, Queens, a long way from Byzantium: "What are you going to do in life?" Most of the answers remain a blur, but someone said she was going to be a novelist and someone said he'd write a play, or for the movies. I remember waiting; I was last to answer: "I am certain I am a poet." Then Miss Green said, "I knew it. You, Stanley, are a bronze satyr," and she whacked my erect penis with a twelve-inch Board of Education wooden ruler.

I ran home in a fury at my parents. They had never told me I was a satyr. My mother's explanation, "You know what a hard time I had giving birth to you. Why do you think every time I hit you it hurts my hand? You had whooping cough the first six months of your life. The doctor said no human being could survive that. Even so, when you were three months old in your crib, you knocked your five-year-old sister unconscious. Nothing ever fits you, not your shoes, not your pants, not your shirts, nothing. Your feet always hang off the bed." How many times did I hear my mother say, "That kid doesn't know his own strength. You'll injure somebody for life.

Don't hit. Don't hit. The other kids, gentile and Jew, lie. You are mythological."

After the revelation, at dinner, I saw my father—a public high school principal—as an angry centaur. Most evenings he was out herding his mares and women together for song, smell, and conversation. At our dinner table, I knew if I didn't speak, no one would. My fifth summer, my father went to Europe "alone," mostly, I think, to Venice and Vienna. By watching others, I taught myself to swim. When he returned I couldn't look him in the eye. He brought back presents: a wooden bowl which, when lifted, played a Viennese waltz, a bronze ashtray of a boy peeing, after the fountain in Brussels, a silver top on a plunger I could never figure out, a blue necklace for my mother, some etchings of Venetian views and one of Beethoven. We lived in an apartment as desolate as Beethoven's jaw.

Still, on February 7, 1935, with my father on sabbatical leave, we set out as a family aboard the S.S. *Statendam*, across the stormy waters of the Atlantic, then southeast to the sunny Mediterranean. It was the first of many voyages I would take under different circumstances from the moral north to the warm south. For the first time, I heard the Roman languages of satyrs and satires, then Greek, Hebrew, Arabic, and Turkish. I heard rolling r's, strange j's and h's, sometimes silent, throated on olives, anchovies, and garlic. Until that February, I had entered a house of worship only on special occasions—a Protestant Adirondack church in summer, to attend films—a synagogue, only once, to tell my grandmother on Yom Kippur that my mother was waiting outside in a car—I was thrown out for not wearing a hat, or perhaps because I was a satyr. My mother offered me hers, a brown, broad-brimmed hat with a veil that I refused to wear. Within a month, this satyr stood before *The Nightwatch* in Amsterdam. I read "Franco Franco Franco" on a wall in Malaga, I rode a camel beside the Sphinx, toured the Basilica of San Marco in Venice, watched men praying at the Wailing Wall; I entered the Church of the Nativity and the Holy Sepulcher, heard the "good news" for the first time. I took off my shoes, heard my hooves echo on the green rugs and tiles in the mosque of Santa Sophia and the Blue Mosque. I was photographed with the caryatids on the Acropolis, ran through the Parthenon on a windy February or March day, the Greek sun so bright against the white marble it hurt my eyes.

A few days later, on the Island of Rhodes, I was proud to be nicked in the leg by a ricocheted bullet in a postrevolutionary celebration. When I told the story throughout my childhood, I was shot in the leg in a Greek Revolution; I said I had a scar to prove it—and I do. That spring, I wandered off alone into the red-light district of Algiers. An auburn-haired, tattooed lady smelling of flowers and sweat kissed me for nothing behind a beaded curtain. She touched a naked breast to my lips—I was in paradise. My mother thought I was lost. Soon, in Cairo, late at night, I roused most of the attendants in a hotel, shouting I had leprosy. I was covered with volcanoes of blood. My only comfort, a black dragoman, tribal scars on his face, until my parents returned from a performance of belly dancers and made the discovery that I had been bitten by an army of fire ants. I would not forget the poverty and disease in the slums of Cairo, the crack of whips over the donkeys and horses. I was nine years old, eight years younger than the Soviet Union, changed forever.

Aboard the *Statendam*, I played chess with a thirteen-year-old kid named Matthew. He wore white knickers and traveled with his grandmother. I last saw him crying, kicking, and spitting at my father, who was beating the dickens out of him. I never, in the two-month voyage, saw Matthew or his grandmother again. I asked my mother if Dad threw them overboard; she said, "You're exaggerating again." My father said, "To ask questions is a sign of intelligence, but you ask too many questions. Your mother is the Tower of Babel. You and she are two of a kind."

Now that I could accept and was proud of being a bronze satyr, I remembered when I was a baby in my Aunt Bessie's arms, I took her breasts out of her blouse, thinking "I am pretending to be just a baby, but I am really out for a feel." I wish I had been photographed then with my little victorious, evil satyr smile, instead of the family photo of me in a baby carriage reaching for a cloud. In our family, the beginning of civilization was understood to be the moment Abraham sacrificed the ram instead of his firstborn son. I started one dinner's conversation with, "I think it would have been better to kill Isaac than the ram. I think the ram stands for me. Daddy, you know there's a very thin line between the good shepherd and the butcher."

"Who are you to think!" Whack went my father's Board of Education ruler, a thirty-six-inch weapon. My mother threatened to stab herself in the heart with a kitchen knife like a bronze Lucretia. We were a family of atheists; still, we celebrated an occasional seder with uncles, aunts, and their children, most of whom kept away from me, lest I molest them. What could I do to liven up the evening? I planted a snail and a skeleton of an eel under the parsley and horseradish on my father's seder plate. The moment he passed out the horseradish, everyone saw the snail and eel's skeleton. I said, "Horseradish rhymes with Kaddish." Lightning, my father reached out for me, but he missed. I was ordered out of the house, into the world of wild things.

I had planned one last, beautiful gesture. My mother and Aunt Mabel had a friendly contest—who could make the lightest matzo balls. My mother always lost. I had found my aunt's matzo balls laid out on a platter in the kitchen. I took our little collection of stones and jewels from Jerusalem, and, one by one, I thrust them into the center of each matzo ball: diorite, opal, quartz, limestone, sandstone, onyx. I watched through the window as the matzo balls were served with a spoon, one by one, into the chicken soup. My aunt had a big and loyal constituency that typically gulped their food. Hypocrites, they swallowed the matzo balls with such comments as, "Light as air!" "Like perfume," until my cousin Audrey cried "I broke a tooth on a rock!" I danced my little goat dance outside for joy. For the first and only time in her life, my dear mother was declared a winner.

Whatever the weather, the smoke of battle never cleared. In November, on the anniversary of my grandfather's death, my mother lit a Yarzheit memorial candle in a glass. I believe she prayed. "What would happen," I asked, "if I blew out the flame?" My mother's face saddened that I should ask such an unspeakable question, but she knew my ways. "That would be a sin." She almost never used that word. Now I knew there was a second sin—the first, the greater sin, wasting food. A proper satyr, sin was my pie in the sky. I knew that in one evening Alcibiades had cut the penises off half the herms in Athens. I scouted the neighborhood, and in one evening, with our nineteenth-century American candle-snuffer, I put out the flames of seven Yarzheit candles. I came across a magazine called *Twice a Year*, that introduced me to Rimbaud, Lorca, and Wallace Stevens; they taught me how to survive. Out of a bar of Ivory soap I carved a Virgin Mother with a baby satyr in her lap, then another virgin with a unicorn in her lap. My thought was the unicorn represented not Christ, but my savior—poetry. I cut school and went two or three days a week to the main reading room of the Forty-Second Street Library (a satyr among lions), or the Museum of Modern Art, or to the Apollo Theater to see foreign films. I smoked five-cent *Headline* cigars. One romantic evening I called my father a sadist (the first shot of the forth Punic War). It was then I was banished from Jackson Heights forever.

Hard years. I learned to disguise myself to earn a living. Wherever I went I carried my desperately thin production of poems and Wallace Stevens. I was sure Hitler was anti-satyr. I joined the navy at seventeen. A sword wound and the G.I. Bill got me through college in style. I had a recurring nightmare that, like the satyr Marsyas, I was flayed—just for being a satyr, for no reason at all, not for challenging Apollo at music. I leapt around graduate women's dorms, broke windows and doors. Police were called. I was expelled for "Communist activity." Now history: I was hired by a detective agency to spy on organizing workers. I became a counterspy for Local 65. I sang in a band, played the bass, waited on tables; I was a sailor on a Greek merchant ship (I got the job through Rae Dalven, the translator of Cavafy); I grazed awhile at New Directions; for mysterious reasons, Dylan Thomas and I became passionate friends—I loved his poetry and his deep-throated Christianity. I remember his saying "the truth doesn't hurt." He could and would talk intimately to anyone, regardless of class or education, not a habit of American or English intellectuals. He drank, he told me, because he wasn't useful, which I understood to mean he could not relieve human suffering. Anyone who really cared about him knew how profoundly and simply Christian he was. Dickens was a favorite teacher. He gave away the shirt off his back. The turtleneck sweater he wore in that picture was mine, knitted for me by my Aunt Tilly. We discovered an Italian funeral home on Bleecker Street where, after the bars closed at 4 a.m., we drank whiskey on a gold and onyx coffin. He introduced me to Theodore Roethke, his second favorite living American poet. His favorite was e. e. cummings—"he can write about anything." Dylan, Ted and I spent an evening with townspeople from Laugharne, trolls who whitewashed the town. What a concert of Welsh accents and laughter. Dylan had his boathouse, Roethke his greenhouse, I had my apartment house in Queens.

I met a blonde, green-eyed Catalan beauty named Ana Maria. Full of Spanish poetry and Catalan republican-heretical-anarchistic tragedy, she was a great bad-weather friend. After Barnard College she sailed off to Spain; I followed, after writing a poem called "Sailing from the United States." (I earned the money to follow by wild luck— an old Eighth Street satyr who knew I loved painting gave me an El Greco to sell, a crucifixion with a view of Toledo.) We married at the American consulate in Tangiers. Our witnesses—her mother and two virgin sisters. There was blood on the floor. It turned out that one of her sisters had been given a metal garter with nails by a nun at the *Colegio del Sagrado Corazón* because the nun thought Ana Maria was marrying an American Protestant. A miracle: the sister who wore the garter and shed her blood at my wedding found her way to Philadelphia, married an Orthodox Jew, a painter. They both died too soon and are buried on a hillside overlooking Haifa.

I knew in Rome there was a tradition of centaur teachers—why not satyrs? I made my way to pagan Rome. I taught English and tutored. We lived facing the temple of the Vestal Virgins across the Tiber. I decided, one August evening, to have a mythological picnic, a cookout for my mythological friends. Of course, it had to be beside the river, on the embankment of the Tiber, because the hippokamps were half-horse, half-fish; the tritons were half-man, half-fish. There were nymphs and maenads. The great god Pan himself came—and the Artemis of Ephesus on a sacred barge. (You understand I could not serve my famous fish soup.) A giraffe crashed the party. He said he was a tree, a sycamore among men, lonely since his nesting birds flew south. He said he envied trees that could lean over a river and see their reflection. Madness I thought, to have a private mythology, but I knew to speak to him I had to accept his metaphor. The symposium began. How did it feel to a man to make love to a fish, how did it feel to a horse to make love to a fish? What was love? Someone complimented Artemis on the beauty of her many breasts. A harpy screeched, "She has no nipples; they are the testicles of sacrificed bulls." We all came out of darkness, hatched from a single egg that was love the enchanting, the brilliant. When we departed, we kissed goodbye in our several heartfelt ways. Some wept because the sirens, as usual, sang their song of how we would be remembered.

I spent years in Rome, happy to eat the leftovers of the gods, reading and writing, trying to make a living holding four jobs simultaneously. More than once, drunk on Frascati, I bathed in the Bernini Fountain of the Four Rivers. On summer evenings, I drank from the Nile with a marble tiger. I corresponded with my mother. I received one letter from my father I carried around awhile. Finally I destroyed it, lest God should see it. Out of the blue, I received a postcard from my father, "We will be in Pisa on August 18, 1956, at the Hotel Cavellieri, if you care to see us." Signed, Pop. Never, not once in my life, did I call my father Pop. I arrived on the appointed day, shocked to see how much they had aged. They were fifty-eight. We had lunch in the piazza, the pages of the Bible flapping in the wind. A little peeved that I had learned Italian and Spanish in the passing years, my father had taught himself passing Italian and Spanish to go with his Greek, Latin, and French. He had more than enough Italian to order, as usual, exactly what he wanted. He insisted on having his spaghetti with cinnamon and sugar, no doubt a Litvak recipe out of his mother's kitchen. My mother said my hair was getting straight; did that have anything to do with the Leaning Tower of Pisa? Oh, how I miss my mother's questions. My father spent a cordial week in Italy, my mother another month at our apartment in Trastevere. She slept in a room I usually rented out, in a bed just vacated by Christopher Isherwood and friend. If she had known, would she have slept a wink? My father said, in wishing me goodbye, "If you had only been a bronze horse rearing up once in a while, I could have handled you." What was our mettle, a word I misspelled in my head as m-e-t-a-l? What we were really made of, the years would prove.

Coming out of his thoughts, my father said abruptly, "What I know of poetry I owe to you."

"How so?" I asked suspiciously.

"When I was studying for my principal's exam when you were two or three, I had to memorize passages from Shakespeare. On walks, I would recite the great speeches over your head, and repeat them out loud until I had them: *Hamlet, King Lear, The Tempest.*"

I said, "Perhaps what I know of poetry I owe to you."

He started reciting "O, what a rogue and peasant slave am I" with his large, tin ear. I finished it. I kissed him and said, "Thanks a lot." (A well known actress from a famous acting family once put me down with, "I saw my father play King Lear when I was ten. You couldn't possibly understand the difference between that and studying Shakespeare at Yale." I informed her that I began my Shakespeare studies when I was two.)

I met Ted Roethke again in Rome when I was munching on the review *Botteghe Oscure*. We both had passed dangers. He said I was the best looking satyr in Rome, "in a Bronx way," that my "God Poem" was a "pisser." We hit it off. We met again two years later by chance at a Pinter play in London when I was heading back to the States after Rome fell. We joined up to see *Hamlet* and Gielgud in *The Tempest* (we did not drown our books). Eight seasons past. Ted and Beatrice came to stay with me at Fifty-Seventh Street at a barn I was living in. I gave Ted big breakfasts and my homburg, he gave me his famous raccoon skin coat. He liked my fish and turtle tank in my small dining room. He told me he was once in love with a snake. Ted brought me to dinner at Stanley Kunitz's. I remember that first long, long, long evening. Thinking back, I didn't quite know how lucky I was. They were in their fifties, Stanley had almost fifty years to go, Ted had six. Dylan had crossed the Styx a handful of years before. On still another visit, not after death, Roethke came with his not quite finished manuscript of *The Far Field*. He went off one evening to show it to Stanley Kunitz. He put on a blue serge suit and my homburg for the occasion. Just before dawn, he rolled back in. "What did Stanley say," I asked.

"He liked it a lot." Then a look of pain crossed his face and I knew that Ted, who had been in the mood to be crowned Heavyweight Champion and nothing less, was disheartened. I thought Kunitz had found something not quite right, that he had been demanding and not just celebratory. Suddenly, Ted said, talking half to me and half to the world, "Stanley Kunitz is the most honest man in America." I told this story in an introduction to a book of Kunitz conversations. More years. Roethke long dead, after a formal Roethke celebration at which Kunitz, an aged ex-Roethke sweetheart and I were the only three people in the room who knew him, Kunitz asked me to repeat the story at dinner to a young poet. I was pleased my true Satyr story had touched Stanley.

When my father was soon to die, he spent his last hours in a fury that he hadn't died a year before when he wanted to. His doctor kept saying to me, "He's made of stainless steel. He's made of stainless steel." I understood my bronze self was just a chip off the old block, a mere alloy of tin and copper. What is a satyr, a Turkish brass sieve without moral outrage, a chamberpot that lets the urine through beside my father's moral steel.

My mother divorced my father six months before her death. On her birthday, a month to the day before she died, she saw her second great-granddaughter, who to her joy, was named after her. She never knew she had a grandson. My sister sent our mother's ashes through the U.S. mail. My parents are buried in a garden I made in Water Mill, the graves two unmarked stones, surrounded by Montauk daisies and pink mallow. I didn't think my mother would want the stones too close. Last spring, a swan nested right on the graves. When the eggs hatched, the mother swan paraded with her six gray signets in the bay in front of our house. When I approached, they all jumped on their mother's back, and she swam away with them to safety. My mother would have liked that.

What has any of this to do with poetry or song? If you laughed at any of this, there is poetry in that. The prose, the tears were left to me.

Open City Index (Issues 1–24)

Abreu, Jean Claude and Jorge Jauregui, trans., "The First Visit to the Louvre: Fragments of an Improbable Dialogue" (story) by Rafael Fernández de Villa-Urrutia. *Open City* 16 (2002–2003): 177–181.

Acconci, Vito. Three poems. *Open City* 5 (1997): 99–102.

Adams, Bill. "Interior, Exterior, Portrait, Still-Life, Landscape" (drawings). *Open City* 19 (2004): 73–83.

Alcalá, Rosa, trans., "The Brilliance of Orifices," "Mother of Pearl," "The Anatomy of Paper" (poems) by Cecilia Vicuña. *Open City* 14 (2001–2002): 151–154.

Alcalay, Ammiel, trans., "Hotel," "Precautionary Manifesto" (poems) by Semezdin Mehmedinovic. *Open City* 17 (2003): 141–142.

Allen, Roberta. "Surreal" (story). *Open City* 9 (1999): 53–54.

Alvaraz, A. Two Untitled Poems. *Open City* 3 (1995): 72–74.

Ames, Greg. "Physical Discipline" (story). *Open City* 17 (2003): 209–216.

Ames, Jonathan. "Writer for Hire: A Spencer Johns Story" (story). *Open City* 9 (1999): 55–68.

Anderson, Jack. "Elsewhere," "Believing in Ghosts" (poems). *Open City* 19 (2004): 51–53.

Anderson, Lucy. "Another Fish Poem" (poem). *Open City* 4 (1996): 195–196.

Andoe, Joe. "This Would Be the Day All My Dreams Come True," "Fence," "Seeing Red," "Eighteen-Year-Old Stucco Laborer and White Crosses" (poems). *Open City* 16 (2002–2003): 59–62.

Anderson, Lucy. "Winter Solstice," "Reentry," "What If, Then Nothing" (poems). *Open City* 9 (1999): 141–144.

Antoniadis, Tony. "Rescue 907!" (story). *Open City* 20 (2005): 181–193.

Arnold, Craig. "SSSSSSHHHHHH," "There is a circle drawn around you," "Your friend's arriving on the bus" (poems). *Open City* 16 (2002–2003): 97–105.

Badanes, Jerome. "Change Or Die" (unfinished novel). *Open City* 5 (1997): 159–233.

Badanes, Jerome. "The Man in the Twelve Thousand Rooms" (essay). *Open City* 23 (2007): 1–3.

Badanes, Jerome. "Guinea Golden," "From Day to Day," "Late Night Footsteps on the Staircase" (poems). *Open City* 23 (2007): 5–10.

Bakowski, Peter. "The Width of the World," "We Are So Rarely Out of the Line of Fire" (poems). *Open City* 11 (2000): 95–100.

Balkenhol, Stephan. Drawings. *Open City* 5 (1997): 38–42.

Bar-Nadav, Hadara. "Talking to Strangers" (story). *Open City* 23 (2007): 11–23.

Bar-Nadav, Hadara. "Bricolage and Blood," "I Used to Be Snow White," "To Halve and to Hole" (poems). *Open City* 23 (2007): 25–29.

Bartók-Baratta, Edward. "Walker" (poem). *Open City* 18 (2003–2004): 175.

Baum, Erica. "The Following Information" (photographs). *Open City* 13 (2001): 87–94.

Baumbach, Jonathan. "Lost Car" (story). *Open City* 22 (2006): 27–35.

Baumbach, Nico. "Guilty Pleasure" (story). *Open City* 14 (2001–2002): 39–58.

Beal, Daphne. "Eternal Bliss" (story). *Open City* 12 (2001): 171–190.

Beatty, Paul. "All Aboard" (poem). *Open City* 3 (1995): 245–247.

Becker, Priscilla. "Blue Statuary," "Instrumental" (poems). *Open City* 18 (2003–2004): 151–152.

Becker, Priscilla. "Recurrence of Childhood Paralysis," "Blue Statuary" (poems). *Open City* 19 (2004): 33–34.

Becker, Priscilla. "Typochondria" (essay). *Open City* 22 (2006): 9–12.

Beckman, Joshua and Tomaz Salamun, trans., "VI," "VII" (poems) by Tomaz Salamun. *Open City* 15 (2002): 155–157.

Beckman, Joshua and Matthew Rohrer. "Still Life with Woodpecker," "The Book of Houseplants" (poems). *Open City* 19 (2004): 177–178.

Belcourt, Louise. "Snake, World Drawings" (drawings). *Open City* 14 (2001–2002): 59–67.

Bellamy, Dodie. "From *Cunt-Ups*" (poems). *Open City* 14 (2001–2002): 155–157.

Beller, Thomas. "Vas *Is* Dat?" (story). *Open City* 10 (2000): 51–88.

Bellows, Nathaniel. "At the House on the Lake," "A Certain Dirge," "An Attempt" (poems). *Open City* 16 (2002–2003): 69–73.

Bergman, Alicia. "Visit" (story). *Open City* 10 (2000): 125–134.

Berman, David. "Snow," "Moon" (poems). *Open City* 4 (1996): 45–48.

Berman, David. "Now, II," "A Letter From Isaac Asimov to His Wife, Janet, Written on His Deathbed" (poems). *Open City* 7 (1999): 56–59.

Berman, David. "Classic Water & Other Poems" (poems). *Open City* 5 (1997): 21–26.

Bernard, April. "Praise Psalm of the City Dweller," "Psalm of the Apartment Dweller," "Psalm of the Card Readers" (poems). *Open City* 2 (1993): 47–49.

Berne, Betsy. "Francesca Woodman Remembered" (story). *Open City* 3 (1995): 229–234.

Berrigan, Anselm. "'Something like ten million …'" (poem). *Open City* 14 (2001–2002): 159–161.

Bey, Hakim. "Sumerian Economics" (essay). *Open City* 14 (2001–2002): 195–199.

Bialosky, Jill. "Virgin Snow," "Landscape with Child," "Raping the Nest" (poems). *Open City* 12 (2001): 37–42.

Bialosky, Jill. "Demon Lover" (poem). *Open City* 17 (2003): 149.

Bialosky, Jill. "The Life of a Stone" (story). *Open City* 23 (2007): 31–41.

Bialosky, Jill. "Subterfuge" (poem). *Open City* 23 (2007): 43–44.

Bingham, Robert. "From *Lightning on the Sun*" (novel excerpt). *Open City* 10 (2000): 33–50.

Bingham, Robert. "The Crossing Guard" (story). *Open City* 16 (2002–2003): 29–38.

Blagg, Max. "A Sheep Is a Gift" (story). *Open City* 23 (2007): 45–54.

Blagg, Max. "6/17/04," "6/18/04" (poems). *Open City* 23 (2007): 55–56.

Blake, Rachel. "Elephants" (story). *Open City* 18 (2003–2004): 195–209.

Blash, M. "Ghost Drawings" (drawings). *Open City* 21 (2005–2006): 131–136.

Blaustein, Noah. "Freezing the Shore My Father's Three Thousand Photographs of Point Dume & Paradise Cove" (poem). *Open City* 21 (2005–2006): 13–14.

Bolus, Julia. "Clasp" (poem). *Open City* 17 (2003): 155–156.

Bomer, Paula. "The Mother of His Children" (story). *Open City* 12 (2001): 27–36.

Borland, Polly. "Britain Today" (photographs). *Open City* 4 (1996): 181–185; front and back covers.

Bourbeau, Heather. "The Urban Forester," "The Lighting Designer" (poems). *Open City* 21 (2005–2006): 137–140.

Bove, Emmanuel. "Night Departure" (story). *Open City* 2 (1993): 43–46.

Bowes, David. Illustrations for Carlo McCormick's "The Getaway." *Open City* 3 (1995): 150–154.

Bowers, William. "It Takes a Nation of Millions to Hold Us Back" (story). *Open City* 17 (2003): 67–69.

Bowles, Paul. "17 Quai Voltaire" (story). *Open City* 20 (2005): 223–229.

Bowman, Catherine. "I Want to Be Your Shoebox," "Road Trip" (poems). *Open City* 18 (2003–2004): 75–79.

Boyers, Peg. "Transition: Inheriting Maps" (poem). *Open City* 17 (2003): 163–165

Bradley, George. "Frug Macabre" (poem). *Open City* 4 (1996): 223–237.

Branca, Alba Arikha. "Yellow Slippers" (story). *Open City* 3 (1995): 81–88.

Branca, Alba. "A Friend from London" (story). *Open City* 9 (1999): 43–52.

Brannon, Matthew. "The Unread Unreadable Master of Overviolence" (bookmark). *Open City* 16 (2002–2003): 119–120.

Bridges, Margaret Park. "Looking Out" (story). *Open City* 6 (1998): 47–59.

Broun, Bill. "Heart Machine Time" (story). *Open City* 11 (2000): 111–118.

Bao, Quang. "Date" (poem). *Open City* 8 (1999): 137–140.

Brown, Jason. "North" (story). *Open City* 19 (2004): 1–19.

Brown, Lee Ann. "Discalmer" (introduction). *Open City* 14 (2001–2002): 137–139.

Brownstein, Michael. "The Art of Diplomacy" (story). *Open City* 4 (1996): 153–161.

Brownstein, Michael. "From *World on Fire*" (poetry). *Open City* 14 (2001–2002): 201–218.

Broyard, Bliss. "Snowed In" (story). *Open City* 7 (1999): 22–42.

Brumbaugh, Sam. "Safari Eyes" (story). *Open City* 12 (2001): 49–64.

Bunn, David. "Book Worms" (card catalog art project). *Open City* 16 (2002–2003): 43–57.

Burton, Jeff. "Untitled #87 (chandelier)" (photograph). *Open City* 7 (1999): front cover.

Butler, Robert Olen. "Three Pieces of *Severance*" (stories). *Open City* 19 (2004): 189–191.

Carter, Emily. "Glory Goes and Gets Some" (story). *Open City* 4 (1996): 125–128.

Carter, Emily. "Hampden City" (story). *Open City* 7 (1999): 43–45.

Cattelan, Maurizio. "Choose Your Destination, Have a Museum-Paid Vacation" (postcard). *Open City* 9 (1999): 39–42.

Cavendish, Lucy. "Portrait of an Artist's Studio" (drawings). *Open City* 11 (2000): 101–110.

Chamandy, Susan. "Hannibal Had Elephants with Him" (story). *Open City* 18 (2003–2004): 33–54.

Chan, Paul. "Self-Portrait as a Font" (drawings, text). *Open City* 15 (2002): 111–118.

Chancellor, Alexander. "The Special Relationship" (story). *Open City* 9 (1999): 189–206.

Charles, Bryan. "Dollar Movies" (story). *Open City* 19 (2004): 41–49.

Chase, Heather. "My First Facelift" (story). *Open City* 4 (1996): 23–44.

Chester, Alfred. "Moroccan Letters" (story). *Open City* 3 (1995): 195–219.

Chester, Craig. "Why the Long Face?" (story). *Open City* 14 (2001–2002): 109–127.

Chung, Brian Carey. "Still Life," "Traveling with the Lost" (poems). *Open City* 21 (2005–2006): 1153–156.

Clark, Joseph. "Nature Freak" (story). *Open City* 21 (2005–2006): 121–130.

Clements, Marcelle. "Reliable Alchemy" (story). *Open City* 17 (2003): 239–241.

Cohen, Elizabeth. "X-Ray of My Spine" (poem). *Open City* 2 (1993): 61–62.

Cohen, Marcel. "From *Letter to Antonio Saura*" (story), trans. Raphael Rubinstein. *Open City* 17 (2003): 217–225.

Cole, Lewis. "Push It Out" (story). *Open City* 12 (2001): 205–256.

Connolly, Cyril. "Happy Deathbeds" (story). *Open City* 4 (1996): 53–78.

Cooper, Elisha. Illustrations for Erik Hedegaard's "The La-Z-Boy Position." *Open City* 4 (1996): 117–121.

Corn, Alfred. "Ultra" (poem). *Open City* 20 (2005): 195.

Coultas, Brenda. "To Write It Down" (poem). *Open City* 14 (2001–2002): 185–186.

Cravens, Curtis. Photographs. *Open City* 2 (1993): 71–74.

Creed, Martin. "Work No. 202" (photograph). *Open City* 9 (1999): front cover.

Creevy, Caitlin O'Connor. "Girl Games" (story). *Open City* 8 (1999): 27–44.

Culley, Peter. "House Is a Feeling" (poem). *Open City* 14 (2001–2002): 173–177.

Cunningham, Michael. "The Slap of Love" (story). *Open City* 6 (1998): 175–196.

Curry, Crystal. "The Corporeal Other" (poem). *Open City* 18 (2003–2004): 187.

Curtis, Rebecca. "The Dictator Was Very Pleased," "The Government Eggs" (poems). *Open City* 20 (2005): 143–144.

Cvijanovic, Adam. "Icepaper #3" (paintings). *Open City* 11 (2000): 53–61.

Daniels, René. "Paintings, 1977–1987" (paintings). *Open City* 14 (2001–2002): 187–194.

Dannatt, Adrian. "After a Giselle Freund Photograph," "Utrecht" (poems). *Open City* 2 (1993): 126–127.

Dannatt, Adrian. Introduction to "The House Where I Was Born." *Open City* 7 (1999): 112–115.

Dannatt, Adrian. "Days of Or" (story). *Open City* 8 (1999): 87–96.

Dannatt, Adrian. "Central Park Wet" (story). *Open City* 10 (2000): 103–114.

Dannatt, Trevor. "Night Thoughts (I)," "Night Thoughts (II)" (poems). *Open City* 19 (2004): 133–134.

Daum, Meghan. "Inside the Tube" (essay). *Open City* 12 (2001): 287–304.

David, Stuart. "A Peacock's Wings" (story). *Open City* 13 (2001): 133–138.

Davies, Howell. "The House Where I Was Born" (story). *Open City* 7 (1999): 116–119.

Deller, Jeremy. "The English Civil War (Part II)" (photographs). *Open City* 9 (1999): 159–166.

Delvoye, Wim. Drawings, text. *Open City* 2 (1993): 39–42.

DeMarinis, Rick. "The Life and Times of a Forty-Nine Pound Man" (story). *Open City* 17 (2003): 185–196.

Dermont, Amber. "Number One Tuna" (story). *Open City* 19 (2004): 95–105.

Dezuviria, Sacundo. Photograph. *Open City* 2 (1993): back cover.

Dietrich, Bryan D. "This Island Earth" (poem). *Open City* 16 (2002–2003): 201–202.

Dietrich, Bryan D. "The Thing That Couldn't Die" (poem). *Open City* 21 (2005–2006): 89–90.

Dikeou, Devon. Photographs, drawings, and text. *Open City* 1 (1992): 39–48.

Dikeou, Devon. "Marilyn Monroe Wanted to Be Buried In Pucci" (photographs, drawings, text,). *Open City* 10 (2000): 207–224.

Donnelly, Mary. "Lonely" (poem). *Open City* 12 (2001): 151–152.

Doris, Stacy. "Flight" (play). *Open City* 14 (2001–2002): 147–150.

Dormen, Lesley. "Gladiators" (story). *Open City* 18 (2003–2004): 155–163.

Douglas, Norman. "Male Order" (story). *Open City* 19 (2004): 151–163.

Dowe, Tom. "Legitimation Crisis" (poem). *Open City* 7 (1999): 21.

Doyle, Ben. "And on the First Day" (poem). *Open City* 12 (2001): 203–204.

Duhamel, Denise. "The Frog and the Feather" (story). *Open City* 5 (1997): 115–117.

Dyer, Geoff. "Albert Camus" (story). *Open City* 9 (1999): 23–38.

Grennan, Eamon. "Two Poems" (poems). *Open City* 5 (1997): 137–140.

Eisenegger, Erich. "A Ticket for Kat" (story). *Open City* 16 (2002–2003): 133–141.

Ellison, Lori. "Coffee Drawings" (drawings). *Open City* 13 (2001): 57–66.

Ellison, Lori. Drawing. *Open City* 17 (2003): back cover.

Ellman, Juliana. "Interior, Exterior, Portrait, Still-Life, Landscape" (drawings). *Open City* 19 (2004): 73–83.

Elsayed, Dahlia. "Black and Blue" (story). *Open City* 2 (1993): 29–35.

Elsayed, Dahlia. "Paterson Falls" (story). *Open City* 9 (1999): 153–158.

Engel, Terry. "Sky Blue Ford" (story). *Open City* 3 (1995): 115–128.

Eno, Will. "The Short Story of My Family" (story). *Open City* 13 (2001): 79–86.

Epstein, Daniel Mark. "The Jealous Man" (poem). *Open City* 17 (2003): 135–136.

Erian, Alicia. "Troika" (story). *Open City* 15 (2002): 27–42.

Erian, Alicia. "The Grant" (story). *Open City* 19 (2004): 109–117.

Eurydice. "History Malfunctions" (story). *Open City* 3 (1995): 161–164.

Faison, Ann. Drawings. *Open City* 12 (2001): 197–202.

Fattaruso, Paul. "Breakfast," "It Is I," "On the Stroke and Death of My Grandfather" (poems). *Open City* 20 (2005): 217–221.

Fawkes, Martin, trans., "Rehearsal for a Deserted City" (story) by Giuseppe O. Longo. *Open City* 15 (2002): 95–103.

Fernández de Villa-Urrutia, Rafael. "The First Visit to the Louvre: Fragments of an Improbable Dialogue" (story), trans. Jean Claude Abreu and Jorge Jauregui. *Open City* 16 (2002–2003): 177–181.

Field, Edward. Epilogue for Alfred Chester's "Moroccan Letters." *Open City* 3 (1995): 219.

Fitschen, David A. "Drive" (tour diaries). *Open City* 21 (2005–2006): 167–191.

Fitzgerald, Jack. "A Drop in the Bucket" (story). *Open City* 17 (2003): 99–104.

Fleming, Paul and Elke Siegel, trans., "December 24, 1999–January 1, 2000" (story) by Tim Staffel. *Open City* 12 (2001): 95–118.

Floethe, Victoria. "Object" (story). *Open City* 21 (2005–2006): 107–118.

Fluharty, Matthew. "To Weldon Kees" (poem). *Open City* 19 (2004): 107.

Flynn, Nick. "Bee Poems" (poems). *Open City* 5 (1997): 69–72.

Flynn, Nick. "Welcome to the Year of the Monkey" (essay). *Open City* 23 (2007): 57–72.

Flynn, Nick. "Earth" (poem). *Open City* 23 (2007): 73–77.

Foley, Sylvia. "Dogfight" (story). *Open City* 4 (1996): 135–144.

Foo, Josie. "Waiting" (story); "Garlanded Driftwood" (poem). *Open City* 1 (1992): 16–18.

Forché, Carolyn. "Refuge," "Prayer" (poems). *Open City* 17 (2003): 139–140.

Ford, Ford Madox. "Fun—It's Heaven!" (story). *Open City* 12 (2001): 305–310.

Foreman, Richard. "Eddie Goes to Poetry City" (excerpted story, drawings). *Open City* 2 (1993): 63–70.

Fox, Jason. "Models and Monsters" (paintings, drawings). *Open City* 17 (2003): 51–58.

Francis, Juliana. "The Baddest Natashas" (play). *Open City* 13 (2001): 149–172.

Friedman, Bruce Jay. "Lost" (story). *Open City* 16 (2002–2003): 185–190.

Friedman, Stan. "Male Pattern Baldness" (poem). *Open City* 1 (1992): 13–14.

Fuss, Adam. "Untitled" (photograph). *Open City* 6 (1998): front cover.

Gaddis, Anicée. "Fast and Slow" (story). *Open City* 20 (2005): 123–135.

Gaitskill, Mary. "The Crazy Person" (story). *Open City* 1 (1992): 49–61.

Gaitskill, Mary. "The Rubbed-Away Girl" (story). *Open City* 7 (1999): 137–148.

Gaffney, Elizabeth, trans., "Given" (story) by Alissa Walser. *Open City* 8 (1999): 141–149.

de Ganay, Sebastien. "Überfremdung" (paintings). *Open City* 11 (2000): 189–198.

Garrison, Deborah. "An Idle Thought," "Father, R.I.P., Sums Me Up at Twenty-Three," "A Friendship Enters Phase II" (poems). *Open City* 6 (1998): 21–26.

Garrison, Deborah. "Giving Notice" (letter). *Open City* 23 (2007): 79–80.

Garrison, Deborah. "A Short Skirt on Broadway," "Add One," "Both Square and Round," "The Necklace" (poems). *Open City* 23 (2007): 81–88.

Gerety, Meghan. Drawings. *Open City* 10 (2000): 151–158.

Gersh, Amanda. "On Safari" (story). *Open City* 10 (2000): 135–150.

Gifford, William. "Fight" (story). *Open City* 4 (1996): 207–214.

Gilbert, Josh. "Hack Wars" (story). *Open City* 18 (2003–2004): 55–60.

Gillick, Liam. "Signage for a Four Story Building" (art project). *Open City* 8 (1999): 121–125.

Gillison, Samantha. "Petty Cash" (story). *Open City* 4 (1996): 197–206.

Ginsberg, Allen. Photograph and text. *Open City* 3 (1995): 191–194.

Gizzi, Peter. "Take the 5:01 to Dreamland" (poem). *Open City* 17 (2003): 151–152.

Gold, Herbert. "Next In Line" (story). *Open City* 22 (2006): 65–69.

Goldstein, Jesse. "Dance With Me Ish, Like When You Was a Baby" (story). *Open City* 17 (2003): 197–199.

Gonzalez, Manuel. "The Disappearance of the Sebali Tribe" (story). *Open City* 22 (2006): 49–64.

Gonzalez, Mark. "To You, My Reader" (story). *Open City* 8 (1999): 153–154.

Gonzalez, Wayne. "Interior, Exterior, Portrait, Still-Life, Landscape," "The Carousel Club," "Self-Portrait as a Young Marine" (paintings). *Open City* 19 (2004): 73–83; front and back covers.

Goodyear, Dana. "Things Get Better Before They Get Worse," "Oracle," "Séance at Tennis," "Setting" (poems). *Open City* 16 (2002–2003): 39–42.

Gorham, Sarah. "Bacchus at the Water Tower, Continuing Ed," "Middle Age" (poems). *Open City* 13 (2001): 111–114.

Gorham, Sarah. "The Sacrifice," "*Would you like to see the house?*" (poems). *Open City* 19 (2004): 119–121.

Gray, Peter. "Alley" (poem). *Open City* 16 (2002–2003): 183–184.

Green, Lohren. "From the *Poetical Dictionary*" (poem). *Open City* 16 (2002–2003): 129–132.

Greene, Daniel. "Paul's Universe Blue," "Mother, Worcester, 1953," "Learning to Stand" (poems). *Open City* 15 (2002): 43–47.

Grennan, Eamon. "Glimpse" (poem). *Open City* 17 (2003): 161.

Grove, Elizabeth. "Enough About Me" (story). *Open City* 14 (2001–2002): 97–108.

Hakansson, Henrik. "Incomplete Proposals 1999–" (drawings). *Open City* 12 (2001): 89–94.

Hall, Marcellus. "As Luke Would Have It" (drawings, text). *Open City* 18 (2003–2004): 177–184.

Hanrahan, Catherine. "The Outer-Space Room" (story). *Open City* 18 (2003-2004): 99–114.

Harris, Evan. "Hope from the Third Person" (story). *Open City* 16 (2002–2003): 107–118.

Harris, Zach. "8" (drawings). *Open City* 19 (2004): 169–175.

Harrison, Jim. "Saving the Daylight," "Adding It Up," "Easter Morning," "Endgames" (poems). *Open City* 19 (2004): 20–26.

Harrison, Jim. "Arizona II" (story). *Open City* 23 (2007): 89–93.

Harrison, Jim. "Another Old Mariachi" (poem). *Open City* 23 (2007): 95.

Hart, JoeAnn. "Sawdust" (story). *Open City* 21 (2005–2006): 97–105.

Harvey, Ellen. "Friends and Their Knickers" (paintings). *Open City* 6 (1998): 133–144.

Harvey, Matthea. "Sergio Valente, Sergio Valente, How You Look Tells the World How You Feel," "To Zanzibar By Motorcar" (poems). *Open City* 18 (2003–2004): 97–98.

Haug, James. "Everything's Jake" (poem). *Open City* 18 (2003–2004): 193.

Hauser, Thomas. "Schmetterlinge und Butterblumen" (drawings). *Open City* 12 (2001): 131–136.

Hayashi, Toru. "Equivocal Landscape" (drawings). *Open City* 12 (2001): 43–48.

Hayes, Michael. "Police Blotter." *Open City* 8 (1999): 107–110.

Healey, Steve. "The Asshole of the Immanent," "Tilt" (poems). *Open City* 15 (2002): 77–80.

Healy, Tom. "What the Right Hand Knows" (poem). *Open City* 17 (2003): 113–114.

Heeman, Christoph. "Pencil Drawings" (drawings). *Open City* 17 (2003): 91–98.

Hendriks, Martijn. "Swerve" (story). *Open City* 21 (2005–2006): 31–34.

Henry, Brian. "I Lost My Tooth on the Way to Plymouth (Rock)," "Intro to Lit" (poems). *Open City* 18 (2003–2004): 139–140.

Henry, Max and Sam Samore. "Hobo Deluxe, A Cinema of Poetry" (photographs and text). *Open City* 12 (2001): 257–270.

Henry, Peter. "Thrift" (poem). *Open City* 7 (1999): 136.

Hedegaard, Erik. "The La-Z-Boy Position" (story). *Open City* 4 (1996): 117–121.

Heyd, Suzanne. "Mouth Door I," "Mouth Door II" (poems). *Open City* 20 (2005): 175–179.

Higgs, Matthew. "Three Parts" and "Photograph of a Book (I Married an Artist)" (photographs). *Open City* 16 (2002–2003): 203–210; front and back covers.

Hill, Amy. "Psycho-narratives" (paintings). *Open City* 14 (2001–2002): 89–95.

Hillesland, Ann. "Ultimate Catch" (story). *Open City* 22 (2006): 37–47.

Hocking, Justin. "Dragon" (story). *Open City* 18 (2003–2004): 123–138.

Hoffman, Cynthia Marie. "Dear Commercial Street," (poem). *Open City* 17 (2003): 125–127.

Hofstede, Hilarius. "The Marquis Von Water" (text art project). *Open City* 3 (1995): 135–144.

Hogan, John Brinton. "Vacation" (photographs). *Open City* 20 (2005): 113–120.

Holland, J. Gill. Introduction to "The Journals of Edvard Munch." *Open City* 9 (1999): 229–232.

Holland, Noy. "Time for the Flat-Headed Man" (story). *Open City* 14 (2001–2002): 69–80.

Hollander, Katherine. "Snow Man" (poem). *Open City* 19 (2004): 187–188.

Howe, Fanny. "The Plan," "A Reach" (poems). *Open City* 17 (2003): 119–121.

Humphries, Jacqueline. Paintings. *Open City* 3 (1995): 235–244.

Hubby, Bettina. Illustrations for Susan Perry's "The Final Man." *Open City* 8 (1999): 15–171.

Iovenko, Chris. "The Turnaround" (story). *Open City* 5 (1997): 73–80.

Jack, Rodney. "Many Splendid Thing," "Mutually Exclusive" (poems). *Open City* 18 (2003–2004): 61–66.

Jack, Rodney. "From Nightlife" (story). *Open City* 23 (2007): 97–110.

Jack, Rodney. "Seedbed," "Black-Capped Chickadee Trapped in the Feeder," "Perpetuation" (poems). *Open City* 23 (2007): 111–114.

Jaramillo, Luis. "Jack and the Rotarians" (story). *Open City* 19 (2004): 85–91.

Jarnot, Lisa. "Self-Portrait" (poem). *Open City* 14 (2001–2002): 167.

Jauregui, Jorge and Jean Claude Abreu, trans., "The First Visit to the Louvre: Fragments of an Improbable Dialogue" (story) by Rafael Fernández de Villa-Urrutia. *Open City* 16 (2002–2003): 177–181.

John, Daniel. "The Diagnosis" (poem). *Open City* 19 (2004): 93.

Johnson, David. Image and text. *Open City* 3 (1995): 155–160.

Johnson, Denis. "An Anarchist's Guide to Somalia" (story). *Open City* 4 (1996): 89–116.

Johnson, Joyce. "Postwar" (story). *Open City* 8 (1999): 183–194.

Johnson, Marilyn A. "Her Deflowering" (poem). *Open City* 16 (2002–2003): 191.

Johnston, Bret Anthony. "Waterwalkers" (story). *Open City* 18 (2003–2004): 229–248.

Jones, Hettie. "5:15 p.m. Eastern Standard Time, November," "One Hundred Love Poems for Lisa" (poems). *Open City* 4 (1996): 86–88.

Jones, Sarah. "Dining Room (Francis Place) (III)" (photograph, detail). *Open City* 5 (1997): front cover.

Jones, Stephen Graham. "Bile" (story). *Open City* 14 (2001–2002): 81–88.

Kaplan, Janet. "The List" (poem). *Open City* 19 (2004): 71.

Kay, Hellin. "Moscow & New York, Coming & Going" (photographs, story). *Open City* 15 (2002): 81–92.

Katchadourian, Nina. "Selections from *The Sorted Books Project*" (photographs). *Open City* 16 (2002–2003): 143–153.

Kazanas, Luisa. "Drawings" (drawings). *Open City* 13 (2001): 139–146.

Kean, Steve. Paintings. *Open City* 4 (1996): 129–133.

Kenealy, Ryan. "Yellow and Maroon" (story). *Open City* 7 (1999): 60–70.

Kenealy, Ryan. "Resuscitation of the Shih Tzu" (story). *Open City* 16 (2002–2003): 89–96.

Kenealy, Ryan. "God's New Math" (story). *Open City* 20 (2005): 209–216.

Kennedy, Hunter. "Nice Cool Beds" (story). *Open City* 6 (1998): 162–174.

Kennedy, Hunter. "When Is It That You Feel Good?" (poem). *Open City* 9 (1999): 117–118.

Kennedy, Hunter. "Kitty Hawk" (story). *Open City* 12 (2001): 137–150.

Kharms, Daniil. "Case P-81210, Vol. 2, 1st Edition," "From Kharms's Journal," "A Humorous Division of the World in Half (Second Half)," "Blue Notebook No. 10" (poems). *Open City* 8 (1999): 130–136.

Kidd, Chip. Photographs. *Open City* 3 (1995): 129–133.

Kilimnick, Karen. "Untitled (Acid Is Groovy)" (photographs). *Open City* 9 (1999): 181–186; back cover.

Kim, Suji Kwock. "Aubade Ending with Lines from the Japanese" (poem). *Open City* 17 (2003): 117–118.

Kimball, Michael. "The Birds, the Light, Eating Breakfast, Getting Dressed, and How I Tried to Make It More of a Morning for My Wife" (story). *Open City* 20 (2005): 197–199.

Kinder, Chuck. "The Girl with No Face" (story). *Open City* 17 (2003): 31–38.

Kirby, Matthew. "The Lower Brudeckers" (story). *Open City* 22 (2006): 23–26.

Kirk, Joanna. "Clara" (drawings). *Open City* 11 (2000): 173–184.

Kleiman, Moe. "Tomorrow We Will Meet the Enemy" (poem). *Open City* 15 (2002): 119–120.

Klink, Joanna. "Lodestar" (poem). *Open City* 17 (2003): 109–110.

Knox, Jennifer L. "While Some Elegant Dancers Perched on Wires High Above a Dark, Dark Farm" (poem). *Open City* 19 (2004): 129–130.

Koestenbaum, Wayne. "First Dossier/Welcome Tour" (fiction/nonfiction). *Open City* 23 (2007): 115–124.

Koolhaas, Rem, with Harvard Project on the City. "Pearl River Delta, China" (photographs, graphs, text). *Open City* 6 (1998): 60–76.

Koons, Jeff. Photographs. *Open City* 1 (1992): 24–25.

Körmeling, John. "Drawings" (drawings). *Open City* 14 (2001–2002): 129–136.

Kotzen, Kip. "Skate Dogs" (story). *Open City* 2 (1993): 50–53.

Kotzen, Kip. "Pray For Rain" (story). *Open City* 10 (2000): 159–170.

Kraman, Cynthia. "A Little Rock Memoir, Mostly About Other Things" (story). *Open City* 23 (2007): 125–133.

Kraman, Cynthia. "Little Gingko," "No Noon But Mine, No Heat But Yours," "Summer Night Poem 1," Summer Night Poem 5" (poems). *Open City* 23 (2007): 135–138.

Kujak, Heidi. "Father's Day," "San Francisco Produce Terminal" (poems). *Open City* 15 (2002): 109–110.

Lamb-Shapiro, Jessica. "This Man Is Eating in His Sleep" (story). *Open City* 17 (2003): 167–175.

Lambert, Alix. Untitled photographs. *Open City* 3 (1995): front cover and 34.

Lambert, Alix. "The Mark of Cain" (photographs, text). *Open City* 10 (2000): 183–194.

Lambert, Alix. "I am not like them at all and I cannot pretend" (collage). *Open City* 18 (2003–2004): 81–86.

Larimer, Heather. "Casseroles" (story). *Open City* 12 (2001): 75–88.

Larkin, Joan. "Full Moon Over Brooklyn" (poem). *Open City* 17 (2003): 123.

Larralde, Martin G. Paintings. *Open City* 11 (2000): 87–94.

Larson, Laura and Anne Trubek. "Genius Loci" (photographs, text). *Open City* 7 (1999): 85–94.

Larsson, Victoria. "Sharp Objects" (story). *Open City* 18 (2003–2004): 167–173.

Lasdun, James. "The Natural Order" (story). *Open City* 15 (2002): 201–221.

Lea, Creston. "We Used to Breed Remarkable Percheron Twitch Horses" (poem). *Open City* 12 (2001): 271.

Leckey, Mark. "The Casuals" (drawings, text). *Open City* 9 (1999): 119–128.

Leebron, Fred. "Welcome to Arcadia" (story). *Open City* 8 (1999): 111–119.

Legere, Phoebe. "Ode to Hong Kong" (poem). *Open City* 1 (1992): 23.

Lehman, David. "Eleven Poems for My Birthday" (poems). *Open City* 18 (2003–2004): 225–228.

Lehman, David. "Fast and Slow Sestina," "The Hotel Fiesta Sestina" (poems). *Open City* 20 (2005): 93–96.

LeMay, Patty. "confessions of a touring musician's lady (part 1)," "confessions of a touring musician's lady (part 24)" (poems). *Open City* 18 (2003–2004): 119–122.

Lesser, Guy. "The Good Sportsman, Et Cetera" (story). *Open City* 8 (1999): 75–86.

Levine, Margaret. "In a Dream It Happens," "Dilemma" (poems). *Open City* 16 (2002–2003): 159–160.

Lewinsky, Monica. "I Am a Pizza" (poem). *Open City* 6 (1998): 129.

Lewis, Jeremy. Introduction to "Happy Deathbeds." *Open City* 4 (1996): 49–52.

Lichtenstein, Miranda. "Stills from *The Naked City*" and "Untitled, #4 (Richardson Park)" (photographs). *Open City* 12 (2001): 275–284; front and back covers.

Lichtenstein, Miranda. "Ganzfeld" (photograph). *Open City* 21 (2005–2006): front and back covers.

Lida, David. "Bewitched" (story). *Open City* 9 (1999): 69–90.

Lindbloom, Eric. "Ideas of Order at Key West" (photographs). *Open City* 6 (1998): 155–161.

Lipsyte, Sam. "Shed" (story). *Open City* 3 (1995): 226–227.

Lipsyte, Sam. "Old Soul" (story). *Open City* 7 (1999): 79–84.

Lipsyte, Sam. "Cremains" (story). *Open City* 9 (1999): 167–176.

Lipsyte, Sam. "The Special Cases Lounge" (novel excerpt). *Open City* 13 (2001): 27–40.

Lipsyte, Sam. "Nate's Pain Is Now" (story). *Open City* 22 (2006): 1–8.

Longo, Giuseppe O. "In Zenoburg" (story), trans. David Mendel. *Open City* 12 (2001): 153–160.

Longo, Giuseppe O. "Rehearsal for a Deserted City" (story), trans. Martin Fawkes. *Open City* 15 (2002): 95–103.

Longo, Giuseppe O. "Braised Beef for Three" (story), trans. David Mendel. *Open City* 19 (2004): 135–148.

Lopate, Phillip. "Tea at the Plaza" (essay). *Open City* 21 (2005–2006): 15–20.

Macklin, Elizabeth, trans., "The House Style," "A Qualifier of Superlatives" (poems). *Open City* 7 (1999): 107–111.

Macklin, Elizabeth, trans., "The River," "Visit" (poems) by Kirmen Uribe. *Open City* 17 (2003): 131–134.

Madoo, Ceres. "Drawings" (drawings). *Open City* 20 (2005): 149–154.

Malone, Billy. "Tanasitease" (drawings). *Open City* 21 (2005–2006): 91–96.

Malkmus, Steve. "Bennington College Rap" (poem). *Open City* 7 (1999): 46.

Mamet, David. "Boulder Purey" (poem). *Open City* 3 (1995): 187–188.

Manrique, Jaime. "Twilight at the Equator" (story). *Open City* 2 (1993): 130–134.

Marinovich, Matt. "My Public Places" (story). *Open City* 13 (2001): 67–70.

Marshall, Chan. "Fever Skies" (poem). *Open City* 9 (1999): 187.

Martin, Cameron. "Planes" (paintings). *Open City* 15 (2002): 49–57.

Martin, Cameron, curator. "Interior, Exterior, Portrait, Still-Life, Landscape" (drawings, prints). *Open City* 19 (2004): 73–83.

Marton, Ana. Photographs, text. *Open City* 5 (1997): 141–150.

Marx, Pearson. "Lost Dog" (story). *Open City* 3 (1995): 143–150.

Masini, Donna. "3 Card Monte" (poem). *Open City* 17 (2003): 145–146.

Matthews, Richard. "Hudson" (poem). *Open City* 17 (2003): 107–108.

Maurer United Architects. "Façade" (photographs, images). *Open City* 15 (2002): 189–196.

Maxwell, Glyn. "Our Terrible Belief" (story). *Open City* 23 (2007): 139–148.

Maxwell, Glyn. "Sufficient Time," "Reality," "Decision," "Dust and Flowers," "The Arms of Half," "Fall of Man [Continued]" (poems). *Open City* 23 (2007): 149–156.

Maxwell, Richard. "A–1 Rolling Steak House" (play). *Open City* 13 (2001): 181–187.

McCabe, Patrick. "The Call" (story). *Open City* 3 (1995): 95–103.

McCormick, Carlo. "The Getaway" (story, drawings). *Open City* 3 (1995): 151–154.

McCracken, Chad. "Postcolonial Fat Man," "Second Grade" (poems). *Open City* 19 (2004): 165–167.

McCurtin, William. "Sometimes Skateboarding Is Like Dancing with Criminals" (drawings). *Open City* 20 (2005): 201–208.

McGuane, Thomas. "Bees" (story). *Open City* 4 (1996): 215–222.

McIntyre, Vestal. "Octo" (story). *Open City* 11 (2000): 27–50.

McIntyre, Vestal. "The Trailer at the End of the Driveway" (essay). *Open City* 22 (2006): 1–7.

McKenna, Evie. "Directions to My House" (photographs). *Open City* 12 (2001): 65–72.

McNally, John. "The First of Your Last Chances" (story). *Open City* 11 (2000): 125–140.

McNally, Sean. "Handsome Pants" (story). *Open City* 6 (1998): 131–132.

McPhee, Martha. "Waiting" (story). *Open City* 2 (1993): 109–118.

Mead, Stu. "Devil Milk" and "Untitled" (drawings). *Open City* 17 (2003): 177–185 and front cover.

Means, David. "What They Did" (story). *Open City* 6 (1998): 77–82.

Mehmedinovic, Semezdin. "Hotel Room," "Precautionary Manifesto" (poems), trans. Ammiel Alcaly. *Open City* 17 (2003): 141–142.

Mehta, Diane. "Rezoning in Brooklyn" (poem). *Open City* 7 (1999): 71–72.

Mendel, David, trans., "In Zenoburg" (story) by Giuseppe O. Longo. *Open City* 12 (2001): 153–160.

Mendel, David, trans., "Braised Beef for Three" (story) by Giuseppe O. Longo. *Open City* 19 (2004): 135–148.

Merlis, Jim. "One Man's Theory" (story). *Open City* 10 (2000): 171–182.

Metres, Philip and Tatiana Tulchinsky, trans., "This Is Me" (poem) by Lev Rubinshtein. *Open City* 15 (2002): 121–134.

Michels, Victoria Kohn. "At the Nightingale-Bamford School for Girls" (poem). *Open City* 4 (1996): 166–167.

Middlebrook, Jason. "APL #1 Polar Bear" (drawing). *Open City* 18 (2003–2004): front and back covers.

Milford, Kate. Photographs. *Open City* 2 (1993): 54–56.

Milford, Matthew. "Civil Servants" (paintings, text). *Open City* 7 (1999): 47–55.

Miller, Greg. "Intercessor" (poem). *Open City* 11 (2000): 51.

Miller, Jane. "From *A Palace of Pearls*" (poem). *Open City* 17 (2003): 157–160.

Miller, Matt. "Driver" (poem). *Open City* 12 (2001): 169–170.

Miller, Matt. "Chimera" (poem). *Open City* 21 (2005–2006): 119–120.

Miller, Stephen Paul. "When Listening to the Eighteen-and-a-Half Minute Tape Gap as Electronic Music" (poem). *Open City* 4 (1996): 162.

M.I.M.E. Photographs. *Open City* 9 (1999): 207–218.

Mobilio, Albert. "Adhesiveness: There Was This Guy" (story). *Open City* 5 (1997): 55–56.

Moeckel, Thorpe. "Johnny Stinkbait Bears His Soul" (story). *Open City* 23 (2007): 157–162.

Moeckel, Thorpe. "Dream of My Father," "Nature Poem, Inc.," "Mussels," "At the Co-op," "Beautiful Jazz" (poems). *Open City* 23 (2007): 163–171.

Moody, Rick. "Dead Man Writes," "Domesticity," "Immortality," "Two Sonnets for Stacey" (poems). *Open City* 6 (1998): 83–88.

Moore, Honor. "She Remembers," "The Heron" (poems). *Open City* 13 (2001): 71–78.

Moore, Honor. "In Place of an Introduction" (assemblage). *Open City* 17 (2003): 105–106.

Moore, Honor. "Homage," "Hotel Brindisi," "Tango" (poems). *Open City* 20 (2005): 77–80.

Mortensen, Viggo. "From *Hole in the Sun*" (photographs). *Open City* 18 (2003–2004): 141–150.

Mullen, Harryette. "Unacknowledged Legislator," "Headlines," "Bumper to Bumper" (poems). *Open City* 14 (2001–2002): 141–143.

Munch, Edvard. "Passages from the Journals of Edvard Munch" (text, drawings). *Open City* 9 (1999): 233–250.

Münch, Christopher. Photographs, text. *Open City* 3 (1995): 89–94.

Mycue, Edward. "But the Fifties Really Take Me Home" (poem). *Open City* 11 (2000): 171–172.

Nadin, Peter. Paintings. *Open City* 4 (1996): 147–152.

Myles, Eileen. "Ooh" (poem). *Open City* 17 (2003): 143.

Myles, Eileen. "The Inferno" (story). *Open City* 18 (2003–2004): 67–74.

Nachumi, Ben. "Spring Cabin," "Crows," "Spring Cabin," "Dream House" (poems). *Open City* 21 (2005–2006): 71–76.

Nakanishi, Nadine. "Seriidevüf" (drawings). *Open City* 19 (2004): 122–128.

Nelson, Cynthia. "go ahead and sing your weird arias," "the adoration piles of spring," "i almost get killed" (poems). *Open City* 14 (2001–2002): 169–171.

Nelson, Maggie. "The Poem I Was Working on Before September 11, 2001" (poem). *Open City* 14 (2001–2002): 179–183.

Nester, Daniel. "After Schubert's Sad Cycle of Songs" (poem). *Open City* 15 (2002): 165–168.

Nevers, Mark. "Untitled" (poem). *Open City* 20 (2005): 121.

Newirth, Mike. "Semiprecious" (story). *Open City* 18 (2003–2004): 87–96.

Nutt, David. "Melancholera" (story) *Open City* 21 (2005–2006): 53–69.

O'Brien, Geoffrey. "Roof Garden" (poem). *Open City* 3 (1995): 134.

O'Brien, Geoffrey. "The Blasphemers" (story). *Open City* 5 (1997): 43–54.

O'Brien, Geoffrey. "House Detective" (poem). *Open City* 8 (1999): 120.

O'Brien, Geoffrey. "The Browser's Ecstasy" (story). *Open City* 10 (2000): 195–202.

O'Rourke, Meg. "The Drivers" (story). *Open City* 2 (1993): 93–96.

Ogger, Sara, trans., "Show #7" (story) by Benjamin von Stuckrad-Barre. *Open City* 12 (2001): 119–130.

Okubo, Michiko. "The Glass Garden" (story). *Open City* 14 (2001–2002): 33–38.

Oldham, Will. "Untitled" (poem). *Open City* 7 (1999): 78.

Ortiz, Radames. "The Plea" (poem). *Open City* 18 (2003–2004): 211–212.

Osborne, Lawrence. "Gentle Toys" (story). *Open City* 4 (1996): 186–194.

Ovaldé, Véronique. "Scenes from Family Life" (story), trans. Lorin Stein. *Open City* 21 (2005–2006): 141–152.

Owens, Laura. Drawings *Open City* 9 (1999): 145–152.

Paco. "Clown Speaks" (story). *Open City* 2 (1993): 77–81.

Paco. "Clown White" (story). *Open City* 3 (1995): 103–110.

Paco. "Ing," "Cross and Sundial," "Flares," (stories), "Firecrackers and Sneakers" (poem). *Open City* 9 (1999): 219–226.

Pagk, Paul. Drawings. *Open City* 5 (1997): 89–98.

Panurgias, Basile. "The Sixth Continent" (story). *Open City* 5 (1997): 81–89.

Pape, Eric. "Faces of the Past and the Future" (essay). *Open City* 22 (2006): 13–25.

Passaro, Vince. "Cathedral Parkway" (story). *Open City* 1 (1992): 26–34.

Passaro, Vince. "Adult Content" (story). *Open City* 13 (2001): 227–235.

Passaro, Vince. "Voluntary Tyranny, or Brezhnev at the Mall: Notes from Wartime on the Willful Abdication of the Liberty We Claim We're Busy Promoting Elsewhere" (essay). *Open City* 22 (2006): 39–56.

Patterson, G. E. "Drift Land" (poem). *Open City* 17 (2003): 137–138.

Pavlic, Ed. "You Sound Unseen" (poem). *Open City* 9 (1999): 227.

Pavlic, Ed. "From *Arachnida Speak*" (poem). *Open City* 16 (2002–2003): 155–157.

Pelevin, Victor. "Who By Fire" (story), trans. Matvei Yankelevich. *Open City* 7 (1999): 95–106.

Penone, Giuseppe. "Reversing One's Own Eyes" (photograph). *Open City* 9 (1999): 91–94.

Perry, Susan. "The Final Man" (story). *Open City* 8 (1999): 155–171.

Petrantoni, Lorenzo. "1880" (collages). *Open City* 21 (2005–2006): 21–28.

Phillips, Alex. "Stonemason's Oratory," "Work Shy," "Dressmaker" (poems). *Open City* 21 (2005–2006): 49–51.

Phillips, Robert. Introduction to "T. S. Eliot's Squint" by Delmore Schwartz. *Open City* 5 (1997): 152.

Pierson, Melissa Holbrook. "Night Flight" (poem). *Open City* 13 (2001): 131.

Pinchbeck, Daniel. "Fleck" (story). *Open City* 10 (2000): 239–272.

Pinchbeck, Peter. Paintings. *Open City* 13 (2001): 215–226.

Pitts-Gonzalez, Leland. "The Blue Dot" (story). *Open City* 22 (2006): 71–86.

Poirier, Mark Jude. "Happy Pills" (story). *Open City* 17 (2003): 39–50.

Polito, Robert. "The Last Rock Critic" (story). *Open City* 1 (1992): 71–78.

Polito, Robert. Introduction to "Incident in God's Country." *Open City* 4 (1996): 167–168.

Polito, Robert. "Please Refrain from Talking During the Movie" (poem). *Open City* 17 (2003): 111–112.

Poor, Maggie. "Frog Pond" (story). *Open City* 4 (1996): 163–165.

Porter, Sarah. "The Blood of Familiar Objects" (story). *Open City* 14 (2001–2002): 25–31.

Primack, Gretchen. "It Is Green" (poem). *Open City* 18 (2003–2004): 153–154.

Pritchard, Melissa. "Virgin Blue" (story). *Open City* 11 (2000): 155–170.

Puckette, Elliot. "Silhouettes." *Open City* 8 (1999): 173–181.

Purcell, Greg. "The Taking of the Government Center, 1996–2006" (story). *Open City* 23 (2007): 173–183.

Purcell, Greg. "I Have About a Billion Friends," "A System of Belts and Wheels and Mirrors" (poems). *Open City* 23 (2007): 185–188.

Purdy, James. "Geraldine" (story). *Open City* 6 (1998): 145–154.

Quinones, Paul. "Peter Gek" (story). *Open City* 15 (2002): 105–107.

Raffel, Dawn. "Seven Spells" (story). *Open City* 19 (2004): 181–185.

Raskin, Jimmy. Art project. *Open City* 2 (1993): 57–60.

Raskin, Jimmy. "The Diagram and the Poet" (text, image). *Open City* 7 (1999): 120–126.

Reagan, Siobhan. "Ambassadors" (story). *Open City* 5 (1997): 27–34.

Reagan, Siobhan. "Neck, 17.5" (story). *Open City* 11 (2000): 61–68.

Redel, Victoria. "The Palace of Weep" (poem). *Open City* 17 (2003): 153–154.

Reed, John. "Pop Mythologies" (story). *Open City* 2 (1993): 97–100.

Reising, Andrea. "LaSalle" (poem). *Open City* 11 (2000): 153–154.

Resen, Laura. Photographs. *Open City* 11 (2000): 145–152.

Reynolds, Rebecca. "Casper" (poem). *Open City* 15 (2002): 93–94.

von Rezzori, Gregor. "On the Cliff" (story). *Open City* 11 (2000): 199–240.

Ricketts, Margaret. "Devil's Grass" (poem). *Open City* 11 (2000): 119.

Ritchie, Matthew. "CaCO$_2$" (drawings). *Open City* 6 (1998): 89–96.

Robbins, David. "Springtime" (photographs). *Open City* 8 (1999): 96–105.

Roberts, Anthony. "Wonders," "Two at Night," "Before Daybreak," "Beside the Orkhorn" (poems). *Open City* 20 (2005): 137–148.

Robertson, Thomas, and Rock Rofihe. "Four Round Windows" (drawings, text). *Open City* 19 (2004): 213–222.

Robinson, Lewis. "The Diver" (story). *Open City* 16 (2002–2003): 161–175.

Rofihe, Rick. "Eidetic," "'Feeling Marlene'" (stories). *Open City* 16 (2002–2003): 227–231.

Rofihe, Rick and Thomas Robertson. "Four Round Windows" (drawings, text). *Open City* 19 (2004): 213–222.

Rohrer, Matthew and Joshua Beckman. "Still Life with Woodpecker," "The Book of Houseplants" (poems). *Open City* 19 (2004): 177–178.

Ross, Sally. "Interior, Exterior, Portrait, Still-Life, Landscape" (drawings). *Open City* 19 (2004): 73–83.

Rothman, Richard. "Photographs" (photographs). *Open City* 6 (1998): 116–124.

Rubinshtein, Lev. "This Is Me" (poem), trans. Philip Metres and Tatiana Tulchinsky. *Open City* 15 (2002): 121–134.

Rubinstein, Raphael, trans., "From *Letter to Antonio Saura*" (story) by Marcel Cohen. *Open City* 17 (2003): 217–225.

Ruda, Ed. "The Seer" (story). *Open City* 1 (1992): 15.

Ruppersberg, Allen. "Greetings from L.A." (novel). *Open City* 16 (2002–2003): throughout.

Rush, George. "Interior, Exterior, Portrait, Still-Life, Landscape" (print). *Open City* 19 (2004): 73–83.

Ruvo, Christopher. "Afternoon, 1885" (poem). *Open City* 18 (2003–2004): 185–186.

Rux, Carl Hancock. "Geneva Cottrell, Waiting for the Dog to Die" (play). *Open City* 13 (2001): 189–213.

Salamun, Tomaz. "VI," "VII" (poems), trans. author and Joshua Beckman. *Open City* 15 (2002): 155–157.

Salvatore, Joseph. "Practice Problem" (story). *Open City* 7 (1999): 127–135.

Samore, Sam and Max Henry. "Hobo Deluxe, A Cinema of Poetry" (photographs and text). *Open City* 12 (2001): 257–270.

Samton, Matthew. "Y2K, or How I Learned to Stop Worrying and Love the CD-Rom" (poem). *Open City* 12 (2001): 191–196.

Saroyan, Strawberry. "Popcorn" (story). *Open City* 6 (1998): 125–128.

Sayrafiezadeh, Saïd. "My Mother and the Stranger" (story). *Open City* 17 (2003): 59–66.

Schleinstein, Bruno. "Drawings" (drawings). *Open City* 17 (2003): 227–237.

Schles, Ken. Two untitled photographs. *Open City* 1 (1992): front and back covers.

Schles, Ken. Photography. *Open City* 2 (1993): front cover.

Schles, Ken. Two photographs. *Open City* 10 (2000): front and back covers.

Schles, Ken. "New York City: Street Photographs Following the Terrorist Attack on the World Trade Center, September 2001" (photographs). *Open City* 14 (2001–2002): 219–232.

Schneider, Ryan. "Mattress," "I Will Help You Destroy This, World" (poems). *Open City* 18 (2003–2004): 249–250.

Schoolwerth, Pieter. "Premonitions" (drawings). *Open City* 12 (2001): 161–168.

Schwartz, Delmore. "T. S. Eliot's Squint" (story). *Open City* 5 (1997): 152–157.

Selby, Hubert. "La Vie en Rose" (story). *Open City* 1 (1992): 35–38.

Selwyn, Robert. "Journey" (paintings). *Open City* 21 (2005–2006): 157–165.

Serra, Richard. Paintings. *Open City* 2 (1993): 101–108.

Serra, Shelter. "Drawings (from Dynamo Series)" (drawings). *Open City* 20 (2005): 69–76.

Seshadri, Vijay. "My First Fairy Tale" (essay). *Open City* 23 (2007): 189–193.

Seshadri, Vijay. "Fractured Fairy Tale," "Wolf Soup" (poems). *Open City* 23 (2007): 195–197.

Shapiro, Deborah. "Happens All the Time" (story). *Open City* 16 (2002–2003): 63–67.

Shapiro, Harriet. "The Omelette Pan" (story). *Open City* 18 (2003–2004): 189–191.

Shapiro, Harvey. "Where I Am Now," "History," "How Charley Shaver Died" (poems). *Open City* 8 (1999): 23–25.

Shapiro, Harvey. "Places," "Epitaphs," "Cape Ann," "Confusion at the Wheel" (poems). *Open City* 11 (2000): 185–188.

Shapiro, Harvey. "One Day," "Night in the Hamptons" (poems). *Open City* 19 (2004): 209–211.

Shattuck, Jessica. "Winners" (story). *Open City* 21 (2005–2006): 1–12.

Shaw, Sam. "Peg" (story). *Open City* 20 (2005): 97–111.

Sherman, Rachel. "Keeping Time" (story). *Open City* 20 (2005): 81–91.

Sherman, Rachel. "Two Stories; Single Family; Scenic View" (story). *Open City* 21 (2005–2006): 77–88.

Shirazi, Kamrun. "Shirazi's Problem" (chess maneuvers). *Open City* 2 (1993): 128–129.

Shields, David. "Sports" (story). *Open City* 2 (1993): 119–120.

Shirazi, Said. "The Truce" (story). *Open City* 9 (1999): 107–116.

Shope, Nina. "Platform" (story). *Open City* 19 (2004): 55–61.

Siegel, Elke and Paul Fleming, trans., "December 24, 1999–January 1, 2000" (story) by Tim Staffel. *Open City* 12 (2001): 95–118.

Sigler, Jeremy. "Inner Lumber," "Obscuritea" (poems). *Open City* 20 (2005): 137–141.

Sirowitz, Hal. "Chicken Pox Story and Others" (poems, drawings). *Open City* 7 (1999): 73–77.

Skinner, Jeffrey. "Winn-Dixie," "Survey Says," "Video Vault" (poems). *Open City* 8 (1999): 69–74.

Sledge, Michael. "The Birdlady of Houston" (story). *Open City* 16 (2002–2003): 211–221.

Smith, Charlie. "A Selection Process," "Agents of the Moving Company," "Evasive Action" (poems). *Open City* 6 (1998): 43–46.

Smith, Lee. Two untitled poems. *Open City* 3 (1995): 224–225.

Smith, Lee. "The Balsawood Man" (story). *Open City* 10 (2000): 203–206.

Smith, Molly. "untitled (underlie)" (drawings). *Open City* 21 (2005–2006): 41–48.

Smith, Peter Nolan. "Why I Miss Junkies" (story). *Open City* 13 (2001): 115–129.

Smith, Peter Nolan. "Better Lucky Than Good" (story). *Open City* 19 (2004): 65–70.

Smith, Rod. "Sandaled" (poem). *Open City* 14 (2001–2002): 145.

Snyder, Rick. "No Excuse," "Pop Poem '98" (poems). *Open City* 8 (1999): 151–152.

Smith, Dean. "Head Fake" (poem). *Open City* 1 (1992): 19–20.

Smith, Scott. "The Egg Man" (story). *Open City* 20 (2005): 1–67.

Solotaroff, Ivan. "Love Poem (On 53rd and 5th)" (poem). *Open City* 3 (1995): 228.

Solotaroff, Ivan. "Prince of Darkness" (story). *Open City* 6 (1998): 97–114.

Solotroff, Mike. "Fe·nes·tral Drawings" (drawings). *Open City* 18 (2003–2004): 213–218.

Southern, Nile. "Cargo of Blasted Mainframes" (story, drawings). *Open City* 1 (1992): 62–70.

Southern, Terry. "Twice on Top" (screenplay). *Open City* 2 (1993): 82–92.

Southern, Terry. "*C'est Toi Alors*: Scenario for Existing Props and French Cat" (screenplay). *Open City* 13 (2001): 41–43.

Space3. "Street Report EHV 003-2001" (prints). *Open City* 15 (2002): 159–164.

Staffel, Tim. "December 24, 1999–January 1, 2000" (story), trans. Elke Siegel and Paul Fleming. *Open City* 12 (2001): 95–118.

Stahl, Jerry. "Gordito" (story). *Open City* 22 (2006): 9–14.

Starkey, David. "Poem to Beer" (poem). *Open City* 12 (2001): 73–72.

Stefans, Brian Kim. "Two Pages from *The Screens*" (poem). *Open City* 14 (2001–2002): 163–165.

Stefans, Cindy. Photographs. *Open City* 6 (1998): 37–42.

Stefans, Cindy. Photographs. *Open City* 10 (2000): 115–124.

Stein, Lorin, trans., "Scenes from a Family Life" (story) by Véronique Ovaldé. *Open City* 21 (2005–2006): 141–152.

Stone, Nick. "Their Hearts Were Full of Spring" (photographs, text). *Open City* 10 (2000): 89–94.

Strand, Mark. "Great Dog Poem No. 5" (poem). *Open City* 4 (1996): 145–146.

Stroffolino, Chris. "Nocturne," "Red Tape Sale" (poems). *Open City* 18 (2003–2004): 115–118.

Strouse, James C. "Goodbye, Blue Thunder" (story). *Open City* 19 (2004): 193–208.

von Stuckrad-Barre, Benjamin. "Show #7" (story), trans. Sara Ogger. *Open City* 12 (2001): 119–130.

Swann, Maxine. "I May Look Dumb" (story). *Open City* 20 (2005): 155–174.

Swansea, Ena. "A Set for an Opera About Plants" (photographs). *Open City* 11 (2000): 121–124.

Swartz, Julianne. Drawings. *Open City* 4 (1996): 79–85.

Swartz, Julianne. "Loci" and "Beach with Car, Long Island" (photographs). *Open City* 13 (2001): 26, 40, 56, 78, 130, 188, 236; front and back cover.

Talbot, Toby. "Gone" (story). *Open City* 13 (2001): 95–109.

Talen, Bill. "Free Us From This Freedom: A Reverend Billy Sermon/Rant" (play). *Open City* 13 (2001): 173–180.

Taussig, Michael. "My Cocaine Museum" (essay). *Open City* 11 (2000): 69–86.

Tel, Jonathan. "The Myth of the Frequent Flier" (story). *Open City* 18 (2003–2004): 219–224.

Thomas, Cannon. "Dubrovnik" (story). *Open City* 16 (2002–2003): 75–88.

Thompson, Jim. "Incident in God's Country" (story). *Open City* 4 (1996): 169–180.

Thomson, Mungo. "Notes and Memoranda" (drawings). *Open City* 12 (2001): 311–320.

Thomson, Mungo, curator. Art projects. *Open City* 16 (2002–2003).

Thorpe, Helen. "Killed on the Beat" (story). *Open City* 5 (1997): 118–136.

Torn, Anthony. "Flaubert in Egypt" (poem). *Open City* 1 (1992): 21–22.

Torn, Jonathan. "Arson" (story). *Open City* 1 (1992): 10–12.

Torn, Tony. "Hand of Dust," "Farmers: 3 a.m.," "To Mazatlan" (poems). *Open City* 10 (2000): 225–230.

Tosches, Nick. "My Kind of Loving" (poem). *Open City* 4 (1996): 23.

Tosches, Nick. "*L'uccisore e la Farfalla*," "*Ex Tenebris, Apricus*," "I'm in Love with Your Knees," "A Cigarette with God" (poems). *Open City* 13 (2001): 45–55.

Tosches, Nick. "Proust and the Rat" (story). *Open City* 16 (2002–2003): 223–226.

Tosches, Nick. "Gynæcology" (poem). *Open City* 18 (2003–2004): 165–166.

Tosches, Nick. "The Lectern at Helicarnassus" (poem). *Open City* 21 (2005–2006): 165.

Toulouse, Sophie. "Sexy Clowns" (photographs). *Open City* 17 (2003): 201–208.

Tower, Jon. Photographs, drawings, and text. *Open City* 1 (1992): 79–86.

Trubek, Anne and Laura Larson. "Genius Loci" (photographs, text). *Open City* 7 (1999): 85–94.

Tulchinsky, Tatiana and Paul Metres, trans., "This Is Me" (poem) by Lev Rubinshtein. *Open City* 15 (2002): 121–134.

Uklanski, Piotr. "Queens" (photograph). *Open City* 8 (1999): front and back covers.

Uribe, Kirmen. "The River," "Visit" (poems) trans. Elizabeth Macklin. *Open City* 17 (2003): 131–134.

Vapnyar, Lara. "Mistress" (story). *Open City* 15 (2002): 135–153.

Vapnyar, Lara. "There Are Jews in My House" (story). *Open City* 17 (2003): 243–273.

Vicente, Esteban. Paintings. *Open City* 3 (1995): 75–80.

Vicuña, Cecilia. "The Brilliance of Orifices," "Mother of Pearl," "The Anatomy of Paper" (poems), trans. Rosa Alcalá. *Open City* 14 (2001–2002): 151–154.

Walker, Wendy. "Sophie in the Catacombs" (story). *Open City* 19 (2004): 131–132.

Wallace, David Foster. "Nothing Happened" (story). *Open City* 5 (1997): 63–68.

Walls, Jack. "Hi-fi" (story). *Open City* 13 (2001): 237–252.

Walser, Alissa. "Given" (story), trans. Elizabeth Gaffney. *Open City* 8 (1999): 141–150.

Walsh, J. Patrick III. "It's time to go out on your own." (drawings). *Open City* 19 (2004): 35–40.

Wareham, Dean. "Swedish Fish," "Orange Peel," "Weird and Woozy," "Romantica" (song lyrics). *Open City* 15 (2002): 197–200.

Webb, Charles H. "Vic" (poem). *Open City* 4 (1996): 134.

Weber, Paolina. Two Untitled Poems. *Open City* 3 (1995): 72–74.

Weber, Paolina. "Tape" (poems). *Open City* 9 (1999): 95–106.

Wefali, Amine. "Westchester Burning" (story). *Open City* 15 (2002): 59–75

Weiner, Cynthia. "Amends" (story). *Open City* 17 (2003): 71–89.

Welsh, Irvine. "Eurotrash" (story). *Open City* 3 (1995): 165–186.

Welsh, Irvine. "The Rosewell Incident" (story). *Open City* 5 (1997): 103–114.

Wenderoth, Joe. "Where God Is Glad" (essay). *Open City* 23 (2007): 209–216.

Wenderoth, Joe. "College," "Wedding Vow," "Against Zoning" (poems). *Open City* 23: (2007): 217–219.

Wenthe, William. "Against Witness" (poem). *Open City* 6 (1998): 115.

Wenthe, William. "Against Witness" (poem). *Open City* 12 (2001): 273.

Wenthe, William. "Shopping in Artesia" (poem). *Open City* 19 (2004): 63.

Wetzsteon, Rachel. "Largo," "Gusts" (poems). *Open City* 12 (2001): 285–286.

Weyland, Jocko. "Burrito" (story). *Open City* 6 (1998): 27–36.

Weyland, Jocko. "Swimmer Without a Cause" (story). *Open City* 10 (2000): 231–238.

Weyland, Jocko. "The Elk and the Skateboarder" (story). *Open City* 15 (2002): 169–187.

Weyland, Jocko. "Vietnam Is Number One" (story). *Open City* 22 (2006): 27–37.

Wheeler, Susan. "Barry Lyndon in Spring Lake, 1985" (poem). *Open City* 17 (2003): 115–116.

Willard, Nancy. "The Cookies of Fortune" (essay). *Open City* 23 (2007) 221–222.

Willard, Nancy. "Auction" (poem). *Open City* 23 (2007) 223–224.

Williams, C. K. "The Clause" (poem). *Open City* 17 (2003): 129–130.

Williams, Diane. "Coronation and Other Stories" (stories). *Open City* 1 (1992): 4–9.

Willis, Elizabeth. "Ferns, Mosses, Flags" (poem). *Open City* 17 (2003): 147.

Willis, Elizabeth. "Devil Bush," "Of Which I Shall Have Occasion to Speak Again" (poems). *Open City* 21 (2005–2006): 29–30.

Wilson, Tim. "Private Beach Bitches" (story). *Open City* 16 (2002–2003): 193–199.

Winer, Jody. "Mrs. Sherlock Holmes States Her Case," "How to Arrive at a Motel" (poems). *Open City* 11 (2000): 141–144.

Wolff, Rebecca. "Chinatown, Oh" (poem). *Open City* 5 (1997): 35–37.

Wolff, Rebecca. "Mom Gets Laid" (poem). *Open City* 9 (1999): 177–180.

Wolff, Rebecca. "The Beginners" (story). *Open City* 23 (2007): 225–237.

Wolff, Rebecca. "Literary Agency," "My Daughter," "Only Rhubarb," "The Reductions," "Who Can I Ask for an Honest Assessment?" (poems). *Open City* 23 (2007): 239–243.

Woodman, Francesca. Untitled photographs. *Open City* 3 (1995): 229–234 and back cover.

Wormwood, Rick. "Burt and I" (story). *Open City* 9 (1999): 129–140.

Woychuk-Mlinac, Ava. "Why?" (poem). *Open City* 19 (2004): 179.

Yankelevich, Matvei, trans., "Who By Fire" (story) by Victor Pelevin. *Open City* 7 (1999): 95–106.

Yankelevich, M. E. Introduction to Daniil Kharms. *Open City* 8 (1999): 127–129.

Yankelevich, Matvei. "The Green Bench" (poem). *Open City* 19 (2004): 149–150.

Yas, Joanna. "Boardwalk" (story). *Open City* 10 (2000): 95–102.

Yates, Richard. "Uncertain Times" (unfinished novel). *Open City* 3 (1995): 35–71.

Yau, John. "Forbidden Entries" (story). *Open City* 2 (1993): 75–76.

Young, Kevin. "Encore," "Sorrow Song," "Saxophone Solo," "Muzak" (poems). *Open City* 16 (2002–2003): 121–127.

Zaitzeff, Amine. "Westchester Burning" (story). *Open City* 8 (1999): 45–68.

Zapruder, Matthew. "The Pajamaist" (poem). *Open City* 21 (2005–2006): 35–39.

Zumas, Leni. "Dragons May Be the Way Forward" (story). *Open City* 22 (2006): 15–22.

Zwahlen, Christian. "I Want You to Follow Me Home" (story). *Open City* 19 (2004): 27–32.